TWILIGHT TEAHOUSE

VOL. 1 THROUGH 3

T.J. MICHAELS

CONTENTS

Twilight Teahouse Vol. 1 through 3 ©

"Interesting new world. Hot stuff!" ~Shayla Black, New York Times bestselling author

"CARINIAN'S SEEKER was a highly erotic, thrilling suspenseful, paranormal read that will blow your mind." ~Fallen Angel Reviews

"It had me rooting for their happy-ever-after as much as cheering their kick-ass assignments" ~Just Erotic Romance Reviews

"T.J. MICHAELS has done an astounding job of crafting a steamy hot suspenseful romance—" ~Romance Junkies

---

Spirit Bound Novels

"All in all, [On the Prowl] is a fun and delightful story with spicy sex and great suspense both in the love story and the plot." ~Just Erotic Romance Reviews

"Using heat, danger and tension, Egyptian Voyage will keep you glued to that edge of your seat as you go along for the ride. T.J. Michaels has written a story that will fascinate, horrify and ultimately delight the reader." ~Sensual-Reads.com

---

Forever December

"[Forever December] is a highly erotic, touching and sexy

novella that will have you reaching for a tall, cold glass of water and a fan." ~Romance Divas

"Explosive love scenes will curl your toes and leave you fanning. Readers who love a flare for the dramatic with paranormal elements will certainly become fans of T.J. Michaels." ~Romance Junkies

---

Jaguar's Rule

"The plot is flawlessly executed and the characters remain true." ~The Romance Studio

"T.J. MICHAELS knows how to write plot and passion in a most memorable way!" ~Fallen Angels Reviews

DEDICATION

To my family by blood, sisters from another mister, and brothers from another mother. Tam, Mike, Mindy and CVD, you guys have no idea how much your love and support meant to me while penning this book. Thinking back on all the conversations that led up to the idea for this series, both funny and not-so-funny, be assured there's a little bit of all of you in this novel! Strap in, it's time for takeoff!

To Softrock, Burton and Mizz Lovitt, you are fantastic for simply being wonderful friends for so many years. Your unwavering kindness and willingness to see your friends through thick and thin is immeasurable.

*To EdenB and Wynde for being my MacKenzie's. Thank you so much for exercising great patience while I asked you a bazillion questions (((SMILE))). Oh, and Wyn, you rock for volunteering your husband to paint my motorcycle *wink*!*

To Mr. Austin, without you this book would not have been possible. At all.

And to my readers, especially the ones who catch me on social networking sites—you are all so supportive, funny and lively. This writing thing wouldn't be nearly as much of a blast without you. I am so grateful.

JUICY

*S*olie Shaw had been so deep in thought that the playful 'ding-da-ding-dong' of her phone startled her. She looked around her desk. It was covered with sticky notes of so many colors it was a fair representation of the rainbow. But where was her phone?

"Ah, there it is." It was partially hidden under the newest project plan she'd printed out. Her current tasks outnumbered her brain cells for sure. She had so much to do that there was no way she'd make all the deadlines. But she was totally grateful for the distraction of work given the recent drama that had engulfed her life.

Yes, she'd been tossed upside down by Hurricane Marcais —a wickedly handsome man who'd crashed into her world, burned it down around her, then rained so much *crazy* into the charred remains, she'd been totally swept out to sea and left to drown. The bastard.

Oh, yeah. Phone. She dug it from under the pile of papers and stared at the screen. Her head tilted a hard right as her gut did a freefall.

The caller id read *Marcais Dupree.*

"Damn. Speak of the devil."

The phone continued to play the special tune associated with his contact. All she could do was stare at the danged screen while commanding her stomach to stop running around underneath her skin.

Solie had learned from a friend that her now ex-dude had been trying to hook up with her, behind Solie's back. She'd been the third woman in a three-week span. So after calling him several times, Solie had left a very polite, though tear-filled voice message; ending what was left of their crumbling relationship. Part of her had hoped he would deny the other woman's claims. Again. Yet another part of her was glad to be done with it.

Marcais hadn't answered her very nice "fuck off" message, nor had he bothered to reply to the e-mail she'd sent a week later, wishing him well. She'd even included a special prayer written just for him. Even though she'd been nothing but an expendable replacement for his ex-wife, Solie had experienced a strange mix of pain and relief when he hadn't bothered to respond.

But all of that was weeks ago. It felt like an eon considering they'd lived together and seen each other every day for a year. He'd even talked of taking her with him overseas once he'd learned that the Army was reassigning him.

Finally the ringing stopped.

She took a deep breath and leaned over to scratch her shepherd, Mims, behind the ears. In that moment, Solie accepted a few things as fact.

First, if just seeing the man's name on the caller id could make her want to run and hide in a lockable closet, then she wasn't quite over the hell he'd brought into her life. A line from the famous movie, Tombstone, came to mind. Solie could even picture the snarl on Kurt Russell's face as he played a rather convincing Wyatt Earp. He'd promised a reckoning to a bad guy as he'd bellowed, "And hell's coming with me! You hear?!" Well, Marcais Dupree had been an expert at ushering in emotional infernos.

Second, sheer determination to process the hurt in a healthy manner burst forward and brought her 'mad' along with it. She refused to be defeated, emotionally or otherwise. A few seconds later her phone dinged again—a text message. From *him*. And the damn phone wouldn't let her delete it without opening it first.

She clicked on the message and braced herself.

"Say what?" she asked to her empty office. Solie looked up to the ceiling wondering if she'd just read what she thought she had. Looking at the phone again had her shaking her head. Nope, the message hadn't morphed into something that actually made sense. It simply read, "Thank you for your e-mail. Hope to talk to you soon."

Really? Why now? What did he *really* want from her?

Instead of replying to the text message, Solie decided to do a little investigating. Maybe he'd decided to behave after all? She had no interest whatsoever in getting back together with Marcais, but a part of her still hoped that he'd meant at least one word of all of those declarations of love and care.

"So he couldn't respond to me telling him that I didn't want to see him again because a third woman told me he was chasing her; but he responds to an e-mail with a prayer in it? And a week or two *after* I sent it? Go figure." The words were half-snarled-half-mumbled to herself as her fingertips flew over the keyboard.

She logged into her private Kinkfest profile and skipped over to his page. Perhaps there was something there that would give her a clue as to why he was contacting her now.

There. There it was. His profile.

Solie's hand flew to her mouth on a gasp.

"Oh. My. God. Why do I always have to look? Why?"

Good question, because now she couldn't *unsee* it either. It was the greatest mind fuck of all and she'd walked right into it. She felt like one of the hobbits from the Lord of the Rings. Yep, she was a nosy chick from The Shire who'd looked at something she had no business. Now she was getting smacked by a damn orc for being nosey.

"Son of a bitch," she breathed. Her chest was heavy, as if someone had hit her in the middle of the sternum with Thor's hammer. Her heart beat a mile a minute and adrenaline pumped furiously.

"Fight or flight, Solie. Fight or flight?"

Three times she started to respond to what she saw posted on *his* wall for the world to see. And three times she stopped herself. Instead, she read it again...and again.

"I want to feel everything. I want to see you squirm in anticipation of what I will do to you. I want tease you with my fingers and feel you get wet. I want to feel you grip me as I push in and pull out. I want to see your pretty pussy hold me. When I pull out it looks like it wants to come with me. I want to wrap you in the rope that I bought just for you, to restrict your movements and leave my hands free to massage and tease other parts of your body.

I want to push deep, then deeper so I can watch your eyes widen because no one has ever been to that spot before. I want you to wear the fuck-me pumps I gave you because I can grab the heels and manipulate your legs to open you up. I love to watch your eyes roll back in your head, to hear you take that deep gasp of air as you reach and stretch for things that are not there.

I want you to beg me to fuck you, want to hear the words because you say it just the way I like. I want to flip you over and take you from behind as I spank your perfect ass so I can see the slight redness of my hand print on your skin. I like that I can manhandle you and yet kiss you softly. I want to manipulate you anywhere at any time. I want to hear you scream as your toes curl when you come. I want to gently wipe your tears when you begin to cry from orgasm after orgasm.

And I can do all these things because you trust that I will never hurt you and that I have your best interests at heart. There is only you. I have no need of other toys. We are fluid-bonded and I wear you when we are done just as you wear me. Your scent is on me and mine is entwined with yours. Yes, I wear you. And you drip of me. I want to hold you afterward as you drift in a space that you have only found with me. I want to kiss you on your forehead, wrap my arms around you as I feed you chocolate while we lay on top of the sweat-soaked sheets. Because you are my submissive. And I love you."

She sat there for long moments with her hand over her mouth, eyes wide with disbelief. When emotions were finally a smidge under control, she slammed the laptop closed, stormed out of her office and down the hall. The leash was snatched off the hook near the front door as she headed to the truck with her dog on her heels.

The half-mile to the trails were a forgotten blur as she pulled into the parking area. The sky was as cloudy as her mood as she slipped the leash around her shepherd's thick neck and took off down the nearest path.

Then Solie did what she should have done the moment Marcais' text message had arrived—she hit the speed dial and called one of her very best friends.

Burton picked up on the second ring.

Oh thank God!

"Burton!"

"Solie? You okay?"

"Hell no I'm not okay! Oh my God, I just can't believe he did that. It's just so low and—"

"Whoa, whoa, whoa, what the hell happened?"

"I'm such an idiot, Burt. I just…I just can't believe I did it."

"Woman, what did you do?"

While Burton and Solie had never had a Dominant/submissive relationship—sexual or otherwise—there'd always been an undercurrent of tension in his presence that made her belly feel as if someone tugged on her insides. She still considered both him and Mac as her private play partners though they seldom ever played. Burton always took care of her...including punishing her if she needed it.

"He sent me a text message."

"He? You mean *that guy*? Solie tell me you didn't call him."

"I didn't, I swear. What I did was worse."

"Huh?"

"Instead of answering his call or responding to his text, I went and perved his Kinkfest profile. And he'd written a poem-like thing. Only it wasn't a poem. It was a story. About me."

"What?"

"You heard me. He started it off by saying, 'I want to...' but then everything after that was a recital of what happened between us in the bedroom."

"Are you shitting me?"

"No! I wish I was." Her eyes stung with tears, but she'd never get through the story if she started to cry now. After what Marcais had written she had every right to bawl her brains out, but that would have to come later. Right now, she had a confession to make. Solie picked up the pace, though she was practically running already.

"Look, Burt, he wrote a journal entry as if it was something that he wanted to happen between him and someone else. He didn't use my name of course—"

"Of course."

"But the facial expressions that he says he wants to see during this act of supposed love were *my* facial expressions. *My* body language. *My* words. He practically described the way I orgasm, the cheap bastard."

"Oh man. That sounds brutal."

"Yeah, but that's not the worst part. He put at the end of it that this person should know that he has her best interest at heart because, and I quote, 'You are my submissive and I love you.'"

Burt's low whistle filled the line. Yeah. She knew exactly what he was thinking.

"And the women he's been collecting like fucking baseball cards had filled his profile with all kinds of sappy shit. They were all like, 'oh, that's so sweet,' and 'oh I wish it were me' and 'oh she's so lucky' and all of this royal bullshit. I stood in my office and screamed."

"You mean kind of like you're screaming now?" Burton asked. And he was right. She was screaming at the top of her lungs. Hadn't even flinched when a terrified flock of birds burst into flight as she'd stormed past the tree they were roosting in. Must have scared them with her banshee impersonation. Even her dog looked at her as if she'd left her brains back at home in her office.

So much for control.

"Sorry," she mumbled.

"No worries. You have every right to yell to the rafters. He's basically taken something that was special and intimate between you two and turned it into bait for some other woman."

That pretty much summed it up.

"I wanted to call him up and tell him off. I wanted to send him a private message or reply to his text in all caps telling him what a mind-fuck it was, the bastard. I wanted to scream, 'Hey asshole, I did that. I gave that. I fucking earned that! But you never loved me. You just came home to me late at night while you spent your afternoons and evenings sticking your dick into anything with a hole!'"

She really was losing it now, but she just couldn't help it.

A guy riding past her on a bike must surely think she was crazy. Solie didn't give a rat's rear end. Not at all.

"Well you know you shouldn't have looked, right Solie?"

Aw man. Burt had turned on his Dom-ly voice, which meant she was actually in trouble. And if she'd been thinking clearly she would have seen this coming. Must be Solie-The-Idiot Day or something. First, she'd walked right into a mind fuck of epic proportions with her ex-dude, and now she'd told all her business to one of the few people that could actually make her sorry—one her best friends and protectors, Burton Khrys.

"Solie?"

"Yes, I know I shouldn't have looked but—"

"There's a *'but'* in there somewhere? Really, woman?"

She kept her mouth shut. Smartest thing she'd done all day.

"You're well aware that this man is a textbook sociopath, yes?"

Sigh.

"Solie, I asked you a question." The words were spoken quietly, but there was no way in hell she missed the steel behind them.

"Yes, I'm aware he's a sociopath," she grumbled.

"And I've shared my experiences with you about people who have this disorder, which lines up with your own research. It's to be expected for a sociopath to pull some kind of shenanigan or another, right?"

She should write a song called, "Yet another sigh." Bleh. Instead, she growled out a plain old, "Yes."

"I'm not even going to ask you what you were thinking, Solie, but I will say that I'm sure you know better."

Oh here we go.

"Are you still going to the vendor fair at the C.S.P. tomorrow?" he asked.

That was a no brainer. The vendor fair at the Community for Sex Positivity was a twice a year event that she and her other best friend, MacKenzie, didn't miss. Many of the vendors were different each time, so there was always something cool and unique to be had.

"Yep, I'm going to the fair. Mac promised my niece that we'd get some new toys for her play bag."

"Okay. So, when I see you tomorrow I'm going to spank your ass for doing what you know you shouldn't have, which was perv *that guy's* profile. Agreed?"

Damn. She could simply say no. Burton wouldn't do anything without her consent. But she was in the wrong. There were no two ways about it. Not only had she connected the sociopathic dots when her relationship with Marcais began to head south, but Burt had confirmed her suspicion because he'd had plenty of experience with people like her former dude.

To make matters worse, Solie had reached out to Marcais' ex-wife to learn exactly what she was dealing with. That woman, who'd turned out to be a fabulous person, had also told her to expect the man to do something to re-establish communication with her. And if he couldn't do that, he would pull a mind fuck.

So yep, Solie had known the moment she'd read his message that Marcais wouldn't have reached out to her for the hell of it. He had a purpose, always. For someone like him it wasn't about love. It was about winning. About control.

In the end, Solie had royally worked herself into a tizzy behind something that could have been avoided. All she'd had to do was exercise a little restraint and stop long enough to think about what she was doing. Basically, she could have simply ignored *he who should not be named*. But nooo-ho-ho-ho. She just had to go and be nosy. Just *had* to see what Marcais was pitching when she knew she shouldn't.

And now, she'd tattled on herself to Burton? Forehead, meet desk. Yeah. That.

"Solie? I asked if you agree to the punishment."

Ugh. Burt knew she was so *not* an exhibitionist, regardless of her love of kink. So public spanking equaled absolute punishment in her book. Hell, she totally had this coming.

"Yes. I agree."

"And I'll spank your ass every time you perv his Kinkfest profile. Agreed?"

"Fine," she snarled into the phone.

"In fact, I'm driving down to Seattle just for you, darlin."

"Yay. I feel so special." The words were dead pan. Burton's responding laughter lifted her mood a bit.

Then he said, "But you are special, Solie. Just because a pathological liar and a serial cheater didn't treat you right, doesn't mean you deserved it. Woman, you should be treated like the amazing catch that you are. You're a queen bee and you know it."

She smiled a bit brighter. But still...

"Well I don't feel like a damn queen. I feel like an idiot. An idiot for not seeing the red flags earlier. For not cutting him off earlier. For not totally ignoring him. Look where it got me."

"Solie, don't be ridiculous. Sociopaths and narcissists aren't stupid. They're very smooth, charming and look like the perfect guy or gal. Why? Because they are experts at manipulation. Didn't his ex say he cheated on her for almost eight years? And didn't she compliment you for cutting him off after barely one year? Can you imagine how hard it was for her to admit that?"

Still, it didn't make her feel any better. Her ego was beyond bruised. And now she was going to have a tender ass on top of that.

Just great.

WITH HER PHONE PLASTERED TO HER HEAD YET AGAIN, SOLIE peered out the window of her office. The soft summer breeze had blown out the earlier clouds to reveal a clear blue sky. It reflected off of the waters of the Puget Sound and reminded her of her favorite piece of sparkling, deep-blue, topaz jewelry.

She twirled lazily in her office chair. Joy was instantaneous when the number she'd dialed was answered on the third ring, and a voice that brought to mind her favorite jazz singer greeted her with an upbeat "hello".

"Hey Mac! I totally agreed to let Burton spank me. Publicly."

"What? You agreed to let that Sasquatch put his hands on you? On your bare ass? Girl, you're a brave one." MacKenzie Ivers burst into a deep laugh that had the sides of Solie's mouth pulling up into a smile. Mac was a female version of Burton—best friends until one of them kicked and left the world for good.

"Girlfriend, you know he's not going to hold back. And his line of work makes him awfully strong."

Solie just sat and shook her head at herself as Mac reminded her that because Burton built houses and supervised work crews, he was a very strong man. Sometimes he had to do the suit and tie bit; when he met with his architects and clients. Other days it was ripped jeans, hard hats, work boots and lots of fantastically defined muscle.

Mac had introduced her to kink and protected her fiercely to this day. Many people thought BDSM was all about sex. For Solie, it was all about trust.

As such, Solie had explored the lifestyle for a few years before ever playing with anyone. Instead of wading into the deep without knowing how to float, she'd taken the time to learn what she liked and didn't like; as well as accept the advice and guidance of her friends. This lifestyle was like anything else—with the good and the bad; ups and downs; sane people and nutballs.

She'd also discovered that although she was a bad ass in the boardroom, she didn't prefer to be one at home. Solie owned a business and had a knack for running things. On the flip side, there existed a submissive side that was greatly satisfied by serving and giving to others. The result was Solie's most cherished nickname given to her by MacKenzie —the "fantabulous alpha bitch submissive of the universe".

When she'd finally been ready to actually jump into physical play, Mac, her very best girlfriend, had been the first to give her a flogger tasting. It had been the most fabulous birthday present ever. For days, Solie had preened in front of her mirror and grinned over the pretty marks left on her skin.

But right now her brow pulled down into a frown at the rest of the memory—that night at the Twilight Teahouse had been Solie's first time playing in public. Ever. And Marcais hadn't been there. He'd forgotten her birthday completely and then claimed he'd thought it was a day later.

But he hadn't shown up the next day.

Or the day after that.

Turned out that one of his other women had a birthday the day after Solie's, and he'd spent the weekend with that chick instead. So sure, he'd forgotten Solie's birthday because his mind had been elsewhere. Literally.

Mac and Burton had seen her through the good and the bad, which included the long list of Marcais' betrayals. They'd held their tongues each time Solie forgave the man, and gave advice only when asked for it. Her buds had listened to all the rants, and dried all the tears.

"Stop thinking about him, Solie." Mac's tone snapped her

out of her musings. "I can tell by your silence after my sasquatch crack that you're thinking about *that guy*."

Mac wouldn't even speak Marcais' name, as if it would taint her soul or something. Actually, Mac described him as the shit on the heel of the antichrist, so maybe she did think his asshole-ish-ness was contagious.

"I can't help it, Mac. You know the human psyche doesn't work that way. I can't just turn it off as if it never happened. Besides, it's only been a few weeks since we broke up for good."

"Yes, I know. I just hate that you're in pain and there is nothing I can do about it. I know you have to process it, feel it. But damn it, Solie, I just fucking hate it."

A few moments of silence passed.

"Mac, I appreciate it. You know I love you, right girl?"

"And I love you right back. Damn it, I've gotta go, Sols. My two-thirty appointment is here."

"No worries. Go ahead and work your magic, oh architect extraordinaire," Solie said. The woman was indeed one of the premier and sought-after architects in the Pacific Northwest. "One day I'm going to hire you to design my dream house."

"Hire me? Do you want to add a second spanking to your punishment, you crazy woman? You won't ever hire me. Whatever you need or want is yours. You know that. Now I'm going to ask you to do something that my therapist once suggested to me as I was going through my divorce."

Mac and her husband, Landon, had hit what seemed like an endless rough patch in their ten year marriage. Mac had wanted counseling but Landon voiced loudly and often that he didn't need any help because it was all Mac's fault—it didn't matter what *it* was. Mac had lifted her head, refused to be stomped on, and filed for a divorce that she'd bounced back from like a champ. In fact she'd processed that madness so completely that her husband, Landon, couldn't help but notice. He followed Mac's example, came to his senses and sought some good therapy. In the end, he'd come crawling back to Mac on hands and knees. Literally. Now, to everyone's grand relief, they were the happiest couple Solie knew.

"I want you to write down how you feel, Sols. No holds barred, no editing or altering. Just write it down. All of it. You're heartbroken and I understand better than anyone. You know that." Yes, she did know. Not too long ago, Mac had been through her own journey through the Seventh level's East Side of Hell. "And I know I told you to stop thinking about him, but that was a knee-jerk reaction. I'm sorry for that. Forgive me?"

"Of course, woman. So, what do you want me to do? Just write about my feelings?"

"Yes, but rather than dwell on all the ways this guy screwed you, concentrate on what you actually feel. So no 'he did this or that'. Instead make it, 'I, Solie, feel…', then fill in the blanks. Make sense?"

"Yep."

"And you don't have to share it, Solie. You're allowed to keep your own counsel and play this as close to the vest as you want. This is your thing. Yours. You own it; do it the way you see fit as long as you stay on this side of functional. No dysfunctional bullshit. Agreed?"

"Agreed."

"Okay, I gotta run. Catch you later?"

"I know we're going to the fair together, but will you stick around for…you know?"

"Do you honestly think I'd miss the chance to watch Burton paddle your ass?"

"No paddle. Just bare hand."

"Not the point. The question was, do you think I'd miss that? Hell no!" Mac laughed, full and honestly. "Wouldn't miss it for the world because you know your goofy ass deserves it."

Did her friends have to be right all the damn time? Solie shook her head at herself, said her goodbyes and turned her attention back to work. And every time her brain tried to skip off to "dwell-on-Marcais-land" Solie deliberately squashed those thoughts. Instead, she concentrated on the anomalies between the databases in front of her. Reverse engineering someone else's work was a pain in the ass, but it was necessary if she was going to figure out why the script she'd written to move data from one system to another wasn't working.

Normally it would be annoying as hell to find such huge differences between systems, but right now it was a hell of a welcome distraction. When eyeballs began to cross and hands trembled a bit, Solie looked down at her now-buzzing phone. Earlier during a brief moment of common sense—she seemed to be sorely lacking in that particular area lately— she'd set her alarm for seven o'clock this evening to keep herself from over doing it on her day.

She hadn't actually eaten since she'd gotten back from walking the dog and screaming at Burton at lunchtime. No wonder her stomach felt like an empty, wind-swept cavern.

"Well, at least I remembered to drink water," she grumbled at herself.

Thankfully, Mac knew her so well she'd swung by a couple of hours ago on her way to Twilight Teahouse. The woman had run in, waved as she passed Solie's office, said something about plugging in a crockpot and then run out again.

Solie had peeked out of her window and caught a glimpse of Mac's outfit as she jumped back into her car—black knee high boots with buckles up the side, a burgundy leather corset with matching bolero jacket over a sleek black cat suit.

My goodness, it was a combination of Selene the Under-world Death-dealer and a sexy, flogger-toting Hollywood starlet. Mac had pulled out of the driveway and was gone as quickly as she'd arrived.

After a quick pit-stop to the bathroom for a wash-up, Solie found that crockpot on her kitchen counter and happily dished up a big bowl of steak chili. This time, when she returned to her office, it was for some self-healing rather than work.

She'd suppressed her thoughts all day. Now she followed Mac's advice and wrote it down. She called her journal entry, Heartbreak and Monkey Balls.

Heartbreak and Monkey Balls

HEARTBREAK SUCKS HAIRY MONKEY BALLS AND MAKES THIS GIRL wish that people came with warning labels, including myself. But you know what else heartbreak does?

It makes you want to crawl into your hole and never come out again, though you know you have too much shit to do to hide yourself away.

Makes you scream, "Big girls don't cry!" while you blow through a box of tissues and a pint of Ben and Jerry's.

Makes you want to scream, "I hate you!" while your heart bleeds and cries, "I love you."

Makes you wonder what you did to deserve this, when you already know the answer is 'nothing'.

Makes you wonder why you aren't good enough. Even while others tell you how awesome you are, in your mind you're thinking, "Yeah, sure - I'm so awesome that I wasn't worth keeping or fighting for."

Makes you want to shank him in the face, yet have the gauze, cloth tape and peroxide ready to sooth him.

Makes you want to put up a "Fuck You and Your Mama!" sign, though you know you were put here to serve and upgrade your partner, family and community.

Makes you wonder why he would stray and end up with nothing, when you'd already given heart, home, money, love, body, mind...everything.

Makes you want to close the door, even while you know you must keep the door open to allow your blessings to come through.

Makes you feel like a used piece of tissue, tossed away for a new piece of temporary ass, even though you know you are spun silk, gold and frankincense. Priceless.

Makes you want to become the ultimate dysfunctional bitch persona with a closed heart, even when you know you're not capable of doing so.

Makes you want to hold and nurse a grudge...when in truth, you've already forgiven.

Makes you want to run for the hills while you long for second chances.

Makes you want to know why, yet makes you NEVER want to know.

Makes you want to yell and scream...but you can't move past the hurt to get to the anger that would allow you to do so.

Makes you wish you were a crazy vindictive bitch, though you just don't have it in you.

Makes you want to punch people in the face who say, "Don't worry, you'll find someone better" when what you wanted...was him.

Makes you want him to admit that he doesn't care about you, even while you never want him to ever admit such a thing.

Makes your stomach tie in knots knowing he'll simply go on to the next one, while you still hope he truly finds happiness.

Makes you feel sorry for yourself because you are alone yet again, and sorry for him because there is no one else in the world like you...and he has lost you forever and has no idea why.

―――――――

YEP, THAT SUMMED IT UP PRETTY WELL.

And Mac had been right. When Solie pressed the save button, closed her journal and turned off her computer, she felt just a tad bit better.

2

*S*aturday rolled around much too quickly.

Mac swung by, picked Solie up and they headed into the city. As they rode, Mac chatted about this, that and the other. Solie appreciated that Mac just let her sit there quietly and ride along to the upbeat music she had pumping through her speakers. There was no need to point out her case of nerves. The fact that Solie was so quiet was a minor miracle in itself.

Mac had even pulled off the freeway and queued into a drive-through, yet Solie hadn't noticed until a hot cup was pressed into her hand followed by a half-dozen nom-noms in a warm open bag.

"Salted caramel Krispy Kreme's? Oooh, yummily. Woman, you are a goddess."

"Yes, I am," Mac said. "And I have ice in a cooler in the backseat in case your ass needs it after your Burton spanking," Mac joked. "Oh, and I have some paddled-butt-be-gone cream, too."

Solie laughed at that one, took another bite of delicious

sugar-coma-in-a-bag and chased it down with piping hot coffee.

"No butt-be-gone for you?" Mac asked. "How about some anti-sasquatch-big-scary-paddle-hand spray?"

Solie choked on her coffee.

The levity helped, but she was still nervous. Was it because she'd be getting a public spanking or because Burton was the one giving it? She totally trusted the man. Had for years. He was ridiculously handsome and something about him had always drawn her although they'd never been intimate in more than a "bestie" kind of way.

Now, with the culmination of all the recent theatre in her life, she stopped to take inventory of her emotions. And with Burton, there was no doubt of a spark of…something. Often she thought on the sound of his voice as he spoke, his quiet but compelling manner. And the impact of his Caribbean Sea-colored gaze when all his attention was on her.

He was an alpha, through and through. Dominant. All the time. It was his nature. Not one of the dark and broody types, yet it still wasn't something he had to tell or declare to anyone. It was just who he was.

And now she had something else to consider—Burton's hands on her skin, caressing her flesh to deliver a mix of what she needed, wanted and feared.

At six-feet even, Burton was perfectly proportioned, a bit on the stocky side and *more* than a bit on the handsome side. In fact, the man was all kinds of pretty, in a Marine "hoorah" kind of way. Known for his skill with floggers, paddles, dragon tail whips and even Hojōjutsu rope technique, Burton Khrys was in demand. His ability to read the needs of his partner, whether they were male or female, was downright uncanny. He could have damn near any woman he wanted in their local kink community. In fact, he'd been constantly sought after since he'd removed his collar from his last submissive.

But Burt was picky. He believed in wholeheartedly and thoroughly caring for those he considered his. He put a lot of time and energy into his relationships, whether they were of a sexual nature or not. As such, he was very selective about who he gave all that energy to. He didn't believe in casual anything. With Solie, Mac and very few others, Burton cared in action, not just word.

He really was the complete package.

Parked right across the street from the Community for Sex Positivity building, Solie took a deep breath and climbed out of Mac's car. Maybe she was twitchy because it was a punishment scene? Nah. It wasn't as if she'd never been in trouble before with her own Dominant. Well, former Dominant.

So, what was this gut-with-butterflies-in-flight thing going on here?

Passing the tables of vendors, a set of sterling silver claws caught her eye.

"Oooh, Mac, look at those. Tooty would love the ones with the red powder finish," Solie said quietly.

"Speaking of Tooty, where is your niece anyway? I'm surprised she isn't here to witness this ass paddling?"

"She wanted to be here. I still can't believe I told her about it considering she thinks I should have snagged Burton years ago. She can't believe we're still just friends."

As they stood admiring the wares on the table, a couple of guys she'd seen at Twilight Teahouse walked past. She couldn't remember their names, but they were always together and dressed in head-to-toe black leather with spikes and crap everywhere. She almost laughed when one of them looked at her, then whispered to the other, "Hey, isn't that the bossy control freak chick that makes Doms quake in their boots? I heard she was a scary bitch."

Mac pinned them with a glare. They glared right back but kept on moving.

Well, Solie could be a lot to handle. She readily admitted that. But those who knew her well understood where she was coming from. She was the chick who got shit done. The end. It was a valuable trait in a submissive who was born to be more than a damn doormat.

Mac picked up a paddle. The handle was beaten metal with leather wrapped around it. She handed it to Solie. This time, she did laugh at the words "feisty bitch" carved into the wood.

"This is awesome, Sols. Maybe the claws and this paddle? I know the people who operate that particular armory. All their stuff is handmade. They have their own forges and everything. Ever want a tour of the place, let me know. Oh! There's our guy."

Solie gazed toward the other end of the large banquet style space to where Mac was looking. Burton stood there, leaning casually with one shoulder against a wall watching her. The moment their eyes met, he began moving toward them. Breath stuck in her throat at the huge, genuinely brilliant smile he sported as he took her in. It totally undid her.

"Nice outfit."

She looked down her body at the tasteful, but short, little red dress she'd sported today. The top was hand embroidered with swirls and little flowers done in a darker hue than the dress itself. Mid-thigh, the cut was tasteful yet sassy. Matching red strappy sandals completed the ensemble.

"Thank you." She gave him a hug, as was their habit. The moment he'd touched her, the jangling nerves quieted. Huh. She'd have to give that some thought...after. The typical warmth and safety of being in Burt's arms remained even after he'd gone on to hug Mac.

"See anything interesting today?" he asked. "How's your bag full before you've even seen the whole place?" he asked, then took a swig from a tall paper cup. The faint scent of coffee and caramel declared his favorite poison—caramel macchiato with double whipped cream.

"I saw a cool set of surgical steel fingertip claws for my niece—"

"Yeah, and that's probably the only thing she didn't buy yet," Mac teased.

"Oh hush. Anyway, I got a unique pair of cuffs, too. I've never seen leather cuffs in that particular shade before. And they were so pretty next to some red bamboo rope I'm determined to try out."

"Rope? You want to be a rigger?" Burt asked.

"Nah, but I wouldn't mind being a rope bunny. I figure if I have my own rope it'll be good energy to attract someone who isn't crazy but is good with rope just the same."

"Hmm." And that was all Burton said. If his eyes were any indication, he wasn't all that excited about the idea. Interesting.

The three of them made their way past a number of booths, chatting as they went. At this moment, this seemed like any other time they'd hung out together—the three of them making small talk, cracking jokes and making plans for the following weekend.

Finally they made it into the building's main play room; which was large and open, with lots of stations throughout. There were winches for rope suspension, tables for everything from massage to fire cupping. For the edge players, there were spots for impact play, padded X's called Saint Andrews Crosses, as well as a crap-ton of spanking benches, which reminded Solie of little padded picnic tables. For a moment, she imagined a polka dot table cloth spread over one of them with her laid out on top as she waited to be served as a main course...to Burton.

Shaking her head to clear it of the unsettling thought, Solie looked around, just as she did every time she came to this particular event.

The place was nothing like the Twilight Teahouse, but it wasn't expected to be. The C.S.P. was one of the Seattle area's best known kinky spots. It was located, of all places, partially under an old freeway. The space was comfy in a 'worn old pair of slippers' kind of way, while the Twilight was more like kitten heels.

"Are you ready, Solie?" Burt asked.

What the hell kind of question was that? Of course she wasn't ready. This man, her very best friend and confidante, had big, thuddy, paddle hands. A woman would have to be nuts if she weren't at least a little apprehensive about having those hands on her bare ass.

She'd watched him play at the local dungeons and the man was an expert at giving a spanking, for both punishment and pleasure. Was she afraid he'd hurt her? Not in the least—she totally trusted Burt. But she also knew that she'd been in the wrong. So, no, she was nowhere near ready. But a deal was a deal.

With a huff and a sigh, she said, "Okay, let's do this."

And in a flash, Burt moved.

"Get up on the fucking bench, Solie."

Solie straddled the spanking bench and allowed Burt to push and pull her into the position he wanted her using her hair as a modern day steering wheel. In this moment he was the epitome of a gentleman who wasn't a gentle man.

"Now, you know why you're getting a spanking don't you, Solie?"

The words were a forceful growl against her ear, spoken

just loud enough for her to hear, but not anyone in the now-gathering crowd. This is what she got for agreeing to get a spanking at the local vendor fair. Nothing like a bit of public humiliation. Bleh.

"Yes. I looked when I shouldn't have."

"Do you agree that he's playing you? Be honest, as always."

"Yes."

"And?"

"And I walked right into it."

"Are you going to do it again?"

"No."

"Why not?"

"Because he doesn't deserve my attention and I don't want my ass set on fire again."

"Good girl. Here we go." He eased her dress up just past her hips so her butt was exposed, but the front of her thighs were covered. Burt burst out laughing once he got a good look at the bulls-eye pattern on her barely-there underwear.

"Wait. Can I have a safe word after you're done laughing?"

"No. This is a punishment. There is no safe word, no warm up and no negotiation. Understand."

Yes, she did. When she'd been particularly bratty with *he who shall not be named,* she'd consented to the same rules. But she was grateful that Burton has asked anyway because in this particular game, one never assumed. Safety was always first.

This was new territory for their friendship. Burton had offered to become her protector the moment he learned how Marcais had been trolling around. But in all the years she'd known him, they'd only ever done some light play together, and never anything sexual.

"Do you consent, Solie?"

"Yes."

"Good. Four on each cheek, okay?"

She nodded and the second her head stopped moving the first blow landed. Solie grunted under the impact. Holy shit, the man spanked hard. And then the second smack landed. Then the third and fourth.

He stopped, leaned down and asked her. "All right?"

She nodded.

Skin warmed quickly as the blood underneath rushed to the areas of impact. On the other cheek, the next smack landed, and with it came a particular sting that reminded her of a flogger more than a bare hand.

When Burton was done, he spoke quietly into her ear again.

"Do you need another one?"

Yes she did. Really, really needed this. Needed the impact to release the tears that welled up in her chest. But they weren't tears of physical pain. They were tears of anguish from the emotional shredding she'd endured at Marcais' hands, both in and after their relationship. Tears of healing. Even tears of joy that it was over and she'd survived.

"Yes, please," she whispered.

After a few more smacks, Burton gently pulled down her dress and helped her up off the spanking bench.

"You did good, Sol," Mac said.

She threw her arms around Burt's waist, buried her head against his chest and sobbed her heart out.

"That's it," Burt said. "Let it out. Release it. Holding it inside isn't good for you."

After a few moments, he asked, "So, tell me why you're crying."

Her words were muffled against the damp fabric of his shirt. "I feel like such an idiot. I can't believe I was so stupid. I fell for a charmer who could give two shits about me, and then I go and look to see what he's up to and he's busy writing about me to impress someone else. Several someone else's. And he didn't love me, Burt!" She sobbed. "He said that the person in the writing was his sub and he loved her. But he didn't love me. Before he moved out he said he loved me, but he didn't." She knew she was practically screeching but now that the dam had burst, she couldn't plug it up again.

"He didn't love me, Burt. He didn't. He didn't! God, he was so mean to me. He yelled and screamed at me when all I did was give and give and give. He treated me like shit. And he cheated with the very types of women he swore he didn't want. Were they so much better than me? Did they have something that I didn't? Why? Why would he do that to me?"

And she cried until she was exhausted and in need a German chocolate cake. And perhaps a new pair of shoes.

And after she got herself together, Solie's two best friends took her to go get both.

SOLIE TOOK THE LEASH OFF HER SHEPHERD AND THE BOTH OF them hopped back into the SUV and were home in less than five minutes. "This is becoming a habit, Burton. Don't get me wrong, I'm enjoying the summer sun and trail walking, but the circumstances suck ass."

"Well, I'm not happy that you're still in contact with him, Solie."

She stomped to a halt just inside her front door. Wait. Had she left it unlocked? Must have. Whatever. She was too pissed to care right now.

"No. Just no. I am not going to let you accuse me of something I did not do. I am *not* in communication with him, damn it. I reached out to this latest chick in hopes that she'd seen some of my jewelry. Actually, it's my niece Tooty's jewelry. It's all Native American beadwork. Handmade stuff that can't be replaced. We've been collecting it for twenty years."

"Why do you think he took it?"

"Other than the fact that it was in the same garage as his stuff, and it disappeared when he moved out? Or maybe the fact that he's a pathological liar and a thief? He thinks I don't know that he once gave his ex-wife some jewelry that belonged to someone else. Or that I don't know that the motorcycle jacket he gave me, you know, the one that he tried to take with him when he moved out, actually belonged to his ex-wife. It's her fucking coat. And he gave it to me as if he'd bought it for me. There's so much he thinks I don't know. In fact, I know enough to write a fucking horror novel. He'd have a mutated cow if he knew that because of his foolishness, his ex-wife and I—"

"What's her name again?"

"His ex-wife? Her name's Whitney. And she and I have become fast friends. In fact, she's as cool as I don't know what."

"Okay, then who's this latest girl on Kinkfest?" Burt asked.

"Her name is Karen. I sent her a note because she was a friend of a friend of a friend. I swear I didn't know she was literally fucking Marcais. After I found out, I sent her another note telling her that I was his ex because I didn't want her to feel as if I'd been trying to play her."

"That's fair. Thoughtful, actually," Burt said.

"Well I agree, or I did agree until she told me that she thought I looked familiar. She'd seen pictures of me on Marcais' Facebook page."

"Excuse me?"

"Yeah, that's what I thought. Whitney told me that he was probably still on Facebook doing dirty, but was hiding it from me, but I didn't want to believe it in spite of all the other crap I knew he'd done. Marcais swore from the moment we got together that Facebook was off limits for him. So why would he let this Karen chick be friends with him there, but hide it from me?"

"Let me guess, because he had a bunch of other chicks on there, too, right?"

"Right." More than right. In fact, Karen had told her that she'd been seeing Marcais for quite a while and how wonderful he was and how sad she was about the fact that the military was sending him overseas and how she'd miss him and blah, blah, blah.

"Damn it, Burt, I swear it seems every time I think I'm progressing, healing and moving on, I get some new piece of information that keeps this man as front and center in my life. He's like a wet booger…just stuck on me and I can't wipe him off! Why can't it be over already?"

To hear Karen talk of how they'd fallen so deeply for each other while he'd been living in Solie's house had cut her anew. Never mind the fact that they were supposed to be a monogamous couple. It made the acid churn in her stomach to know that a woman Marcais was cheating with had fallen in love with his monkey ass. Just like Solie had fallen in love with him.

"You know what's going to happen, Sol. Marcais is going to drop this Karen girl like a hot rock as soon as he finds out the two of you had a conversation. Why? Because she was supposed to be a secret. The only one who didn't know it was her. If he doesn't dump her now, he'll dump her as soon as the next one is in place. That's the MO. It's what sociopaths do."

"Doesn't make me feel any better, Burton."

"Just remember that to a man, pussy is very different from love. She was just a lay."

Solie knew Burton was right and she almost felt sorry for Karen. Almost.

But her compassion for the other woman was damn near on empty because Karen admitted that she'd *known* Marcais was in a relationship with someone else…with Solie. But she hadn't given a rat's ass. Instead, she'd spent time with Marcais anyway. Slept with him anyway. Got hooked on him anyway. Took pictures of her having sex with him anyway.

"Mac bring you lunch today, Sols?"

"Yep. It's homemade clam chowder." She spooned up a big bowl while talking to Burton. Now, sat down at her desk, took a bite and moaned in appreciation. Fog had rolled in and it had gone from sunny to chilly. The thick creamy soup, made hearty with a ton of seafood, potatoes, savory spices and herbs, warmed her tummy.

"Good to hear you're not skipping meals. It's a bad habit and it's something you do way too often."

"I'm working on it, Burt. Seriously."

"Work harder. I'd hate to have to dole out more punishment."

She giggled when he said, "Then again, you have such a perfect ass I may have to make up something to get you in trouble just to get my hands on you again."

Burton. Was. Flirting!

And she had no idea what to do with it, other than acknowledge the wiggle in her tummy that signaled an impending bout of giddiness.

Then she remembered what they'd been talking about.

"You know what, Burt? I wonder if Karen knows that Marcais posted pics of them on the internet having unprotected anal sex."

She closed her eyes and shook her head trying to dislodge the image—Marcais' thick cock disappearing into Karen's willing body. The woman had held herself open for him, little pools of sweat gathered at the base of her spine. Her own fingers dug into her flesh. One of her fake fingernails had been broken, while the others were coated with glittery-blue polish. Marcais' cock had been slick with her juices. And no condom.

It was forever branded into Solie's brain.

A brain she wished she could just pluck from her head, sit down somewhere else and let it cool off for a while. Because in addition to the hurt, Solie was mad as hell.

Her dude—correction, *former* dude—had had unprotected sex with another woman, taken a picture of it, and was stupid enough to post it online. And yes, the date on the photo was *before* Solie had broken it off for good.

"It doesn't matter, Sols. As soon as he finds out that Karen spoke to you, she's history."

The next day, Burton was proven right.

After her typical early-morning wake-up ritual of show-ering, throwing on whatever she felt like, then practically dunking her head in a pot of coffee, Solie walked into her office. Karen's note was the first one in her email inbox. The woman had sent her a message telling her that Marcais was angry because the two women had spoken with one another. He was livid that Karen had told Solie the truth. And after he'd told the woman off as if she were some two-bit crack whore, he'd blocked her on Kinkfest and all the other social media sites.

Poor thing. Solie almost felt bad.

Until her phone rang just before lunch.

It was her doctor.

Marcais was the gift that just kept on giving...which unfortunately included a sexually transmitted disease.

An angry and hurt Solie transformed into a nuclear-hot Solie. The doctor had to report her condition to the state and the state would report it to the Center for Disease Control.

After firing off a note to inform Marcais that he'd infected her, Solie headed to the pharmacy. One hour and a massive dose of antibiotics later, Solie pondered an issue that had been tapping at her brain since the doctor had called earlier.

She knew that Marcais was *not* going to return her calls or her texts. How could she make sure he got tested and treated? There had to be a way to keep him from pretending that none of this was happening.

Mind made up she made a few calls to some friends who happened to be stationed at the same Army base as him. Shortly after, Solie was voice-to-voice with Marcais' First Sergeant. And she didn't hesitate to lay out all the dirt, down to the last detail.

Thankfully, the sergeant was willing to help Solie out. The man wasn't happy that one of his soldiers was smack dab in the middle of such foolishness, had passed her cooties and played her dirty. Not to mention that particular soldier was soon headed out of the country to get away with it all.

But not anymore. He was going to have to face the music now that his command was aware of what he'd been up to.

Yep. Karma was one saucy bitch...and today she was Solie's best friend.

Sitting in her office like a zombie, Solie stared at a blank computer screen with the events of the day playing over in her mind like a bad B-movie. She picked up the phone and called Mac, who was quickly angry on her behalf.

And though she felt a bit better after Mac threatened to slip a castration pill into Marcais' food somehow, it didn't make the tight knot in the middle of her chest go away.

She needed something, someone else.

An hour later her doorbell rang.

She opened the door and her mouth dropped wide open.

It was Burton, who promptly informed her that dinner was on its way before shooing her into the living room.

Mac came in right behind him with her arms full of said dinner. She pecked Solie on the cheek and disappeared into the kitchen

Solie's eyes were instantly filled with tears. "You guys are too much."

"We care about you, woman. Now sit." Burton pointed to the couch and gave her the I-dare-you-to-argue look.

Burton turned on a movie that they'd all seen a million times so they could talk if they wanted to. Fifteen minutes later, Mac shoved a plate into her hands. The last thing she wanted was food, but she didn't fuss. Besides, she just didn't have the bandwidth for a fight. At all.

With dinner done and some blow-'em-up action movie exploding in the background Solie broke down and the tears poured out of her.

Pulled into Burt's lap, Solie found herself wrapped in strong arms as he whispered his care and concern into her ear.

The anger melted away, leaving a pool of bubbling pain in its place. And for the second time in as many days, Solie bawled her eyes out and soaked the front of Burton's shirt.

God, she was so damn tired of crying over someone who wasn't worthy to sniff her farts. Someone who was currently pretending as if she'd never existed. Someone who was a total douche canoe.

This was it. The last time she would give the memory of Sir Hell the power to level her. As of now, she was done.

Would she hurt awhile longer? Probably so. Denial would get her nowhere. But would she allow all her thoughts and emotions to be focused on the searing pain of betrayal? Hell no.

So Solie let it out and cried until she had no tears left. Cried until she was so worn out she fell asleep in Burt's lap. The last thing she remembered was hearing Mac say that

Landon had come to pick her up. She'd sweetly pecked Solie on the cheek as Burton tucked her into bed.

And Solie passed into a world of dreams filled with darkness, lava and fire with *he who should not be named* at the receiving end of a red hot poker up the ass.

Ah, justice.

3

*T*he bedroom was always chilly this early in the morning. Today, Solie didn't feel any of it. Soothing energy rolled off of the man next to her—a man who'd tucked her in last night and stayed with her to make sure she was okay.

And Burton's presence warmed her from the inside out while his solid body warmed her from the outside in.

Yep, best of both worlds.

Solie ducked her head under the covers, mashed her face into his chest and wrapped her arms around him.

She took a deep breath. Fabric softener from her blankets and the natural masculine scent of her best friend filled her until she was drunk-n-drowsy. This wasn't the first time one of her friends had slept over, however this particular buddy had never slept in her bed. Especially not with her in it.

As she snuggled closer, the first thought that came to her muzzy mind was…safety. Not in a physical sense, though surely Burt could take care of her in that way, but this was more of an inner peace. A "my head and heart are safe with this guy" kind of thing. It was a knowing that unfurled in her belly. Rang in her head. Filled her up.

And the second thought? Well, that was easy—*damn he's hawt!*

"Solie? Wake up, honey."

Solie stretched with a half-smile-half-frown. "No wanna wake up. Comfy."

Burton's arms loosened as if he were about to get up. It was obvious he didn't really want to when his hold tightened again.

And the thought that he wanted to stay exactly where he was made Solie feel all manner of gooey inside—something she'd never quite experienced with *that other guy*. She wondered why considering that she'd loved Marcais. Truly loved him. But there was a piece of herself that she hadn't truly given over. Perhaps she'd known all along that he was playing her while a part of her soul hoped she'd been wrong.

"THIS IS INTERESTING," BURT WHISPERED AGAINST HER HAIR before dropping a gentle kiss on the top of her bed-head. "We've been friends for years and now, I—"

Solie stiffened, unsure of whether to eagerly anticipate what he was going to say, or prepare to flee. Burt stopped mid-sentence, took in a deep unsteady breath and blew it out. Arms tightened more around her body, then he let go and got out of bed.

Solie sat up, pulled the cover to her chin and pulled her knees up to her chest. Suddenly she felt so...cute.

"Why the blush, Sols?"

She didn't answer. Instead she simply shrugged and kept her mouth shut. This *kawaii* thing wasn't something typical. After all, she was a bitch on wheels every day, all day long as she ran her company. Sexy? Sure. Kick ass? Yep. Cute? Not so much. But there was no disputing that Burton just seemed to bring it out of her. Or maybe it was the Hello Kitty shorts-and-tank top pajamas she wore. A set given to her by the very man peering down at her from beside the bed.

God, something about Burt rang her bell. And right now, she didn't really care what it was or why. In spite of the emotional roller-coaster she'd been on, there was one truth she didn't bother to dispute—she trusted this man. Completely.

He'd been her friend through all her ridiculous bullshit even while in the midst of his own heartbreak. While Mac was going through her on-again-off-again divorce with her husband, Landon, Burt was there. He was the genuine article when it came to loyalty minus naiveté or games.

And here he stood in her bedroom looking all kinds of yummy in a pair of tented—whoa, wait, *tented!*—boxers and a fabulously formed bare chest sprinkled with fine black down that arrowed to a very, very happy trail.

Oh my God, definitely tented boxers.

Burton's hair was a mop of jet black waves, cut short on the sides and a little longer on top. She almost smiled at the way it stuck up all over his head, glossy and inviting to her fingertips. Eyes so clear and crystalline blue they brought to mind one of those deep pools at the top of a glacial mountain under a clear sky.

Had she noticed how gorgeous he was before? Sure. But she'd never allowed herself to dwell. He'd belonged to someone else...and so had she.

But now she looked her fill after having spent the night being consoled in his arms. And Burton Khrys was just...wow.

And did she mention the tented boxers? The package beneath the fabric seemed long, thick and inviting. And it was all for her? Then again, maybe he always had some serious morning wood and it had nothing to do with her at all?

"Stay there. I'll be right back," he said.

A certain something about Burton—a something she'd been able to ignore before—seemed so close to the skin that it was almost tangible. And when he left the room, it left with him. And just that quickly, she missed it. Him. Whatever.

Six minutes later—but who was counting right?—Burton walked back into the bedroom and brought the scent of toothpaste and that certain *whoosh* of masculine energy with him.

He motioned with his head and said, "Scoot."

She immediately moved over and he set a tray down in front of her. Burt snatched some tissues out of the box next to the bed, pressed them into her fingers, and then put his attention back on the tray.

Solie looked down at her hand and back up at Burton.

"You're going to need it, Sol."

She was going to need tissue? This couldn't possibly be good.

Before she could ask why, he picked up her favorite porcelain mug and a small glass of half and half off the breakfast tray. A splash of cream soon joined what smelled like Italian roast coffee.

He handed the hot mug to her and said, "No sugar for you. Do you need to test your blood sugar first?" Yep—a gentleman who, beneath the skin, was not a gentle man. And she loved the contrast. Always had.

Solie tried not to compare him to her former dude but it was impossible. Why? Because Marcais knew she was diabetic but had never once asked if she needed to check her blood sugar or anything else, for that matter. Instead, he'd bring her all manner of sugary crap as gifts, then get mad at her when she couldn't eat it.

Okay, squash that. Back to the present.

"No, I'm fine. My doctor told me that a lot of times my fasting blood sugar doesn't really measure how well I'm doing. It's what happens after I eat that tells her whether my body is doing what it should or not."

While she made small talk, Burt was busy grabbing a little brown bottle off the nightstand, retrieved a single tablet and pressed it into her palm.

"Thank you," she said as she popped the medicine into her mouth and chased it down with a gulp of coffee bean heaven. She moaned as she swallowed and then peeked over the rim of her mug at her friend. As she sipped, Solie almost smiled into the brew at Burt's lopsided, but totally smug, grin.

He was racking up brownie points. And he knew it.

Cheeky bastard.

With the tray moved over to the dresser, Burton sat down right in front of her and looked her square in the eye. Her cup paused halfway to her mouth.

"Listen, Solie. I know when you look at me you see someone who's been active in the BDSM community for years, someone who enjoys impact play and being a basic mean old man…"

Old? He was one year older than her? She raised an inquisitive brow, but didn't interrupt.

"I also know that you know me better than anyone else. And I have a proposition for you, none the less."

A prop-a-what? Was he serious?

She braced herself. Hard. But not out of fear like with Marc…

No. Nope. Keep it here, Solie.

And she would remind herself a million times a day if that's what it took to move on toward healing.

"I know you're on the rebound. But if I can take your pain, any of it, Solie, I want to do that for you. You could use the release, the catharsis."

Well he was right on that particular point, but there was more to this than Burt's desire to help her relieve the big ball of emotional tension she'd been carrying around. So she sipped her coffee and waited for the other shoe to drop. And God, she hoped that particular shoe was her size—nine medium, thank you very much.

"I've always been honest with you, Sols. It's been a long time since we discussed any feelings for each other, and understandably so. We've both been in relationships with others for years. I'm grateful because it allowed us to be good friends with no physical baggage between us. Still, you know I've found you attractive in every way, for a very long time. My timing is shitty, I'm sure, but it's the truth."

No wonder he'd handed her the tissue a few moments ago. Damn eyes were starting to tear up without her permission.

"Please tell me those are tears of happiness."

She cocked her head in genuine surprise.

"I may be able to anticipate some of your needs, woman, but I'm nowhere near a mind reader. I have no idea what's running through your head, or whether I'm making you happy or sad right now."

So she smiled because that's all she could manage just now.

"Okay, happy then?"

She nodded.

"Good," he said with a relieved sigh. "Back to my little monologue…. Shit!" Then he jumped up and flew out the door.

"Well, wow," she grumbled to herself. The snarl turned into a grin when the smoke detector blared. In fact, Solie stifled a very unladylike snort. Neither of them had ever been good at cooking. Thankfully Mac and her husband,

Landon, usually took care of that particular task whenever they had dinner and movie night at any of their homes.

Back in the bedroom, Burton presented her with a small plate of perfectly crisp bacon and two of the most burnt English muffins she'd ever seen.

She laughed. Just couldn't help it. And thankfully, Burt had a good sense of humor and joined in.

"Uh, since this is still smoking I think I'll just leave the bacon and go toss the rest." He picked up the charred bread with a napkin and started to head out again. "Be right back. Windows are open in the kitchen."

Before he could get up, Solie's free hand shot out and took him by the wrist. The moment he stilled she snatched her hand back. She hadn't meant to snatch him like that, but there was no way he could leave the room. Not now.

His expression was wide open and she was glad to see that he wasn't offended that she'd grabbed him like he owed her money. Instead, he simply stood and waited for her to say whatever was on her mind.

"Wait, Burt. I-I really need to finish this conversation. Please."

Instead of leaving, burnt bits were tossed into the little waste basket next to the nightstand and he sat back down.

"What are you thinking about?" he asked.

"I want to know when your feelings for me moved past friendship."

"Beautiful, they've always been past friendship. But I was with someone else at the time, and so were you. I don't cheat, and I wouldn't disrespect you or the person I was dating at the time by asking you to be the 'other woman'. Having you as a friend wasn't my way of settling for what I couldn't have. It was important to me to be a good friend to you because you deserve it. And you've been a good friend to me right back. Been there for me. Saw me through all kinds of ridiculous drama with idiots in the lifestyle. And we've had some good times, too."

He gently traced her jaw with one hand, and snatched another tissue out of the box to dab at her tears with the other. "And there's no denying that the attraction between you and I has always been there, just kind of buzzing beneath the surface."

She blew her nose and took a bite of bacon. How did he make perfect bacon but manage to burn water? Solie sipped a bit more coffee, and then offered him the cup.

She felt all kinds of special when he took it, gulped without hesitation and set it down with a smile.

"While you're healing from your relationship with Wonder Dick, I hope to have a chance to play with you, then perhaps be more."

"Wonder Dick?" Solie snarfed her coffee and started coughing. Burt just shook his head at her and pounded her on her back.

"As I was saying, when you're ready, I want to talk about where this zing thing between us could go. What we could possibly grow to be to each other. So think about it, Solie?"

"But, but I have cooties!" she wailed. She never wailed... except for last night...in Burton's arms after learning about just how deep Marcais' dishonesty went. She'd been so upset that Mac fed her coconut brownies after dinner. Okay, so maybe she did occasionally wail. Whatever.

Burton looked at her with a mix of compassion and anger. "Luckily the cooties he gave you are curable. You had your massive dose of antibiotics yesterday. Seven days of no sex and you're good."

She knew this, but still she felt...tainted. Unclean. She tested clean before *and* after being with Marcais. In fact, he'd shown her his paperwork, so she knew he'd tested clean, too.

So for him to give her an STI now meant he'd picked it up outside of their relationship. Obviously.

"Solie, stop it. I know what you're thinking."

"I thought you said you couldn't read minds," she snapped.

"Really?" he growled as he gave her "that look". She rolled her eyes and mumbled an apology.

"You did everything you were supposed to do, Solie. You're not at fault here. If you'd been the one slinging your pussy around to any and every one without protection, then yes, I'd blame you for this. But you didn't. That's all on him. I can't tell you not to feel angry or hurt, but I can remind you that this is not your fault. And it doesn't change how I feel about you."

She didn't say anything. Couldn't form the words past the lump in her throat.

"Do you hear me, Solie?"

She lifted her chin and looked at Burton as she had so many times over the years. Even while baring the most vulnerable parts of himself, the man was still a force of nature. Right now, Solie drew on that special energy of his and let it settle into herself. Chest loosened, upper lip stiffened and suddenly it was as if the tears of last night, and the sniffles of three minutes ago never existed.

Strength. It's what he gave her. Though she had plenty of her own, this was a different kind of fortitude. This wasn't boardroom-politics strength. This was more of a weather-a-shredded-heart kind of determination. She was more intimidated right now in her pj's trying to fathom letting her guard down the tiniest bit to let Burton in, than she would be if she were standing toe-to-toe with someone who threatened to take over her company.

He was in no way asking for all of her—not her heart, and perhaps not even her body. She knew that BDSM play wasn't all about sex with Burton. Sure, he enjoyed impact play with floggers, crops, rope and cuffs; however, what he loved most was getting into his play partner's head. And still, he hadn't even asked for that.

He'd only asked to give her what she needed...and she would be the one to decide what that was. And later, if she wanted to, he was open to moving into something a bit more...personal.

Slipping her hand into Burton's, Solie said exactly what was on her mind.

"Burt, I don't need to think about it."

"What are you saying, Solie," he asked with quiet surety. "No beating around the bush. Just let me have it."

"I want to explore this zing between us, B. And I'm ready to explore it now. Yes, I will admit I'm on the rebound, but we both know that. And right now, I want you more than anything or anyone else I can think of."

"More than a new souped-up gaming computer?" he teased, poking at her nerdy side.

"That's kind of pushing it, but yes, more than a new gaming computer. And more than World of WarCraft. And more than non-burnt English muffins. I want to be with you more than I want a bare handed, over the knee spanking."

"Now that's hard to believe," he quipped back. "But I think we can do something about that. Last I heard, there was nothing like a spanking from Mr. Big Thuddy Paddle Hands."

Solie's mouth fell open. "Mac told you about that?"

"Of course she did. And she had no shame in admitting that she's the one who came up with that loving little title for me while you wholeheartedly agreed. So I'll take that as a compliment."

Solie fell backwards onto her pillow laughing like she hadn't in weeks...hell, months even. She could tell Burton was seriously restraining himself from tickling her. When she caught her breath, she sat back up and smiled as he fed her more bacon.

"So what's the next step, Burt?"

"That depends. What do you want? I may be a Dominant, but I'm not a bully. You set the tone and the pace here, Sols. After that last D.I.N.O.—"

"D.I.N.O.? What's a D.I.N.O.?"

"Dominant-In-Name-Only."

"Oh." She chuckled and rolled her eyes. Didn't that about sum it up?

"Neither of us are into casual dating, but after *he who must not be named*, you may not even want a D/s dynamic, hon. And this may sound fucked up, but I want you happy, even if it's not with me. I can give you what you need until you decide that what you need isn't me."

"Not want a D/s dynamic? Oh, I definitely want it, Burt. I need it, actually. That's part of why that last thing was so disappointing and destructive. He knew what I needed, but his narcissism was more important. And now that I understand sociopaths, I get that it wasn't personal. Hey, did you know that he was actually convicted of domestic violence while we were living together?"

"What the fuck, Solie?!"

"Hey, I just found out myself. I knew he was going back and forth to court for some stuff with his ex-wife, but I thought it was simple post-divorce proceedings. He kept all the nasty details to himself. Straight up lied, actually."

"So he was living with you, was going back and forth to court for ex-wife stuff and ended up convicted? Fucking convicted, Solie? For domestic violence against…who? The ex?"

"Yep. And she's terrified of him, Burt."

"Damn. Talk about bullet dodged, woman. Given how

aggressive he could be sometimes, and the way he would get up in your face and yell, it could have easily been you pressing charges against him, love."

"No doubt. But he wasn't stupid in that regard." Solie was trained in two different martial arts, plus was proficient with firearms. Hell, she even had a hunter's license and could bag a fully grown elk at two hundred yards. "But back to the question you asked me about next steps. I think the next step is to determine what kind of relationship we want. I want to negotiate, set boundaries and all that, but even still, I want to take it one day at a time. And most important, I want you to be who you are, Burt. And that's alpha to the bone. And I'm not afraid of where that will lead because I know you, and alpha doesn't mean jerk in the Book of Burt."

"Book of Burt? I like that. We should also discuss triggers and things that might set you off given your recent ordeal. I don't want you walking on eggshells and I don't want to tip toe around either. Okay?"

Then Solie got up on her knees and did something she'd never done in all the time she'd known this man—she kissed Burton Khrys. And she put all her hopes, fears and desires into it as if her life depended on it.

HE TASTED OF COFFEE AND HIS OWN DISTINCT FLAVOR OF PURE man—a mix of strength and spicy heat that she hadn't realized she'd been dying to sample…until now.

But Burton didn't sample. He feasted.

One moment she was on her knees pressing her lips to his, and the next she was dragged into his lap and positioned to his liking. He held her tight as he slanted his mouth over hers. She felt the flex of muscle against her body as his arms tightened and released around her.

Suddenly he was pouring himself into the kiss, taking, plundering. She couldn't breathe. Didn't want to.

God, it was like drinking from a bottle of her favorite champagne after it had been shaken, uncorked and then pressed to her lips.

She opened to him. Held nothing back. Let him take what he wished. His tongue tangled with hers—not so much that she felt like she would gag, but just enough to make her want to chase him for more.

Burton pulled back just a bit.

"Let your head fall back, Solie."

She instantly obeyed, trusting him to keep her from tumbling off his lap and onto the floor. The second her neck went limp, Burton groaned his appreciation. And the sound was so deep, so masculine it made Solie's thighs quiver—thighs that happened to be pressed against his as she straddled his groin.

Kissed her neck. Nipped her jaw just enough to make her hiss. The bit of sting made her nibble on her own lips in anticipation of what he would do next.

He broke the kiss and whispered quietly into her ear.

"Tell me what you need."

"Hair," she gasped.

His fingers eased into her hair, to glide across the scalp and play with her locs. The gentle press of his fingertips was sweet followed by an exquisite bite of pain as he gathered a hank of it in his hand and squeezed. Hard.

Her hair, bundled in his hands as if his fingers were a scrunchy, reminded her of the man himself—tightly controlled, bundled strength.

Then thought faded away completely as she sank deeper into the kiss, further under this soul-satisfying spell, to *feel* rather than wonder at it all.

"What else, Sols? Now."

Without hesitation, the words tumbled from her lips between thick gasps. "Bite me. Please."

"Where?"

"Here." She touched the spot just beneath her ear and slid her fingers down her neck to a certain spot on just shy of her shoulder.

"Cross your arms behind your back and hold your elbows."

The moment she did, Burton yanked her head sideways and then nibbled along the path that her fingers had shown him. Suddenly his teeth sank into the muscle between neck and shoulder and Solie's eyes rolled back into her head.

"Oh my God," she gasped.

It was her sweet spot—the one place on her upper body where sensation could drive her to the brink of orgasm.

Fingers tightened even more at her scalp as he began to suck earnestly. Then he was biting again, then sucking. And all she could think of was…more.

He didn't try to touch her anywhere else, but focused only on what she'd said she needed. The sting of scalp and skin, mixed with the intimacy of his lips on hers was indescribably delicious.

And Solie was quickly heating up to a point where this bit of play wasn't enough.

Her hips went wild and there was nothing she could do to control them. The thick ridge of his cock pressed against her core, made her squirm and pant as he continued to bite her neck. Gasps became moans. Moans became cries. Cries became pleas.

She wasn't sure what she begged for, but whatever it was, only Burton could deliver it.

Lips left her skin and when Burt spoke Solie was pleased to hear he was just as winded as she was.

"I do believe kissing you has made my day, and it's only seven o'clock in the morning," he said. "But no sex. Not yet."

Solie started to withdraw, to sink down into a pool of disappointment as she was reminded of the sexually transmitted infection she'd been treated for just yesterday. But Burton Khrys wouldn't let her pull away.

"No sex, but not only because of your condition, Solie. I don't want to move too fast or rush you in any way. Understand?"

His consideration ramped her right back up to boiling. Arms twined around his neck, she held on for dear life. Solie's ears heard the words, but her brain wasn't processing them.

"Sols, I need to go. We'll finish this later."

But she was dialed up and eager. She ground her Hello Kitty jammy bottoms against his cock, reached for the little bit of sensation that would take her over the edge. She could come without sex, right? Hell yes! All she needed was just a little bit more. Just...

"Solie Alise Shaw." Uh oh. No one but her grandmother said her entire name, and only if she was in trouble.

Burt sank his fingers into her thigh with just enough pressure to deliver his message without actually hurting her. Solie stilled immediately.

"You're not speaking, but I'm not missing a single thing that your eyes or your sexy and oh-so-tempting body are saying. We will talk this out Solie. Starting tonight. You game?"

Game? Hell yes. She nodded her agreement.

"Use your words, Solie. Are you game?"

"Yes."

"Meet me at Twilight this evening. No working late for you. Six thirty sharp."

"Okay." He stood up with her still in his lap, then turned

and eased back into bed. Head on his chest, Solie relaxed under gentle strokes that calmed and brought her down from that brink of delicious madness.

They shared the rest of the jumbo mug of coffee along with some comfortable small talk. Burt grabbed the remote off the nightstand and Solie found herself sharing a very "normal" morning with her friend as they watched the day's weather forecast on TV.

A few minutes later, a sexy, nicely caffeinated Burton climbed out of bed and pressed a kiss to her forehead.

His gaze took her all in as he said, "I'm all yours as of this moment, Sols."

She gawked as he grinned at her and backed into her bathroom. A few minutes later he was dressed and gone, and Solie headed into a scalding hot shower.

Her whole body hummed—every spot he'd touched and even the ones he hadn't. It was as if her very blood shimmered beneath the skin.

For a woman who managed a corporation on a daily basis and planned damn near everything to the nth degree, this thing with Burt she hadn't seen coming.

She moaned aloud as the water sluiced over the bruises forming on her neck where Burton had been so very thorough. It was tender to the touch and the thought made Solie smile like a loon.

She looked up at the ceiling, watched the steam swirl around as it rose. Then she let out the elation bubbling in her gut as she screamed, "Oh my God, I haz a boyfriend! Burton Khrys is mine! Wheeee!"

She twirled until she almost fell and busted her ass on the slick tiles. And even then, Solie couldn't stop the wild grin from spreading across her lips, nor the flash of anticipation from dancing around in her belly.

And she didn't want to control it. Not in the slightest.

4

"*K*onbanwa. Welcome to Twilight Teahouse. Would you please confirm your preference for this evening, Miss Solie?"

Solie beamed and executed a formal bow. "Yes, thank you, Kuri. I'll be having both dinner and dessert." She didn't bother asking about a reservation, knowing that Burton would have seen to it if he'd told her to be here.

"Wonderful, Miss Solie. Please wait here. Your table is almost ready. Mina will be along to escort you in a moment."

"*Arigato gozaimasu*," Solie replied, thanking her hostess in perfect Japanese.

Kuri bowed and then turned to greet other guests. Her traditional kimono was a gentle swish of purple silk covered with delicate-looking cherry blossoms. Solie was always amazed at how every attendant always had every single hair in place and perfectly coifed. Elegance and class with a dose of kink described Twilight Teahouse perfectly.

For dinner she'd have a shrimp salad and fresh yellowtail sashimi. If she was brave enough, dessert, would be the St.

Andrew's cross in the far corner of the play space upstairs in the Hall of Mirrors.

Yes, this place had become her personal crack. Japanese teahouse in the front, and a world-class, well-equipped, totally not-somebody's-converted-basement dungeon on the upper floors.

As she stood in the waiting area, Solie looked around. Being here once again brought a mix of giddy anticipation and inner-growly annoyance.

The last time she'd played here was when one of the area's premier rope Tops had agreed to give Marcais flogging and rope lessons as a favor to Solie. That Friday night, Solie had gladly been both the rope bunny and the flog bunny.

Even now, the details of that time started out bright and shiny in her memory, then unrolled themselves like a stained cheap carpet.

The play had been fabulous. In fact, she and Marcais had gone home and played some more that night, and then did yet another scene on Saturday morning. It had been a wonderful way to begin a weekend and each session had gone just the way she'd hoped. The buzz-like floaty experience had been followed by standing in front of the mirror and admiring the pretty deep purple marks left on her skin.

A smile played over her lips as she recalled Mac's words —*"Solie, you look like a cinnamon tiger with a rainbow-striped ass!"*

But then Sunday rolled around and Solie had hit bottom. Hard.

Just as one sometimes experienced subspace, or endorphin rushes, after heavy impact play, Solie found herself living the polar opposite—an endorphin crash, or sub-drop. And she'd "dropped" so deeply into a funky depression, she'd wanted to stick her head out the window and slam it closed on the back of her neck. It was like falling down a deep pit full of spikes...and just never getting to the spikes. When she'd tried to call Marcais, he'd been incognito. Gone. Dropped off the face of the planet. Wouldn't answer his phone nor return her texts.

By evening, she'd hit full-blown subby distress, and was completely out of chocolate, damn it. Thank God for Mac and Burt. Those two had come over to keep her company and both were livid by the time Marcais finally got back to her late that night. And Burton was beyond pissed, had even snatched the phone and torn Marcais a new one after Marcais had finally admitted that he didn't know what sub-drop was, hence his lack of urgency in getting back to her.

Solie had been amazed. Marcais was the first to ever get her to a place where subspace bliss had occurred. So he was also the first she'd experienced sub-drop with. And though it had been her first sub-drop, she'd at least known what the hell was happening to her and why.

How did a person just tool around in this lifestyle and not bother to learn how their actions could physically affect the person they Topped? And how had he hidden something so significant as his lack of knowledge for so long?

He'd lied. Skillfully and often.

Just...goddammit.

As the memory rolled through her, Solie recalled her reaction when she'd learned that while she'd been in sub-drop hell, her so-called Dominant had been chatting up one of the attendants right here at the Teahouse. While trying to talk the woman into having coffee with him, he'd used the same cheesy line he'd used on Solie when they'd first met.

"Are you single or am I too late?"

Yeah, that.

She hated the memories of it all, hated that it flashed into her brain as she stood at the threshold of the Twilight Teahouse's inner sanctum awaiting the man of her fucking dreams. It had only been a month since what felt like the ulti-mate heartbreak by a world class man-whore, yet a part of her felt like she should be further along. Instead, it was all still so very fresh in her mind.

Usually she liked fresh things.

But this? Not so much.

Solie knew herself. Knew exactly where she stood in regard to her emotional and psychological recovery—she had a long way to go in the mending process. And a trip to the Twilight Teahouse with Burton was the ticket. Or at least the beginning.

Right then, one of Solie's favorite service Tops rolled in looking like a decadent breath of fresh air. Rachelle served others by Topping them in the manner they required, and she was damn good at it. Handing her large black duffel off to one of the male attendants, the woman made a beeline for Solie.

Arms spread wide, she said, "Ah, So-leee, how are jew daaahling? So vunderful to see jew!" The words were full of joy and wrapped in Rachelle's smooth French accent as she pulled Solie into a fierce hug.

Solie grinned and tried to answer, but her face was smashed between the taller woman's breasts. So instead, she simply inhaled Rachelle's floral light perfume and let the comradery flow over her. After all, the woman offered to castrate Marcais if he ever showed his face at the TT again. Yes, it was good to be back here for sure.

No surprise that Rachelle knew what Marcais had done. In fact, it may as well have been on the local news consid-ering how many women had come forward after word of his trifling behavior had gone viral. There were too many to count that had either been approached by him or had slept with him. And yes, they'd known about Solie, but Solie hadn't known about any of them.

"Well, I knew he was seeing some people, but I was seeing some people too, so I didn't really think much of it."

Which basically meant that that particular bitch hadn't cared that Marcais was cheating on Solie and had been happy to be "the other woman". Another had claimed that she and Marcais had fallen so hard for each other and she just loved him so much, and blah, blah, blah.

Solie hugged Rachelle back as the other woman kissed each cheek and offered some slow-motion castration for Marcais. One thing was certain—good friends with encouraging words, cuddles and chocolate were greatly appreciated at times like this. Take those same friends and add floggers and the occasional paddle, and you had a total god-send.

Rachelle was skipping dinner tonight and headed directly to one of the banks of private elevators strictly for club members. Moments later she was greeted by yet another club regular, and another.

Perhaps Mac and Burton were right and she'd truly been missed in the local community?

As if conjured, Burton's big warm hand slipped around her waist.

She turned her head to meet the gaze of the one of the most darkly gorgeous men on planet Earth. And he happened to be grinning at her as if he'd won the lottery. Perhaps, in his mind, he had.

Body heat radiated through his clothes as he pressed close to her from behind, wrapped his arms around her, and placed a soft kiss on her check.

"Good evening, beautiful. I love this dress on you," he whispered in her ear as he discretely traipsed a finger up the spine exposed by the knee-length red and black backless number.

"I'm glad you like it." Lord, she was almost breathless just from that simple touch; as this morning's kisses replayed themselves over again in her mind. Oh man, she had it bad. "You gave it to me for Christmas last year, and Mac gave me the matching shoes."

He looked down at her feet to the red suede heels, and when his gaze once again met hers, it smoldered until she was sure her panties would catch fire. She'd seen that look before, but it had never been directed at her.

Burton moved deeper into her personal space, and was almost lip-to-lip when he said, "Baby, those shoes are meant to be airborne. Damn, we have good taste."

And they did indeed considering he was dressed impeccably. Black slacks and a black silk pullover knit sweater set off his mesmerizing blues until they shone like jewels. Dark, hard, and a twinkle of a smile made this man number one on the delish list.

Having Burt's full attention did funny things to her organs—the damn things just seemed to dance all over the place. And after the recent hell she'd been through, she was happy to let them do the mambo if they wanted to. Why? Because there was one thing she knew—Burton was sincere. If he'd been anything over the years, it was honest. Sometimes brutally so.

There was quite a line waiting to be seated by the time their attendant arrived a few minutes later.

"Good evening, Miss Solie," Mina said. Then she turned to Burt with the same graceful bow and said, "Master Burton."

"Good evening, Mina. Thank you for seeing to us this evening." Burton bowed, then took Mina's hand and planted a chaste kiss. Solie hid a smile as the hostess blushed and giggled, a bit flustered and put out as she motioned for them to follow her.

As they were led down the silk-lined hallway and through the thick double doors into the dining area, Solie wondered why it felt so new. She'd been down these same hallways a bazillion times; eaten and played here, even danced and partied here plenty. But tonight, in this moment, it felt…

She took in a deep breath as the light bulb went on. This was a new chapter in her life, and who better to accompany her on a new journey than an old friend?

As they walked, Burt's hand settled on her lower back and her stomach dove down into the soles of her feet.

Wow. Tummy wiggles and goose bumps? Heh.

"What are you smiling at, Sols? Looks like you have a secret."

"Oh, nothing," she lied. Burt's raised brow let her know that he wasn't buying it, but he was obviously letting her get away with it…for now.

Once through the main dining-room doors, they stopped at the shoe station, slipped off their shoes and placed them in the little wooden bin with their table number on it. Twilight Teahouse provided traditional tabi socks or slippers for each guest. Tonight Solie chose a pair that matched her dress. Burt followed suit and chose a gray pair of men's slippers.

The slippers were so comfortable, Solie almost didn't look forward to getting her own shoes back.

Shoji screens separated each booth, where classily dressed people sat and enjoyed their meals. Candlelight cast a romantic glow off the highly polished wooden table tops. The aroma of various teas filled the air, complementing the scents from the dishes that were being delivered to those who were dining.

Once at their table, Solie automatically slid into the booth, but not before Burton pressed the sweetest kiss to her lips—a kiss that finished the story his eyes had begun to tell when they met up in the lobby only moments before. It was a tale of possibilities. Very, very good ones.

They made small talk about their day until the waiter arrived with tea…and no menu. With a bow and a smile, he turned and left.

Solie looked after him wondering why he hadn't bothered to take her order. She was dying for some fresh Ahi, damn it. She opened her mouth to call him back, then snapped it shut at Burt's word.

"Don't worry. I ordered ahead."

Her pissy side reared its head, but she smacked it back down. She knew what she was getting into the moment she'd accepted his offer this morning. Or at least she *thought* she knew.

Besides, this wasn't anything new. Burton liked to order the food for their table. Always had. Even Mac occasionally let him get away with it and that woman didn't have a submissive bone in her body.

"Stop glaring at me and take your meds, Solie. Dinner will be here pretty quickly."

She didn't stop glaring, but she did do as he asked and fished her diabetes medicine out of her purse and gulped it down with some tea.

He took a sip of water and sat back even as she leaned forward with her arms crossed on the table. The shift in their relationship dynamic was swift and had her tilting her head at a hard right. Add hunger to the mix and you had a less-than-giddy Solie.

"I thought we were going to talk tonight." Oooh, she hadn't meant to snarl, but she was hungry, damn it.

Like some people were unpleasant drunks, Solie was an unhappy hungry person. In her head, she was like the little old lady she'd seen in a movie. The woman sat waiting for her lunch while her waiter talked on the phone, laughed and cracked jokes with whoever was on the other end. Meanwhile the lady, who was also diabetic, sat and waited. And waited. And waited some more. Finally she'd tossed aside the entire table, yelled, "Where is my food?!", and then chased the waiter around the restaurant and finally out the front door.

"And we will talk. After we eat." He gave her a moment of silence and simply watched. Too closely. "Are you having second thoughts about being with me? As a friend, I know I can be somewhat bossy."

She almost choked and snarfed water through her nose. *Somewhat* bossy? Really?

"As a lover," he continued, "I am even more demanding. But it will work for you."

"Really? And why is that?" she asked. A bit of growl still laced the words though she was trying hard to get her hunger-induced annoyance under control.

"Because what you really crave is to be in service to someone. Don't interrupt, Solie." She snapped her mouth shut and reached for the tea pot as if that's what she'd meant to do all along. She poured quickly and then lifted the small traditional cup to her lips.

It was so hot she almost burned her mouth off, but no way she'd let him know by yowling.

"As I was saying, you wish to be in service to someone. But to someone who not only appreciates all that you do, but who gives you a reason to continue doing it. For example, that time when Marcais needed work done on his truck, but the dumbass had no idea how to handle it. You did the research and took care of it. Not because you're a control freak, but because that's what he needed."

Truth. And nothing but.

"However, he hadn't appreciated it. Gave you no reason to continue serving him. I remember that you saved his grown ass several times because of his own stupidity. Bottom line is Solie, he lost your respect a long time ago. He may have known his way around a spanking, but he didn't know *you*, the woman."

She had nothing to say to that. Couldn't find a single thing to dispute...and she was trying really, *really* hard to think of something redeeming about that whole situation. Other than Marcais delivering some really good sex, nothing came to mind.

How depressing.

Thankfully she didn't have to reply because dinner arrived quickly, just as Burton promised.

And he'd ordered her favorites. All of them.

By the time she was done stuffing her face, she'd inhaled what must have surely been a bucket-full of fresh Ahi, salmon, yellow tail and prawns, a trough of wakame seaweed salad, and enough pickled mango, wasabi and ginger for ten people. She wasn't one of those women who didn't eat when out on a date. In fact, she still had a bit of room and would have kept right on going if Burton hadn't reminded her that dessert was still forthcoming.

As soon as the dishes were cleared, Mina returned.

"Where would you like your dessert served, Master Burton? There are open seats on floor one off to the right of the ankle stocks, and another on the small loveseat near the spanking bench."

"Which spanking bench?" Solie asked.

"The burgundy leather one, ma'am. If you prefer some privacy, the bamboo room is also free."

Her stomach did a free fall at the thought of being alone with Burt in the bamboo room. There was absolutely nothing in there but a huge beanbag-like chair big enough for literally five people. The reason it was called the bamboo room was because the door that led inside was made of bamboo poles and you could see right inside.

She'd never taken advantage of that particular space before, other than when invited to watch others indulge. She pictured herself laying in Burt's arms in a cuddle puddle and felt her cheeks heat. But not because she was embarrassed at all, but because the thought of all that solid flesh pressed against her set a fire down south that might require an extinguisher.

Suddenly an image of Burton dressed like a firefighter popped into her head.

Pulling her mind out of the proverbial gutter, Solie turned to Burt.

He was looking at her as if he knew exactly what she was thinking. Her breathing hitched. Burt's eyes lit up like Christmas trees. A subtle, but very *there* smile tilted up one side of his mouth. Guess she hadn't been successful in hiding her reaction over such a little thing as picking a spot for dessert.

She cleared her throat and asked, "Do you have a preference as to where we have dessert?"

His words and tone were totally smooth when he replied, "Not really. You choose."

And just like that his gaze had her pinned in place. Did he really want her to choose, or was he waiting to see if she would defer to him? It wasn't something she typically worried about with Burton, but it was a game Marcais played. Often.

Burt tilted his head. "Solie, you okay, hon?"

Ripping her gaze away from his deep blues, she simply said, "Yes, I'm fine. Up to you. Lead the way please."

And she refused to look at him again until they were seated next to each other near one of the stations where an expert flogger was using a Florentine double-handed technique. He was very smooth and practiced, almost like a martial artist demonstrating how to use a staff or bo. The result of his flogging was even stripes on the back of the women who held onto a pair of large thick rings.

Her arms and legs were spread. Fingers wrapped around the steel attached to the top of the wooden structure. She wasn't tied or secured in any way, her partner trusting her to keep her fingers exactly where they were.

Their dessert arrived just as the strokes began to fall a bit faster and harder. The volume of the woman's moans, quiet and barely there at first, rose with the intensity of the strikes.

A part of Solie wanted to be the woman on the receiving end of the flogging. Part of her resented that she wasn't that woman because the man who should be flogging her was surely laying up with yet another woman by now. Then she felt guilty because she was thinking about the former dude rather than the man sharing her dessert right here, right now.

"Okay, tell me what's going on." The words were quietly spoken, but were clearly nothing short of an order, given the steel infused in them.

"What?" she asked.

"You went weird on me after I gave you the choice of where we would have dessert. Tell me."

Shit. So much for wishing he'd missed that.

She took in a deep breath and looked Burton right in the eye. All she could do was suck it up and be honest. So she told him how she'd slipped back into Marcais-induced behavior, wondering if Burt really wanted her to pick, or if he was just looking for a reason to start a fight and be a dick.

"Are you mad?" she asked.

"Can't be. That's where you are right now. And if I'm any kind of a man I have to meet you where you are, not where I want you to be. I told you this morning that I knew you were in the early stages of getting over all this madness and I'm willing to be what you need. Luckily, what you need is a mean old man. I've got you covered."

Oh good grief. She snorted a laugh.

"So, tell me about the phone call from *he who must not be named's* commanding officer."

Saved by Burt's intuition on when to change a subject. She wished she had the man's gift. But on the other hand, no one was perfect considering Burt had also had his fill of dealing with cuh-ray-zee.

"Marcais' First Sergeant walked into his office in front of all his co-workers, made him stop what he was doing, and escorted him directly to the medical facility. He was tested and treated on the spot."

Burt whistled and then grinned like a loon. "Back to that whole karma thing, right? I told you this guy should have been Sméagol."

Solie looked up at the server and murmured her thanks as a crystal mug of hot tea was set down on their small table. "Smee-who?"

"You know, Sméagol from the Lord of the Rings." Then in a completely terrible accent, he said, "I told you he was tricksy. I told you he was false. Stupid fat hobbit!"

They both laughed until she was damn near out of breath.

Finally Burt said, "Now, on to us."

She cleared her throat and jumped in with both feet.

"Okay. I want to put this out there now, up front. After a while..." She paused, took a sip of tea for fortification—this time it wasn't lava-lip-burning hot—and then laid out her one true desire. "If our relationship is working the way we want, I want a collar out of this deal."

She watched the blood drain from his face. But she was proud of herself for not taking it personally. Solie knew exactly what was going through the man's mind. The last woman he'd given his collar to was supposed to become his wife. Burton Khrys didn't play around when it came to intimate relationships. When he realized that regardless of what he did, said or gave, he just wasn't what that woman needed, he'd ended it. Tore his heart out in the process.

But Solie wasn't going to be less than honest. She was tired of trying relationships on for size with open-ended expectations. She wanted something permanent with someone she was compatible with.

"Well," she said, "looks like you're the one that needs to give it some thought, eh?" she said with her typical sass.

"Smart ass," he grumbled.

"Damn right."

"You know you're going to pay for that at some point right?"

"Of course I do." But they hadn't negotiated anything yet, so she knew it was safe to be as much of a brat as she wanted. It felt damn good considering she typically spent her days being a hard ass. *Not* being in control, *not* making all the decisions was like a refreshing cool breeze on a hot summer day to her. And right now, she was basking in it.

"Let's get the negotiations out of the way. I'm suddenly eager to get started," Burt said.

Out of the blue, Mac appeared and sat down with them.

"Am I late?"

"Late for what?" Solie asked before the shock could truly register.

"I, my dear girl, am going to mediate your negotiation with Mr. Thuddy here."

"Excuse me?" Solie gasped.

"Not forever. Just for tonight," Mac clarified.

Burt grinned until Solie was sure she saw little horns start growing out of his forehead as he said, "Let the games begin."

THE NEGOTIATIONS WENT SMOOTHLY AS THEY BOTH LAID OUT what they would and wouldn't tolerate as they explored this new facet of an old relationship. As soon as limits were set, Landon walked over. The whole crew smiled her way as Mac's husband sat an oversized piece of seven layer chocolate decadence in front of her, along with a steaming hot pot of aromatic jasmine tea.

Being surrounded by people who cared for her made Solie feel as if the sun had risen over her little spot at the table. She knew this was a safe place where she could say any and everything, and it would remain in confidence.

"So what's your poison tonight?" Mac asked with a fairly wicked grin.

With a tired sigh, Solie simply replied, "Nothing."

Mac took both her hands while Burton sat back and let the moment happen. Energy hummed off of him and she knew he was up to something. The man was so good at being unobtrusive yet bossy at the same time. And how did he manage to pull that off, anyway?

"Solie, listen, you can't be so hard on yourself," Mac said as Landon handed her a fork and poured her tea as his wife tried to set her straight. "There's no way you could have known what he was. Sociopaths are experts at concealing the truth. Pros at charming people out of anything and everything. For them there's no empathy. It's not about emotions. It's about winning."

"But I think I did know. I just didn't stop long enough to really analyze what I was seeing, hearing and feeling. Instead I just went ahead and jumped into it, choosing to believe him rather than stepping back to think for a minute."

"Well, you know, or rather you know *now*, that sociopaths move in fast. They push the relationships quickly for a reason—while they're laying on the charm and manipulating you, they get you addicted to their special kind of attention.

You're in it before you know what hit you. I mean, look at the other women who've come forward. And the one that's still involved with him, even though she knows she was his little secret."

"It doesn't change the fact that he pretty much told me what he was and I walked into the shit anyway."

Burt sat forward now, humming with an energy that was a bit more on the darker side. Edgy. And focused. "Solie, what are you saying?" he asked in that super calm voice of his —the one that *sounded* nonchalant but was deadly serious and no-nonsense to boot.

"I'll tell you like I told Marcais. He once told me that his ex-wife hated his flirting, but he kept right on doing it. His wife was the woman he was supposed to love, cherish and protect more than anything. And if he didn't stop flirting for her, what the hell made me think he would do it for me? He told me that he used to lie to his wife about everything, and I mean everything about himself. So if he lied to her, a woman he was with for eight years, why would he tell me the fucking truth?

Mac's eyes went wide in surprise. "Wow, you dropped an F-bomb? In public? All righty then."

Solie let the words continue to rush out. "He once even told me I was expendable."

"What?! I'll kill him."

"No, that's not what I mean, Mac. And sit down and eat some more cake, woman.

Anyway, he once told me that the way to get over one woman was to get another one. Well, he basically all but told me that I was nothing but a distraction to help him get over his ex-wife. And whenever I asked him about his feelings for me, his answer was, 'Well, I don't know you yet.' Yeah, that's key for, 'I don't have deep feelings for you, Solie.' What's worse is that he would tell me that his co-workers at the

Army base would ask him where he always found so many quality women. But he'd only been divorced for a few months when he and I got together. So when did he have time to find all these girls?"

"I see what you're saying."

"I knew you'd get it. He was either messing around on his wife, which she confirmed he did for eight years, or he was messing with a bunch of women while he was scoping me out, which also turned out to be true. Basically, he waved some pretty big red flags in front of my face, and I was so caught up in his charm, I didn't see them."

"I see what you mean. But knowing it wasn't personal should make that particular pill a bit easier to swallow."

"True, but it's still a bitter pill, you guys. Cod liver oil mixed with crushed aspirin bitter. I mean, *dayum*."

Burton rose to his imposing height and held out his hand to her. "Well, if you'd like a bit of medicine that's a tad bit sweeter, come on up to the third floor. I think I have something you might appreciate."

"Should I be scared?"

"It's me we're talking about here, Solie," Burton said in mock outrage.

"Yep, scared. Definitely scared," she said, voice deadpan with mock fear. She even threw in a little shaking and wiping of non-existent tears from her eyes. Inside, she squirmed, wondered if he would ask...no. He wouldn't ask. Had no need to.

Negotiations were done. It had taken next to no time. In fact, he'd simply slid a piece of paper across the table right after Mac had shown up. Listed were the things he believed would be hard limits for her. He'd hit them all dead on, except for one—and that's because while it might have been a no-go with others, she trusted Burton to introduce her to edge play in a way that wouldn't break her.

She glanced over at Burt and caught him and Mac passing a certain look.

"What are you two up to?"

"Do you trust me, Sols?" Burt asked. Forced herself to relax though inside she squirmed, anxious to experience what Burton would do to her. All she had to do…was say yes.

"Of course."

"Then finish your dessert and head up to the Ice Palace. Five minutes." He took her hand and kissed it, keeping his eyes on hers the entire time. Then he turned and walked the hell away.

Mac sat there and sang a song she called "Ode to Mr. Thuddy Paddle Hands" while grinning like a nutball. Solie wanted to smash what was left of her chocolate decadence into her friend's nose. Instead she took her time finishing her yummies and dallied. Well, she dallied as close to five minutes as she could with just enough time to grab her heels from the shoe bin and book it upstairs.

THE PROPRIETOR WHO'D DREAMED UP TWILIGHT TEAHOUSE was brilliant. The entire five-story club was private, except for the restaurant. Solie had inhaled a perfect dinner on the public side of the first floor, and a delectable dessert on the private side. The second floor held a full-service spa, complete with traditional Japanese baths and massage space.

Each floor had its own particular theme, from hot Egyptian nights to sultry Caribbean days. But now, it was time for the icing on her particular cake—The Ice Palace on the third floor, Solie's absolute favorite.

As the elevator moved, she held her own gaze in the mirrored walls. This morning after Burton had left her, she'd washed and braided her hair. Once dry, she took it down to reveal a mop of glossy, dark brown, wavy locs that swung with health every time she turned her head. The bit of gloss she'd worn on her lips was long gone, courtesy of her chocolate dessert and a linen napkin. A touch of waterproof eyeliner finished her off. It was next to nothing in the makeup department, but she never wore much when coming here. It squicked her out to see other people's sweat, tears and makeup streaked over the furniture, so she made sure she didn't leave anything for anyone else to clean up.

Her brain zoned out at the thought of the many spray bottles of disinfectant and clean towels that dotted the place.

The elevator slowed and thoughts of Burton's handsome face pushed the squick from her mind. That edgy smile he'd given her along with his "you've got five minutes" declaration set a different kind of shiver skating over her skin.

"God, girl, you are in over your head." Funny thing was… she liked it. "Maybe you're just as nuts as Marcais?" Laughing at herself, she shook her head and smoothed down her already smooth dress.

Amazing how Burt set her to twitching. Solie stared down directors of multi-billion dollar companies every quarter when it was time for her vendor review, yet one arched eyebrow from Burton made her as nervous as a bug in a henhouse.

He looked at her just like that, too. Like he wanted to devour her.

"Yep. Definitely in over your head. And you're talking to yourself in an empty elevator while staring at your reflection in a mirror." So why the hell was she grinning like she'd just had a shot of pure endorphin right into her brain?

Humans. Such complex creatures. Surely they were the only animals on Earth that could be happy, excited and terrified all at the same time…and like it.

Sigh.

The elevator doors parted with a quiet swoosh. On the other side, Burton stood between her and the exit with an outstretched hand. He seemed to love holding hands. Interesting she hadn't noticed before. Even when watching his interactions with his ex, he'd never given off this "I want to snuggle" vibe before.

Hard ass mixed with cuddle puddle?

I think I can work with this.

They passed several stations with spanking benches and massage tables, and rooms that appeared to be wide open but could be closed off with screens or by simply sliding the embedded glass doors shut and drawing the curtains.

It was like tooling through a crystal palace in a science fiction movie. There weren't any scaly, green women up here, but endless white—white walls, white tiled floors and one-way glass. Secrets were safe within; even with all the lights on in the darkness of night, no one could see inside from the street.

Mirrored pillars topped with marble and crystal sculptures reflected light in a mix of rainbow-prism arcs and edges. Muted brilliance filled the room until you swore you were inside a sparkling masterpiece of ice, minus the bone-chilling cold.

A quick glance at her watch. It was still early, especially for a Monday night. No surprise that they passed no one as Burton led her to a semi-open space with three walls.

"In you go," he said quietly.

Solie took off her shoes. The tile of the walkway was cool against the soles of her feet as she stepped off the main floor and onto the carpet of their play room for the evening. It was almost completely empty. One wall had a number of D-rings and assorted attachments for ropes, cuffs and things. A dark blue, overstuffed chair provided the only splash of color; and looked like it would have been more at home in her living room in front of the big-screen TV. Off to the side was a long table covered with a white cloth. Burton stooped, dragged a huge black duffel out from underneath and set it on the table with a loud "thunk".

The thoughts in her head were mirthful. She'd seen this man in action, and every time she did it made her equal parts jealous and equal parts happy that she wasn't on the receiving end. Burton could indeed be a deliciously mean old man.

And it was what she wanted. Craved. God, she *needed*.

Gently, he put a hand on each cheek and kissed her. Then, fingers tensed on her jaw. Soft gentle touch morphed into a firm, unyielding grip. Enough to get her attention but not enough to bruise or cause true discomfort. Something flared in his gaze and Solie found herself facing an entirely different person. In the blink of an eye, this was another man —this was *the* Burton Khrys.

Uh, maybe I should start backing away. Slowly.

Too late.

"I want you to pick ten things out of this bag that you want me to use on you. Put them right here." He motioned to the table top. "Place them in order with the ones you're not quite sure of or want to try for the first time on the far left, and the ones you like most on the right."

She started to nod. Burton gave her the Mr. Spock one-raised-eyebrow look.

Words, woman. Use your words. Funny she never had this problem with anyone but this guy. Solie opened her mouth with a simple, "Okay."

"Are you sure? If you're not ready, we can wait. I think you need this, but in the end you hold the control here...until you give it to me."

"I'm fine, it's just I'm not a big impact player like you are and I'm not sure if I can..."

He crowded into her space, cornered her with his big body.

"Baby, I can give you exactly what you need. I've got you, okay?" Suddenly she wanted to lower her gaze, look anywhere but at him. But before the thought could complete in her head, Burt lifted her chin with a single finger, looked deeply into her eyes. Captured her gaze until there was nowhere to go, nowhere to look, but right back at him.

Then the man pulled her close, wrapped her securely in his arms. Kissed the wind right out of her sails. Her response, instant and uncontrolled. Leaning in, she took all he had to offer with that mouth, those hands.

With each pass of his tongue against hers, Solie sank just a bit further into her need. Burton buried his fingers into her locs as he deepened the contact. He pulled gently. Tilted her head a bit to the left. Solie sighed into his mouth, loving that all she had to do was stand there and let him direct her where he wanted her to go.

Mmm. He tasted of chocolate decadence, coffee and a touch of mint. The flex of muscles in his arms ratcheted up her anxiousness. Not because she was afraid, but because she hadn't realized—or wanted to admit—just how much stress she'd been carrying around until she'd started to let go of some of it.

He pulled harder, just enough to cause her to gasp at the bit of sting at her scalp. A moan edged up out of her throat at the delicious trail of dampness left behind as Burton nibbled his way down one side of her neck and up the other.

By the time he reached her opposite ear, Solie was damn near panting.

Teeth tugged on an earring and then he whispered. "Strip. Keep the panties on. Ten minutes."

Once again he turned to leave, but not before he pulled a

pair of shoji screens into position at the arched entranceway to give her some privacy.

She tossed her shoes off to the side. Must have had too much sugar given the way her fingers trembled as she undid the clasp at her neck that held up her dress.

A quiet tap on the screen.

"Sols, it's me. Can I come in?"

Mac.

"Of course." Solie turned, holding her dress up with one hand. "Whatcha up to? Doing a scene with Landon tonight?"

"Nope." Mac dropped Solie's personal play bag next to the blue cushy chair.

"First you appear to magically mediate negotiations and now you have my play bag? Woman, when the hell did you manage to get your hands on that?" Solie demanded. She knew exactly what was in that bag, and right now she wasn't sure how she felt about it.

Mac grinned and attempted to look innocent. She failed miserably.

"I stopped by your house on my way over here to drop off a casserole. This was sitting in the hallway all lonesome and such." She motioned to the royal blue and black designer bag on the floor while she dropped her ass into the chair. "Oh, I checked your back door, which you'd left unlocked by the way. And I fed your horse-sized dog, too."

Solie snorted and rolled her eyes. "And I did not leave my door unlocked, and my German shepherd is supposed to be horse sized. The better to bite your backside with."

"Need help with that dress?"

"Nah." Solie paused. "You look awful comfy. You staying?"

"Yep. I'm your protector tonight, so I made sure to bring all the goodies."

Dress forgotten, it fell of completely and hit the floor as Solie braced her hands on her hips. Temper flared as she glared at her best friend. Understanding dawned in her mind —she'd been blessed...or something, with the two most caring, nosey ass people in the universe.

"And who the hell decided you were going to look after me while doing a scene? In fact, who said I was playing tonight at all?" Solie snapped.

"You did."

"Excuse me?"

Mac was up out of that chair and in Solie's face, standing toe to toe...or boots to toe. Whatever.

"You heard me, woman. You chose me as your protector the moment you said yes to Burton Khrys this morning!"

Solie's grumble became a growl. "He told you about that? What are you two, a couple of teenaged girls who talk on the phone at all hours of the night?"

"If being a teenaged girl means Burton cared enough to call me this morning to ask me to be here in case you needed me, then fuck yes, I'm a teenaged girl," MacKenzie snapped right back.

Really?

"Mac, you're a fucking mother hen, is what. Isn't it enough that you feed me several times a week, damn it?"

"You're my best friend, Solie Shaw. And I love you to pieces. And so what if I feed you several times a week? You're always working and it's what you need, damn it. Now move your ass. You're down to six minutes."

Aw hell. And she hadn't chosen a single thing out of Burton's stuffed-to-the-hilt bag.

Solie stepped out of the red and black fabric puddle. Mac swiped it up, walked her sexy ass back to the oversized chair and started pulling stuff out of Solie's personal bag. "I've got your fluffy blanket here for after, as well as some chocolate and plenty of water for you. So take care of your task. I've got the rest of this. Oh, and take off the jewelry, just in case."

Handing over her watch, earrings and necklace, Solie hustled over to Burt's bag and grabbed five things she was familiar with. The rest, she just guessed at their purpose and quickly laid them out on the table in the order she'd been instructed to.

"Nervous?" Mac asked. "Okay, never mind. I know that 'duh' look when I see it, Solie. We knew you'd be a bit nervous after your recent not-so-great experience and that's why Burt asked me to be here. Just to be reassurance for you. You know, a second set of eyes and ears."

"I appreciate it, Mac. I do. This is all just so intense and so very…I don't know." She sucked in a deep breath and tried to relax. It wasn't working so she did the next best thing—she changed the subject. "What I'd love is to watch you and Landon. It's been awhile since I've seen you two play."

Marcais hadn't ever wanted to come to the club on the same nights as her friends. She'd never noticed just how much he'd separated her from the people who cared about her. Controlled where she went and with whom. And so smoothly, Solie hadn't noticed until Mac mentioned it some months back.

But Solie had started paying very close attention and had been shocked at the corner she'd allowed herself to be manipulated into.

Then she'd gotten out. Fast.

Just not quite fast enough, damn it.

Some of the deepest wounds a person could inflict on another were the kind that were unseen—like words that cut to the bone. Solie only hoped she was strong enough, healed enough to choose to accept this chance to have who and what she really wanted.

Mac was her favorite kinky bitch on heels, and occasionally submitted to her husband in the sack. Yet as much as she admired her good friend, Solie didn't want what Mac had.

She didn't want to Top her man. She didn't want to be in charge in the bedroom. Actually, she didn't want to be in charge at home, period. Running her office and all her consultants was enough, thank you verra much.

And speaking of "in charge", where the hell was Burton?

"Good grief, woman, will you stop pacing? Your boobs are very distracting bouncing around like that."

Solie rounded on her friend, but the expression on Mac's face brought her up short. The woman was sprawled, one leg over the arm of the big chair, with a huge teasing grin on her face. Busted. Solie was indeed pacing. Definitely not the norm for her, but it seemed her feet were trying to catch up with the fucking pterodactyls flipping around in her gut.

And why was she so nervous? This wasn't her first rodeo, after all. And she was going to be playing with a man she'd known for years and years. So…what was she so concerned about?

Perhaps she really was messed up in the head?

"No you're not," Burton said from the doorway.

Shit. Had she said that out loud?

"Yes, Solie. You said that out loud. Mac, give us a minute. I'll call you in when we're ready to get started."

Without a word, Mac nodded at Burton, winked at Solie and showed herself out.

Burton came fully into the room and for some reason, Solie couldn't meet his gaze. A part of her felt…diminished. Not quite herself. Unsure. Unsettled.

Unworthy.

Burton sat in the chair while she stood off to the side. Here she was, damn near naked, in a pair of red and black polka dot panties that showcased her body to perfection. Yet in her head, she stood at a wall with her face practically wedged in a corner.

"Come here, Solie."

Her brain said, "no wanna" but she forced her feet to move anyway. When she was just a few inches away, he motioned to his lap and simply said, "Sit."

She sat stiffly on one of his knees, her gaze focused on the table full of toys that she wasn't sure she could enjoy tonight. God, but she wanted to. She really did.

Arms wrapped around her, he pulled her back against his chest and nuzzled the top of her head as he spoke.

"This isn't about sex, Sols. It's about you. Understand?"

She nodded.

He smacked her lightly on her ass. "Words, Solie."

"Fine. Bossy ass…"

He smacked her again.

She yelped, "Yes. I understand."

"Good. Give me your wrist."

Without lifting her head, she held up one hand. Her thoughts scattered at what felt like a stiff leather cuff being tightened and secured. She shuddered.

She tried to remind herself why she was here, why she'd agreed to be his, to be with Burton.

I want this. I want him…

But you're not good enough. Even a sociopath didn't want you.

"Look at your wrists. Look at how the leather seems to fit just right." Words, quietly spoken. The breath warm against her forehead.

She glanced up and stilled.

They did fit just right…because they were hers. Mac must have slipped them to Burt when she wasn't looking. Boy, when those two conspired, they really went all out.

"I've seen you wear these on plenty of occasions. Watched from a distance as the white leather caressed that beautiful cinnamon skin. I always liked how the brown piping and trim matched your skin perfectly. The buckles used to catch the light whenever your arms were suspended. Beautiful."

But seeing the leather buckled in place again, surrounding her wrists made her feel…ill. Her brain tilted sideways at the memories that washed through her head, so fast if it had been a flood of water, she'd have drowned.

Thoughts of Marcais putting these same cuffs on her, telling her he loved her, calling her the perfect submissive… and then treating her as less than the dirt on the bottom of his combat boots. Not with the bondage, or the flogging or the spanking. But with his cheating, lying and subversion. The fucker.

"Now," Burton said, "I want you to take the cuffs off, and throw them in the trash over there." He pointed to a little wastebasket near the entrance to the space that she hadn't noticed before.

"Throw them away? But…why?"

"Do it. I'll tell you after."

A mix of anger and sadness had her biting back some choice expletives, not to mention a few tears.

When she was done, she turned to find Burton next to the table, waiting.

She didn't have to be told to go to him. She was far from stupid…well, on most days.

Standing in front of him, Solie pictured a corner and the wall again. Why? Because she knew the man saw more than she wanted him to.

He held out a hand. She wanted to hide rather than put hers in it, but from somewhere inside she made that arm stretch out to her new man, and stay there.

Without a word, Burton put new cuffs around her wrists and tightened them just to the point of discomfort. The leather was unmarred. No tension marks or "broken in" areas. They were flawless, and surprisingly, matched the outfit she'd been wearing—red leather with black trim and bronze buckles.

He passed some red rope through the D-rings until her hands were loosely bound, and then led her over to one of the hooks secured to the wall. Burton pointed to one of the hooks that reminded her of something she'd hang a set of keys or a picture on—easy on, easy off.

"Loop the rope over the hook and face me."

Wait, what? He wasn't going to tie or secure her to anything? Didn't he think she could handle it, goddamn it?

"I had you throw away the other cuffs because they represented your old relationship, that guy's claim on your heart. His influence on your thoughts, feelings and emotions. I asked you to toss them, Sols, but bottom line is that you had to *choose* to do it. Just like you have to choose to accept these new cuffs from me. It's not a collar, but you will wear them when we're together."

Hmmm. Not quite what she had in mind, but Solie didn't say anything. Just glared at him, hating the memories the old cuffs had dredged up, and waited to see where this would go.

"Tell me how you felt when I put the old cuffs on you."

No. Couldn't form the words. Couldn't get them past the lump in her throat. Tears she'd effortlessly kept in check came spilling down her cheeks.

Burton didn't comfort her. Simply stood and waited for her to get herself under control. It was the greatest gift he could have given her. It meant that he believed she was strong enough to get her shit together enough to have a conversation about this very painful subject.

After a few moments, she cleared her throat.

"May I have some tissue, please?"

Burton fished around in her play bag and brought her tissue. Solie unhooked herself from the wall and reached for it.

"Did I give you permission to release the rope from the hook?"

Shit. Just that quickly she'd forgotten that in this space and anytime they were together in private, he was boss. Hell, she even had it in writing as part of their earlier negotiations.

Solie put her hands back over her head, hooked the rope on the little hook on the wall.

Burton gently cleaned up her face and even held the tissue to her nose.

"Blow."

No way. That was just nasty. This morning when she'd let the waterworks loose, she'd taken care of her own snot rockets, thank you very much.

Burton cocked his head sideways. "Blow," he repeated.

She shook her head.

"Yes, Solie."

Frowned and turned her head away with a simple, "Nu-uh."

"Alright." The man was completely calm, neither face nor words held any trace of anger. But when he calmly said, "Put your clothes on. We're done here," panic, sheer and unmistakable, filled her chest. The word, "No!" came out in a rush as her heart pounded up into her throat.

"Excuse me?"

"I mean, I'll let you clean my nose. I don't want to go home. Not yet. Please."

"Solie, you know me, right?"

"Yes."

"And what would my typical response be?"

His gaze lasered to hers. His expression was unwavering, with body language to match. He was not happy with her just now. But he was being incredibly patient as well.

"Your typical response would be, too bad. We'd be leaving. Right now."

"I will say this and I will only say it once. I am not a D.I.N.O."

"I know, Burt, I just…"

"Do not interrupt."

Fingers wrapped around the rope between the cuffs and she held on for dear life, thankful for the knots on the ends. Her gut screamed that this moment would make or break what she wanted with this man.

"I am your friend, Solie. Will always be. But when I tell you to do something and your response is 'No', there is no negotiation at that point. If we're in the middle of a scene, the scene is done. To me, refusing an order is the same as screaming a safe word. Understand?"

"Yes. I understand."

Without taking his eyes off of her, he called out and Mac ducked back into the room. From her periphery, she saw Mac tilt her head as she looked back and forth between herself and Burton, but Solie didn't dare take her eyes off of his.

Thankfully, the other woman sat without a word and Burton continued as if there'd been no interruption at all.

And this time when he put the tissue to her nose, no matter how much it made her feel like she was five years old, she blew.

"Why didn't you want to blow your nose, Solie?"

"You're going to get mad at me."

No response. Just…quiet. God, she'd give her left kidney for a little bit of white noise just now. Finally, she sucked in a deep breath and forced the words out.

"Because Marcais would yell at me when I cried. Made me feel like shit. Even if he was the reason for the tears, he would scream 'Stop fucking crying' like I'd physically harmed him or like I was crying for the hell of it or something."

The silent tears of a few moments ago became a gut-wrenching bawl. And Burton wiped her nose again. And she kept her hands exactly where they were supposed to be though it took all her effort not to snatch that box of tissue from his hands and run for it.

"Solie, you don't have to be strong all the fucking time," he growled. "I'm your port of harbor, your safe place to let it all out, like I have been for all the years you've known me. Turn around and face the wall."

The moment she did, his hands were on the bare skin of her back. The touch quieted, but not quite comforted. Eased up and down along either side of her spine, careful not to touch her tickle spots. Fingers pressed deeply into tense muscle at her neck and shoulders.

When her skin felt warm and her muscles loose and languid, the first light strike fell. Solie gasped. She could tell by the weight and impact, that it was a warm up flogger. The wash of pleasure was twofold—one, it just fucking felt good and two, it was only going to get better as he took her on tonight's journey.

Her mind took a quick trip down memory lane of what she'd put on that table. The three floggers ranged from very light leather to heavy strips of rubber. Of the two crops, one was your typical stiff one with a thin shaft covered with leather. The other had an ornate end of thick, pink, heart shaped plastic with little studs on it. It reminded her of the back of the mats people put on the floor of their cars.

Her mind flipped back to the present by the next strike. The impact was thuddy rather than stingy, followed by a gentle caress of his free hand on her skin, along the same path of the blows.

The dam she'd erected to protect her heart after the Marcais disaster began to strain under the pressure of the waves of desire for Burton that rolled up against it.

Desire was stoked and fostered by Burton's knowing hand and the energy he brought. Tonight, she was going to take it slow. Tonight, she was going to ease her way back into this part of her life. Right?

"Control your breathing, Solie."

What? Why? This was cake, nothing hard or...

"It's too soon. You're already starting to float away and we haven't really gotten started yet," Burt said.

Taking stock of herself, she ignored him. There wasn't any pain, no reason for alarm. She heard someone talking off in the distance. Sounded like they said something about someone floating away. Well, good for them. As for herself, she liked the way this felt. She hadn't had anyone touch her like this, or put a flogger to her skin in so very, very long, and it was just so good, and...

Smack!

"Ouch!" she yelped.

Burton had changed up his strokes, broken the rhythm and the force of the blows to yank her back from the sub-space edge.

"Well that certainly worked," she grumbled, her head clearing of any residual fog as he turned her to face him.

She glanced over at the table. He'd only made it to the fourth toy and she was toast. Damn.

"I want you to hear what I'm saying, Solie. Tell me you hear me."

It took a couple of tries, but she finally said, "I hear you. Loud and clear."

"Solie Shaw, you are the most desirable, together female I've ever met. You're loving, caring, giving."

Then his fingers were around her throat. Tightened just enough to make her aware of their presence, then a little bit more until she was keenly aware of exactly how much breath she was being allowed.

"You take care of your friends better than you take care of yourself." He lowered his head for a passion-filled kiss that set her body on fire. The weight of his hand against her skin, the total control he had over her as he collared her neck with his fingers, made her feel safe, secure and sexy in a way that nothing else did.

"You have your shit together and don't you dare allow the memory of some asshat to make you feel less than the spectacular woman you are."

He nipped her tongue and then her bottom lip as he deepened the contact. Held her tight so that his chest pressed against hers, his silk against her bare skin. Rubbed back and forth until her nipples pebbled and ached. Breath soughed in and out of her lungs.

The palm of his free hand skated over a bare breast. Up, down. Back and forth. Then a tug and a gentle pull with thumb and forefinger.

"Does that feel good?" he asked.

He knew it did, but one of the rules was that she must always answer a question, even if she thought it was stupid. So she gasped out, "Yes."

Then he tugged hard, harder, until the nipple throbbed and stung. The he stepped back just a bit to reach for something.

A second later, a riding crop tapped the tender skin of her breast. One, then the other, and back again. Over and over.

She squeezed her thighs together. Shifted up on her toes and back down, trying not to tug on the barely-there hook that her rope was laid over.

"Still good?"

"Oh god, yes. So good," she babbled, unable to quite catch her breath as the hand around her neck forced her head to the right.

Then he bit her.

"Ah god!"

Her determination to take it slow tonight slid down the

river of her sensual desire. The moment the thick clear-pink heart with the little spiky things landed on the side of her ass cheek, her determination went clear out of sight.

She cried out.

"Sssh. Breathe through it, baby. You can do it." Burton's voice with just the right mix of encouragement and bossiness. The heart landed again, and again. She was sure to have bruises. The thought made her smile.

She would call that particular toy, "Brunhilda" from now on because it was one tough bitch.

Another blow. Burton wedged his knee between her thighs so that it rubbed against her clit.

It was over.

The wall around her vulnerability failed all together; and her emotions, infused with her true and natural sexuality, overflowed the banks of her need.

And she let it. Let it go. Let it take the path that it wanted to.

Until all she knew was the sensation of her man's hands around her neck, teasing and tormenting her breasts, skating over her stomach and her panty-clad ass. Brunhilda's sting on her glutes, her thighs. Burton's lips on her skin—sucking, nipping and biting.

Until knees began to buckle and...

"Please. Oh please, Burt," she begged.

Burt lifted the rope from the little keychain hook thingy, picked her up and eased down into the oversized chair with her in his lap again.

Suddenly a blanket was over them as Burt rocked her back and forth.

A thought poofed into her head—Burt with others. Flickers of his landing a flogger or a whip across someone else's skin. She'd even watched him create a butterfly pattern out of color-tipped needles on a woman's back before.

But Solie had never seen him give anyone aftercare when a scene was over. No one.

Yet that's exactly what he was doing with her. Using his hands to soothe, wrapping the blanket over her skin so she wouldn't get chilled. Holding a piece of chocolate to her mouth, encouraging her to eat it. Telling her how well she'd done after such a long time out of the scene. Even massaging her scalp a bit as she fell backward into the endorphin-laced waters of her mind.

5

*I*t had been a hell of a week, but all her deadlines were met for her current clients, she'd picked up a new contract, and had even sent off a congratulatory email to the consultants in Japan who'd landed the new business.

All hail geeks, because without people like Solie, the world just didn't turn. And that meant a nice living for her and her employees.

A glance out the window revealed an uncharacteristically clear day for the Pacific Northwest in early summer. Sunlight sparkled off the Sound and there wasn't a bit of fog to be seen.

She wasn't responsible for the weather, but that fact didn't keep a happy sigh from slipping past her lips as she linked her fingers behind her head, leaned back in her chair and actually put her feet up on her desk.

Yes, I fucking rock.

Add to that, she had a new-but-old fantabulous guy who'd given her space when she needed it, and hung around when she needed that, too. Burton had slept over this week and they'd began to develop a feel for each other.

Solie now automatically slipped on her new cuffs—which she loved, by the way—the moment he walked in the door. She'd learned that he liked to be greeted with a deep, passion filled kiss rather than a "hello" or a "how was your day".

And he'd learned that while she could plan the hell out of a business trip-for-two, she was never going to be the domestic type. Good thing she had sense enough to have a housekeeper or she'd be up to her neck in at least a year's worth of laundry.

She loved sharing her space with Burton. After she bought this place, Mac had designed her a Japanese bath, and Burton's company had built it. Glass brick walls and shoji screens made the space bright and airy. Tiled floors and big windows kept it comfortably cool even when steam filled up the room.

Each evening after a dinner that thankfully neither she nor Burton had prepared, they'd soaked in her Jacuzzi tub until they were limp noodles and relaxed from the stress of their day. Then Burton had let her wash him from stem to stern, which was a delicious journey all on its own.

Skin heated as she thought of how she'd oiled and massaged all that golden, tanned mountain of a man. Burton had muscles on top of muscles, or at least that's what it felt like under her fingers.

She'd sat, perched on his ass, worked coconut oil into the sculpted planes of his back, and along his ribs—he was ticklish, too—and down his hamstrings. Solie had paid special attention to his feet knowing that some days he spent a good deal of his day on them.

By the time she'd worked her way around to his front and down his thighs, his cock had been waving at her. God, she'd practically salivated with the desire to taste him. His natural scent mixed with the coconut oil had been like inhaling a pina colada. He just smelled so…juicy.

He's not even here and my mouth is watering right now. Gah!

Her reward for a job well done? Spankings. Lots and lots of spankings, followed by spooning until she'd fallen asleep. Burton knew she was two kinds of whores—a total shoe whore and a spanking whore. And this man delivered in both those areas.

What she really loved was that the man wasn't interested in turning her into someone she wasn't. He was interested in having her submission from her heart, not some contrived fake version of herself. And that rocked because that *other* guy...

Aw who cared about that other guy?

She now spent her time with Mr. Tall, Dark, and Domly. The up-close experience revealed exactly what kind of mojo he was packing. And Burton brought more to the table than she'd ever imagined.

She thought back on his words at Twilight Teahouse when he'd noticed her shoes and matching outfit. *"Damn, those sexy shoes are meant to be airborne."*

Solie had smiled then. And couldn't help but smile now.

She bounced out of her chair, happy with both her professional and personal lives. This called for dancing, which meant a flail of arms and legs around her office in some semblance of the Running Man. Her body felt light and her spirit even lighter. Add the growing heat in her flesh as a result of Burton's, uh, special focus on her. Damn near every night. All week long.

And, to top off her wonderful week, Solie had quietly made a visit to her doctor to make sure that her seven days of no sex were truly up. And yes, as of yesterday afternoon, sex with Burton was a-okay. After all the delicious attention he'd showered on her all week, she really, *really* wanted to share the ultimate intimacy with this man.

So now, it was Friday. Time to play.

But first, Solie logged onto Kinkfest.com, something she hadn't done since the last time she'd peeked at a certain someone's profile and ended up taking her battered heart from bruised to bloody, as well as getting her ass warmed in public.

Today she noticed a particular note on the "Today's Favorites" page. The person who wrote the post asked, "Why do some people feel the need to test your affection, push you away just to see if you come back? Perform destructive actions repeatedly to hurt themselves and the bond they have with you? Is it that they don't feel they deserve to be happy? That if they have a good, fulfilling and happy relationship that there is something dark hidden? To those people, I say that if you're trying to sink the boat, have the basic decency to let others out of the boat first before you go down with it like some poor suffering martyred soul."

Solie understood exactly where this woman was coming from. But unlike this female, Solie didn't need to ask this question—she already had the answer. The time she'd spent over the last few weeks with both herself and her friends had helped blow out the fog of post-breakup pain-n-rage brain. Today, she was centered, clear headed. Perhaps even half-way in control of her life.

Solie re-read the woman's post and smiled. Burt was right —Solie loved to be of service if she could. So she focused on her inner self, considered the woman's questions, and then poured her heart into an answer.

She wrote, "I read your post and I hope what I have to say is helpful without sounding preachy. I recently went through something similar, and here's what I truly believe—some people are just plain old broken. Common sense doesn't apply because they don't understand themselves. They are walking, damaged, abused, drama creators who are convinced it's everyone's fault but their own.

"It's Kinkfest.com's fault. It's Facebook's fault. It's their mama's fault. Their ex's fault. It's the UPS guy's fault. The weather man's fault. When it comes to the pain they cause others, you could stand before them bleeding from a hundred cuts yet they will swear it wasn't them who did the cutting; even though they're holding the sword with your blood dripping from it.

"Some are narcissists. Some are sociopaths. Some are cyberpaths. Some are psychopaths. Some are just plain predators who specialize in sabotaging themselves and you. They cultivate uncertainty and are good at keeping you off-balance by sowing seeds of doubt. Next thing you know, you begin to second guess yourself in areas where you'd always been confident. And a place like Kinkfest.com is attractive to those types. They are, in various forms, psychological, emotional, even financial and physical predators.

"For a large portion of the population, there is no explanation for why these people "poke you with a stick" other than the most common reason—dysfunction. The end.

"Is this everyone? Nope. Not at all. But I do believe, after having contact with these types, that it is a plausible answer to your question. Learn the signs and if you find yourself ready to commit, run instead. And if you're already in the boat, jump overboard and swim for shore."

A quick check for typos and Solie hit the send button.

Amazing, the lift a few shared words could do for a person—and not the one receiving, but the one giving. With a spring in her step and a dash of pep in her attitude, Solie left the computer exactly as it was, grabbed the house keys off the hook, patted her shepherd on the head and headed out the door.

A broad grin spread across her lips even as the pack of drunk butterflies dive bombed her gut because Burton stood on the front porch.

How the hell a man could make leaning against a deck railing look sexy, she would never know. Her moment of surprise morphed into giddy expectation...and giddy was not a word she associated with herself. Ever.

But Burton just seemed to bring the "little" out in her sometimes.

She didn't bother asking why he'd come here instead of meeting her at the local patisserie for lunch. Whatever his reasons, she didn't really care. Solie just stood there and took him in for a moment. Yep, the man standing on her porch looked good enough to *be* her lunch rather than the soup and sandwich she'd planned to order shortly.

She still felt the impact of those mesmerizing blue eyes, even when hidden behind dark shades. God, he just hummed with a crazy vibrancy that made the skin on her arms erupt in goose bumps. Arms crossed a wide chest that was tastefully covered in his favorite, royal purple silk. He must be off work today. No pressed slacks or suit. Instead he sported a pair of jeans that fit so perfectly she wondered if they were tailored.

Her next thought was curiosity as to where he preferred to have his things cleaned. Solie pulled back from that thought. She and Burton had already negotiated that point— she would not be taking on any domestic tasks for him.

For now, it was all about her, and her emotional and physical needs. Period. And the stubborn ass man wouldn't be moved from that point no matter how much she insisted that she could handle more.

So as he waited for her to come down the steps she was back to ogling the muscled forearms that peeked out from beneath the short sleeves. They were ropey and well-formed, sprinkled with the same dark hair that was on his head and...

"Keep looking at me like that, Sols, and we won't make it out of here."

"Uh, and that's bad?"

"Smart ass." Then he just stood and waited with that damn brow raised. Solie bit her lip to keep from smiling but it didn't really work. He grinned right back as she greeted him with the kiss he wanted, and the kiss she was beginning to love to give. Up on her toes, she simply said, "Hi", and then poured herself into a lip lock that she hoped curled his toes.

When his arms wrapped around her and lifted her against his body with a moan, she lit up inside knowing that the simple contact had him making that delicious sound.

Set back on her feet, Burton stepped back as his fingers trailed over the skin of her neck. He took off his shades and Solie gulped. Oh man, the look he laid on her as he backed away, walked around to the passenger side of his truck and opened the door for her stopped the breath in her lungs.

"Stop eyeballing me, woman, and move your ass."

After all, they were on a schedule and he still hadn't told her why he'd come to pick her up for lunch instead of meeting her at the eatery as planned. But the moment she got a good look at the sparkling mischief in his eyes, she was sure it would be an afternoon to remember.

"You're always in such control. You don't really have a choice, and I'm sorry for that. I know you long to relax, but you just don't have the time, or the chance…or a person who will *make* you."

He was right…but she didn't particularly feel like admitting it just now so she sat, put on her "Me no need nobody" face and sipped her cola in silence.

"Today, I'm that person, Solie."

He snatched her glass and slid his lemon water over to

her side of the table. Head tilted a hard left as she started to open her mouth.

"Unless this is your diabetic cheat day, you'll have lemon water with your food. Period."

Fuck. And she really wanted that cola, more for the kick than anything else. After all, her successful week came with the sacrifice of a nice chunk of sleep. Even if the man across the table was responsible for some of those lost zzzz's and late nights, if Solie was honest with herself—which she made a habit of doing—she needed neither the sugar nor the caffeine.

Burt sat back, all long legs, wide buffed chest and healthy tanned skin. So tall, it looked like someone had folded him into that chair. Add piercing blue eyes against the backdrop of jet black stylish hair, and he looked so delicious, she wanted to just gobble him up and skip lunch all together.

God, it was nice to look at a man and not have to fight that sick sinking feeling of betrayal in her gut, or that anxious knot lodged in her throat almost cutting off her air.

Taking in Burton Khrys was an exercise in decadence, plain and simple.

"Now, where were we? Oh yes, today I'm going to get you to think on nothing but us and what we're doing together. No work. No clients."

He'd reached across the table again, but this time work roughened fingers massaged her palm as he held her gaze. The words were smooth as silk, quietly spoken so only she heard, but her gut did a freefall at the underlying steel of his tone. And suddenly, all of the need to display her everyday bad-assness just...melted away. It felt wonderful.

"What I'm going to tell you to do will push the boundaries of our friendship and our new relationship. Do you trust me?"

For a second her brain got stuck on the words "tell you to do".

Burton Khrys? Alpha boss to her alpha bitch. A different animal. Primal. Earthy. He seriously flipped her subby switch. So instead of calling him on his "tells" rather than "asks", Solie answered his question.

"Yes, I trust you."

"Do you believe that I'd never do anything to harm you?"

She took a sip of lemon water. It was actually pretty refreshing. Good call on his part. Another swallow, then she said, "Burt, I trust you and I agree to whatever it is you're going to ask me to do." She'd deliberately said *ask* instead of *tell* and then bit back a smile when he gave her the raised eyebrow and stern look. "You don't have to keep asking me that. I meant it when I answered you the first time."

"You giving me attitude, Sols?"

"Nope. I'm just sayin'." Besides, every woman had to push her boundaries every now and again. His fingers still stroked her palm, stoking a fire low in her belly that trickled clear down to her toes.

"Do we need to negotiate, woman?"

"Nope. Bring it."

Oh, she was really feeling her Wheaties just now, but she knew she wouldn't regret it. From the stern set of his jaw, it appeared that nice Burton—*oxymoron*—was gone and Mr. Thuddy Paddle-hands was in attendance. Actually, now that she thought about, he was always present. Just not always quite so…

"Well all-righty then." He handed her a little black plastic bag. "Here you go. Off to the bathroom. You'll know what to do with it. See you when you get back."

The bathroom? Oh my goodness.

She rose on wobbly legs with a feeling of both excitement and impending doom. She must be crazy because the thought made her smile inside. When she opened the bag in the ladies room, boy was she glad she'd worn a pair of regular panties instead of a sexy thong or something.

Back at the table, Solie sat gingerly and stared at the man across the table from her. Her yoga pants felt a bit more snug just now.

"Give me the remote." She wasn't stupid enough to mistake it for anything other than what it was—an order.

She handed it over, and watched closely as he fiddled with it in his lap, and then gave it right back to her.

"Turn it on."

"But there are no batteries in it. I already che…" She flipped the switch and went still as the toy she'd inserted into her pussy fired up and her nerve endings went full tilt.

So that's what he was doing. Putting batteries in the thing.

"Turn it half way up and let's go get our food."

Then he winked and left her sitting there?

Was he nucking futs? Go get food? They were at a Mongolian grill where she had to serve up her own veggies and meat, and then take it to the cook to grill it. How was she supposed to do that with a vibrator humming away in her pants?

And Burton was over at the buffet filling his bowl. She sat and stared. The man didn't even turn and look to see if she was coming.

Oh, you'll be coming, all right.

Damn it, she could do this…quaking knees and all. Maybe it was her ego talking, but who knew? She wanted to pass this little test for two reasons—she wanted to prove she could keep her shit together while being totally distracted, and she wanted to please her guy.

Solie sucked in a breath, rose from her seat, ever grateful she'd worn tennis shoes today, and hustled on over to the buffet.

Just keep breathing, just keep breathing. You know, like the blue fish in that Nemo movie. Just keep swimming, just keep swimming.

By the time she made it back to her seat, her palms were sweaty and her hands were shaking about as fast as the little silver bullet stuffed up her pussy.

Burt sat down, turned somewhat sideways in his chair and crossed his legs. Chopsticks in hand, he began to tuck in. "Turn it all the way up. Now talk to me."

Talk to him? Hell she could barely eat her...whatever it was she had in her bowl. Damn chopsticks hit the tabletop three times before he took mercy on her and handed her a fork.

God, it felt like she had a sign propped on top of her head that said, "I have a vibrator stuffed up my hoo-haa. It's flipped to *high* and I want to come SO bad!" On the other hand, she also wanted to kick Burton under the table for coming up with the idea, and then run for it. Maybe that would wipe the shit-eating grin off of his face...but somehow she doubted it.

"Are you close to coming, Solie?" he asked, then popped a piece of grilled shrimp into his mouth. She wondered if it was delicious considering everything she had on her plate tasted the same—like out-of-reach-orgasm, if she had to give the flavor a name.

Sitting back in her chair, Solie pushed away the food she'd been picking over, and gave up fighting the sensations coursing through her body.

She could feel the hum everywhere. Her inner thighs quivered, ass cheeks clenched, knees locked tight. Toes were prepared to curl inside her tennis shoes. Because an orgasm was coming. And it wasn't sneaking up on her. No, it was chasing her, barreling down on her like a cargo train.

Burt had said something. Had asked her a question.

Her brain ran to catch up to the rest of her body. It was losing the race. Badly.

"Solie, no coming without permission," he whispered.

"Huh?" She knew her eyes had begun to droop to half-mast. Didn't care. At all.

"Solie?" He reached under the table, grabbed her knee and squeezed hard.

She jerked in her seat, but it wasn't quite enough to bring her around. So he did it again.

Three times must be the charm because finally she raised her gaze to meet his. Even her eyes felt...wobbly.

"Baby, you look absolutely adorable and goofy."

Well that was enough to pull her completely back from the brink.

Goofy? As if.

Burton laughed out loud.

Solie glanced around. Burton's laugh had caught the attention of a few diners. In fact, several women watched him as he watched Solie.

A swift wind of anxiety kicked up and blew away a bit more of the fog in her horny brain. And just as quickly, she pushed back and chose to sink into the cocoon of need that Burton weaved around her with his words and wicked grin.

After all, he wasn't looking at those women, or returning their attention. This was her best friend, and he'd never been a cheater. He'd pledged himself to *her* a week ago. Had given *her* his unwavering friendship years ago. His toy hummed inside of *her*. And when they left, he'd be going with *her*.

"Any plans for this afternoon, Sols?" he asked, chugging the last of his, uh, her cola.

She shook her head. "Took the rest of the day off."

"Good. Leave your plate. By the time we get to TT, you're going to beg me to come."

TT? He was taking her to Twilight Teahouse in the

middle of the day? Well, they did have a light luncheon tea and menu. But they'd just eaten. Was he taking her to the upper floors? She knew they were available for play at this hour, but she'd just never taken the time to go up to Seattle at mid-day. The traffic alone was a total buzz kill.

Would she have to sit through an agonizingly long bumper-to-bumper ride with a buzzing toy stuffed up her cooch? This gave a whole new meaning to the term "crotch rocket".

Oh god, Solie wasn't sure she could take it.

Burton was on his feet staring at her with a receipt in his hand. When had he paid the bill? Holy hell, she really was drifting in and out of it, whatever "it" was. Just now she had no words.

She grasped the hand extended to her.

"Come along, my googly-eyed beauty."

She snorted, but didn't even bother trying to talk. Googly eyed? Pffft.

Her head said, "Fuck you." But there was no denying that her body said, "Fuck me!"

6

*S*olie handed over the remote when asked, then buckled herself in. She barely noticed the movement of the truck as they sped along, unless Burton hit a bump in the road. Those, she felt profoundly.

God, her fingers trembled. Legs were restless. Skin felt stretched too tight. Pussy was on fire.

Not being allowed to come was exquisite torture. The entire ride from their lunch spot to downtown Seattle, Solie experienced longing, rage and every emotion in between, courtesy of Burton and that fucking remote control.

Every time she thought her mind was about to completely slip, Burton upped the ante.

"A little added sensation, beautiful," he drawled right before a thick fist delivered a thuddy blow to the thickest part of her thigh muscle. The impact of his hand combined with the sizzle of the nerve endings from the sensual sensation was, God, just delightful.

She was going to come. Just couldn't help it.

Right before detonation, Burton dialed the vibrator down

to the lowest setting and all the movement in her channel came to a halt.

"Fuck!" She screamed. Yelled. Practically sobbed. Then he was slapping her thigh again, a lovely and calculated combination of thuddy and stingy blows.

"I've been counting the days, Solie. My dick is about to burst thinking about that sweet pussy. Waking up to the scent of your arousal and not being able to have you has been killing me. So I want to drive you absolutely crazy. Promise I'll join you there shortly after."

He steered his beast-of-a-truck with one hand, and the other was buried in her locs.

"I love your hair. I love that I can pull on your dreads, yank them the way you like, and you won't scream about how I mess up your hair-do." Now his fingers drew circles on her scalp. Round and round. Up and down. Soft strokes followed by the easy *scratch, scratch, scratch* of short blunt nails.

And then he pulled.

Solie slammed her eyes shut, squeezed her thighs together and bit down on her lip to keep from yelling out her pleasure. He hadn't told her to keep quiet. There was just a bit of stubborn in her that was still trying to hold it together.

Finally, she gasped, "Oh God, please!"

"Almost there, baby. Just hold on. Almost there, I promise." Burt's words were barely a whisper, yet the impact could be felt from eyebrows to baby toes.

And she wasn't the only one in sorry shape. Her man wasn't immune to what he was doing to her. The evidence was in the barely-there hitch of his breath when she'd screamed. The dampness on his palm as he ran his free hand up and down her forearm.

Knowing that his desire was being pushed and pummeled by hers only sent her trip higher.

Crazy? Yes, that pretty much summed up where she was right now. She was in Loonyville. Tooty in the head. Brimming with bonkers. Coo-coo for Cocoa Puffs.

By the time they pulled into the underground parking garage at Twilight Teahouse, Solie was damn near ready to pass out.

Burton walked around to the passenger side and opened her door. Could her legs even support her weight? The better question was, did she care? Burton was big enough, and certainly strong enough to carry her without any problem so she decided to let him.

He switched the vibrator back on for a split second, then turned it off again.

Solie went still. Held her breath and waited to see if he would change his mind. Again. The last thing she needed was to think she was in the clear, step out of the car and then fall flat on her face when the sensation kicked back in.

Hey, she'd made a rhyme. Such a talented lady at multitasking.

Oh wait. Not a rhyme. Just her brain cells imploding.

She laughed, cackled actually.

"Need a second?" Burt asked as she swung her legs around so she could hop out of the vehicle.

A second passed. Then two. Solie made no move to actually get out.

Burt grinned. "I'd offer to carry you, but even in your current sorry state—"

"Sorry?" she hissed. "You put me in this state, by the way."

"—I still don't think you'd let me carry you anywhere."

Well he had that right. It didn't matter that she'd just told herself that she'd let him toss her over his shoulder if he wanted. Now that he'd pushed her particular "independent woman" button, she would walk on her own two feet until the moment that she couldn't stand up any longer. And based on the experience so far, she just might reach that point pretty soon.

She looked around the parking lot that was for private club members only. No public parking to be had—not even for those who came to enjoy the unique and delicious fare in Twilight Teahouse.

"Quite a few more cars here than I'd expect for a mid-day romp. What are we doing here, Burton?"

"Don't worry. I wouldn't invite anyone into our play unless we'd discussed it. And honestly I'm not anxious to share you at all. As for today, you've done so well denying yourself multiple orgasms, I think you deserve a treat."

She eyeballed him but didn't ask what kind of treat. Besides, he knew full well that she was curious, and if he wanted to tell her, then he would.

"I asked Kuri to hold a play room for us, just in case we made it out here today. Fourth floor. Japanese baths."

An unfamiliar sound erupted out of Solie's throat. It kind of sounded like a…squeal. Solie was sure she'd never made that sound before, but immediately didn't care. Out of the car, not only were her legs steady, she practically ran Burton over trying to get to the elevator.

Solie and Mac took advantage of the spa on the second floor at least once a month. Nothing kinky, just a slice of mani-pedi heaven. However, the fourth floor was couples only—no exceptions. She'd wanted to experience the Japanese themed play space forever, but the ex-dude hadn't been interested. Solie learned later that one of the many women he'd slept around with worked up there—big surprise. Not!

And now, thanks to Mr. Burton Khrys, here she was at last.

This man is racking up some serious lucky points.

Once inside the sleek elevator, Solie pushed the button

for the fourth floor. Doors slid closed but the elevator didn't move.

Shit.

She didn't have her little magnetized access keycard to the club.

Damn it, damn it, damn it.

Burton reached past her, swiped his keycard and Solie let out a sigh of relief.

Though her sex was heated and throbbing, her underwear was soaked and the damn things were beginning to cool against her skin, the only words in her head were "clothes", "off" and "now".

Relief. She needed it badly. But more than that, Solie needed Burton, the man, not just what he could give her, or do for her. She needed his special kind of tenderness. His own unique brand of care.

Suddenly he was there, pressed against her even as her back was flush against the cool frosted glass of the elevator wall. She drank from his lips as if his kiss were her oasis in the dessert. He'd been raining life on her own particular parched heart for years. She just hadn't realized the depth of it until now. All the love and care he'd shown in their platonic relationship was just as solid and sincere now that they'd decided on an intimate pairing.

And now that she'd had a taste, Solie loved kissing Burt. The man put all his emotion and intention into every kiss, every time.

He'd told her when he'd picked her up for lunch today that she would focus on nothing but the two of them. No work. No clients. The man had been so right—her concentration was on him, *them*. No one and nothing else. Not her past. Nor her future. Hell, not even the present, with the exception of where this elevator was headed.

Burton broke the kiss, but Solie kept her eyes closed and waited to see, *feel*, what was next.

Her man flipped her around, grabbed her by the hair and pulled her head sideways. Then he bit her on *that* spot—the one that made her unsteady and her entire body quiver. He bit her again, then sucked the skin just there. Solie's knees buckled. Burton caught her and lifted her into his strong, brawny arms with no effort. Barely a moment later, the elevator dinged.

God help her, they'd reached the fourth floor already?

Doors slid open and she felt Burton move. Head buried in his chest, she listened to the solid thump of a strong heart, heard him speak briefly to someone, and then they were off again.

A traditional Japanese bath meant scrubbing down in the shower, and then soaking in a deep tub for relaxation. Images floated through her head of Burton's lean and muscular body as she'd washed him in her own bath at home. All that deeply tanned skin, sprinkled with dark hair on ropey defined arms. The sculpted chest slick with ginger soap as she played with the single nipple ring that graced his left pectoral. Solie almost smiled against his shirt just now as she remembered how the thick beautiful cock had tapped her forehead as she'd scrubbed his quads thoroughly. His groans of pleasure as her fingers glided over his perfect ass.

Women would kill for an ass like Burton Khrys. Just...*dayum*.

"Thank you," Burt said with a hearty laugh.

"Huh?"

"You complimented my ass. Glad you like it."

"Wait, what? Oh, never mind. You must be the only man on Earth that makes me say things out loud when I don't mean to." Solie tried to sound grumpy, she really did. But his fingers were teasing the underside of her breast and she tried to bury her face even deeper into his chest as he hurried along.

"Like I said earlier, adorably goofy."

Smart ass.

"Really?" Burt snorted. "I think you've just earned yourself a spanking with your orgasms."

Yep. I'm definitely gone in the brain.

Only she made sure to keep that particular thought to herself.

SOLIE FOUND HERSELF CARRIED INTO AN IMMACULATE CREAM and lapis blue shower that was big enough for at least ten people. A little wooden stool sat in the middle of the space.

Just as Burton set her on her feet an attendant came in.

"I'll see you in the soaking tub shortly, okay Solie?"

She must have looked disappointed because then he said, "I told you this was a treat for you. Not service for me. Not right now. Enjoy your shower and the attendant will bring you to me. Oh, and the bathroom is over there. Go and take care of things, but no touching yourself. That's all mine."

He gave her a quick kiss, and left. After a trip to the bathroom, the evil bullet vibrator was washed and tucked away in her clothing. The attendant already had the water at the perfect temperature when she came out of the restroom. The woman washed her with sugar scrub until she was sure her skin glowed.

Ten minutes later, her entire body felt as solid as a wet noodle as she was led to the soaking room.

Her breath lodged in her throat as she caught sight of her man standing there waiting for her. He wore a traditional blue robe and stood next to a bank of windows that looked out over the city. She caught the glint of sun off the deep blue water of the Sound and swore it was close enough to dive into from here.

The tub was huge, more like a big sunken pool rather than a soaking tub. Burt motioned her into the water, shed his robe and stepped down onto the first step. He wore not a stitch. And that was just the way Solie liked him.

"Come over here, Solie."

She eased into the pool with a sigh. The temperature was perfect—not too hot, not too cool. Solie waded over to him and sat down in a spot that caused the water to level out just below her breasts.

"No, right here."

He pointed to his lap and the dusky pole of a cock that was almost purple at the head.

Oh my goodness. She'd been turned on high for a good part of the day and even though the shower attendant washed her with not a single indication of horniness, Solie was still on a medium simmer.

If she sat on his lap she wouldn't last long.

Wait a minute, what in the world was she thinking? Who said she had to last at all? This man wasn't going to play games with her. He wasn't going to offer her a lollipop and then snatch it away when she reached for it.

No. That was another life. One that didn't deserve her emotional attention.

This was her and Burton's time, and that's where she would keep her thoughts. Period.

So she eased over to him and sat on his lap. With a gasp, she found herself face down over this lovely thighs, with his cock pressing into her stomach.

"First, let's get this out of the way, courtesy of your favorite smart ass."

His palm landed on her ass with a loud *schwack*. Holy fuck! Her skin was wet from both the shower and the quick trip across the tub, and it caused the mother of all stings when his hand connected with the damp flesh.

By the third whack Solie was ready to float away.

Four.

Five.

She was moaning, gasping his name.

Six.

Seven.

Begging was imminent.

Eight.

Nine.

Ten.

"Oh please. Please, Burton..."

She was so boneless her legs just fell open as she panted in an attempt to catch her breath.

"Mmm, look at that. That pussy is so wet and pretty. You're ready aren't you?"

A nod was all she could manage as all the stimulation of the day swirled together and crashed down over her libido like a thunderstorm that had been building in the summer heat.

Just before thick fingers slid into her swelling folds, he stopped. "I'm going to do a wet check, all right?"

"Yes," she breathed.

And then he was stroking her, slipping the pad of his index finger against the resisting ring of muscle at her entrance. The other hand explored the blushing skin of her ass. Solie found herself quickly moving past want into pure, unmistakable need.

With each dip, her hips wound in a larger and larger circle until she was practically humping his hands.

It didn't matter that the silken heat of his cock scalded the skin of her stomach. It didn't matter that he obviously wanted her as much as she wanted him. Burton wouldn't give her what she craved until she asked for it. Nicely.

"P...Please fuck me. Please."

"And why should I do that, Solie?"

"Because I need it."

"And why else?" He pressed two fingers deep into her sex. She almost came on the spot.

"Because I deserve it."

"Deserve what?"

She knew what he was after. It was a conversation that they'd had on more than one occasion throughout their friendship. And Solie knew it to be true, so she didn't hesitate.

"I deserve to be loved without conditions. I deserve to be treated like the queen that I am. I deserve to have what I desire. And in a D/s dynamic, I deserve to be rewarded when I have earned it."

"Good girl. And today, you have definitely earned a reward. You were amazing, kept your sanity long beyond what I expected. And you didn't come. Not once. So let's fix that."

Without another word, Solie found herself in the tub with her chest flat against the cool tiles where Burton had been sitting only moment before.

With an ass cheek in each hand, the man spread her wide, then worked himself inside until he was slick with her juices. Then he was *there*, the entire length of him stretched and filled her, until she swore that if she were looking in a mirror she'd see his cock reflected in her eyes.

One hand buried in her hair and the other stroking every inch of flesh he could reach. And it was so good. Each stroke was better than the last, better than every dream she'd ever had about this man. Better than a new pair of sexy strappy high heeled shoes!

And then she was coming, and coming and coming. Making up for each orgasm she'd denied herself earlier. And when she thought she was all wrung out, Burton proved her wrong twice more.

By the time he found his own pleasure deep inside her pussy, Solie was damn near cross eyed and beyond noddle-boned.

It was the best lunch-date-turned-dinner-date EVAH!

LATER ON THAT NIGHT, SOLIE WOKE ABRUPTLY. SHE ROLLED over and took in the sight of the man next to her. She seldom used the fireplace in her bedroom, but the sunny day had turned into a fog-filled chilly night. The embers glowed just enough to cast the most beautiful light on her best friend.

And grabbed her journal, flipped on a small reading light so as not to wake Burt, and she began to write.

Eight weeks ago she'd been beyond heartbroken, the pain so tangible that when she looked in the mirror it seemed etched into her very skin.

Eight weeks ago, a confidence that had never been in question before had teetered on the ledge of her surety. Why? Because the person that was supposed to love her, treasure her, care for and keep her, had been on the wrong side of everything.

He'd spoken to and about her in a manner that was far beyond unkind.

Had yelled and screamed at her, pushed into her space, gotten in her face. When she'd finally had enough and asked why he treated her in such a manner his response had been, "Because I can."

If she'd been honest, that was the day she knew it was over. Her heart had known what her mind didn't want to accept.

Eight weeks ago she'd learned that the man that had lived in her house, slept in her bed, spent time with her family and friends, had also done those same things with countless other women...all at the same time.

She'd given and given and given—her mind, body, soul, money, food, her trust and her time. All he had to do was ask for it, and it had been his.

It was in her nature to give. It was a part of herself that she couldn't simply turn off, and had no desire to, although at that time she'd wished otherwise, if only to keep some part of herself from being emotionally stomped into the carpet.

Eight weeks ago, she'd tallied up what he'd given her and it amounted to nothing more than a lovely spanking or two, a broken heart...and an STD.

But that was eight weeks ago. And this was now.

Was she still healing? Sure. But the hurt was barely there. The heartache almost completely healed until the cracks in her heart were now full of love for herself and the man whose arm was thrown over her waist. Gone was the fire-driven anger that had been a companion of sorts. Now, there was only pity and compassion for Marcais, a man who would never truly know love.

Solie was free. In every way that she needed to be, she was free.

And not so free.

She was in service to Burton Khrys, his companion and lover. And this bondage was a sort that she welcomed any day of the week.

With that, she tucked away her journal, clicked off the reading light and decided to dream of what she would look like in the new red and white bamboo and silk rope Burton had given her after he'd brought her home from a most wondrous and playful afternoon that faded seamlessly into an equally wondrous night.

7

*J*n the early darkness of the morning, Burton woke her up with tender lovemaking that quickly morphed into the rough-and-tumble loving she craved.

After coming three times, they landed in a hot and deliciously sweaty heap with the sheets a tangle around their feet.

Out of the blue, a final remaining dam Solie hadn't been aware of, broke inside of her.

Burton gathered her into his arms and squeezed tight. "What's wrong, Solie? What is it?"

"Nothing is wrong. It's perfect actually. You've given me back to myself," she sobbed.

"No, darlin', you did that all on your own."

Her mouth dropped open when he eased her away from his body so he could look into her eyes. A solitary tear slid down his cheek. His words were solid without a single waver. If she hadn't been looking at him just now she wouldn't have believed it.

"Here's what Marcais didn't understand, Solie. A Dom isn't just someone that tells you to strip, bends you over the sofa or his knee and gives you forty whacks. The man was obviously never taught to take care of his things. He didn't know the difference between rough sex and being a Dominant, baby. Anyone can Dom a doormat, just like anyone can tie up a woman and then tell her not to move. Me, I'd rather place your arm where I want it, tell you not to move and know that you can move—but won't.

Anyone can declaw a cat and then feel high and mighty because it can't scratch. But honestly, darlin', I'd rather have you just the way you are, claws and all, knowing that you keep them sheathed just for me.

God, I adore you. You're strong and I respect that. That guy's issue had to do with his character, not yours. I guess for some fucked up reason he felt that if he convinced you that you were 'less than', then it would make him feel 'more than'. Solie, you're an amazing woman. And the fact that you submit to me because you choose to makes me the luckiest bastard alive."

"Thank you, Burt. Thank you so much for that." Watery smile and all, she leaned up and kissed him. And Burt being Burt, she soon found herself underneath him moaning out her pleasure before slipping back into a peaceful sleep.

SOMETHING WENT FROM KNOCKED OUT TO FULLY AWAKE IN seconds. Her heart pumped furiously and a chill traveled up the back of her neck. She felt...watched. Like something or someone was in the room with her. Rather than rolling over and jerking herself out of bed to fight, she stretched, rolled over slowly and kept her eyes lashes lowered so that her eyes were mere slits.

Arms over her head, she peeked toward the door and then wrapped her arms around her pillow and snuggled in with what she hoped was a convincing sleepy sigh. She lay there in the dim light of the new dawn and stilled as if she'd fallen back asleep.

And something was wrong. She knew it.

The dog had barked, but as quickly as she'd started up with her deep shepherd voice, loud enough to wake the dead, she'd stopped. Must have been a squirrel outside or something.

Then the bedroom door moved. Slowly. Deliberately. Until it closed with a quiet swish. Maybe it was Burt? Yes, that was it. It was Burt just checking in on her before he left to go get breakfast. No need to be worried, right?

When the tingle wouldn't go away, Solie forced herself to relax and drift back to sleep. Only, sleep wouldn't come, damn it.

After half an hour of pretending to snore with no further noise or door movement, she got up and hit the shower.

"May as well start the day," she grumbled.

Ten minutes and a protein shake later, with leash in hand she headed out to walk the dog.

If there were any farms nearby, she was sure she'd beat the chickens awake, it was so quiet out. The dew on the grass as she jogged began to seep into her shoes to make her socks damp. The fog was thick and the humidity felt good on her face. It was the only skin showing since she'd bundled up against the chilly Pacific Northwest July morning.

"Some summer we're having, right, Mims," she said to the dog. Then she laughed at herself. What a bundle of contradictions she was...well, sometimes.

"Damn. Time to go back Mims. Sorry, girl. I need to get my day moving."

Around the corner from her house, Solie ducked into the wide, clean alley that separated the townhouses down the street from her house. Almost to her back door, she slammed to a halt.

Marcais Dupree, nutball extraordinaire, stood there in the dim light of the dawn watching her.

"What the fuck are you doing here?" she snapped.

"What do you mean what the fuck am I doing here?"

"Why are you near my house?"

"I have a friend in this area. And what's it to you? I can go wherever the fuck I want to go whenever I feel like it."

With each word he walked closer, bowing up his chest at her, his words bitten off at the ends as if he wished he could chew her up and spit her out. His body language screamed violence and she hated that her muscles were tensed for fight or flight.

At one time, she would have never been afraid of this man.

But that was then and this was now.

Mims must have picked up her nervousness because she started to growl. The noise drew Marcais' attention, thankfully.

"Well, have a good day. Come on, Mims." And Solie walked on toward her house taking a wide berth around the man who stared daggers at her.

From behind his words punched her in the back.

"So you left me for that faggot, Burt, I see."

Left him for Burt? Was he out of his mind?

Oh yeah. Sociopath, remember? Duh.

"I didn't leave you for anyone, Marcais. You cheated. You lied. I walked. And I have it on good authority that you're carrying right on with one of your mistresses as if she was always your world rather than your secret. So fuck you. Now if you'll excuse me, I have a jog to finish and work to do."

With that, she forced her legs to jog rather than flee,

pulled her key from her sweatpants pocket before she was even close to the door, and ducked inside at record speed.

Heart pumping, she knew that she'd just defused a time bomb. The expression on his face chilled the marrow in her bones. The anger. The malice. It didn't make any sense, given she'd been nothing but good to the man. The fact that he was angry because he thought she'd left him for Burt was more than unsettling given it had no place in reality whatsoever. It didn't even make any sense.

Wait a minute. How the hell did Marcais know she was seeing Burton? Having Burt at her house was no new thing, even when she'd still been with Marcais, Burt and Mac spent plenty of time over here. He'd been banned from the Twilight Teahouse after they got wind that he was passing cooties around so no one there would dare tell him her business. So how in the hell did he know what she was doing in the privacy of her own home?

Sociopath. She had to keep reminding herself. She slipped the leash off of the dog, toed off her damp sneakers and locked every door in the house.

Mac had used her considerable connections in the Army and learned that Marcais was being reassigned to Germany soon. Well, Germany couldn't get here fast enough, damn it. Yep. He was a time bomb all right—one that needed to completely go away so she didn't have to worry about it detonating anywhere near her.

SHORTLY AFTER SOLIE HAD BOOTED UP HER COMPUTER WITH the determination to concentrate on work, Burt showed up with coffee and Dunkin' Donuts. Work all but forgotten, she left her office, ducked into the bedroom to put on her leather cuffs and grab her meds, and then met her man in the living room.

Burt sat on the couch and Solie chose a spot on the floor between Burt's legs. She sunk her bare feet into the thick plush carpet with a sigh. "Ooh, I think I'm in love," she mumbled around a bit of carb-loaded perfection. "Timing is perfect." She took another bite and followed it down with a gulp of strong coffee. The stuff was so hot it burned all the way down her throat, but it tasted so good she didn't care.

As they ate, Solie told of how surprised she'd been when Marcais appeared like some vengeful spirit out of the fog.

"I don't like that he's hanging around here out of the blue, Solie. You know he's bat-shit crazy from his whacked out behavior with you. And if the stories his ex-wife told you are true, this man can be dangerous."

The doorbell rang. Solie jumped.

"Okay, I really don't like that you're wound up so tight, woman. At all." Burt got up off the couch and walked out of the living room. Mims joined him as he headed to the front door. A few moments later he called out, "Solie, come here, darlin'."

God, she loved when the country-boy came oozing out of his pores. Such a gentleman. Sort of.

At her man's side, Solie smiled at her neighbor from down the street.

"Hi, Miss Solie. Sorry to disturb you this early in the morning, especially on a Saturday, but I wanted to catch you before I head out to the base."

"No problem, Grange. What's up?"

"Well, my wife thinks it's nothing but I'm not so sure so I'm just gonna tell you. We've been seeing a black truck cruising up and down the neighborhood."

Her stomach hit the floor.

"And it seems to slow down near your house and then

keeps going. And a couple of weeks ago I noticed someone coming in and out through your back door when you're not at home. And sometimes it's really late at night, like two and three in the morning.

My wife figured it was your boyfriend or something. But after comparing notes, we realized that it's not the same person." With that he nodded at Burt.

"So, what does this person look like?" Burt asked. Solie braced herself for the reply.

"Tall, about six foot three. Big. You know, muscular big, not fat big. Bald. Dark skin."

"Really?" she asked too brightly. "Well, thanks. I appreciate you looking out for me. But it's all good. No worries."

"Good. I was hoping everything was okay."

"So how long are you down range this time, Grange?"

"Just a quick tour and I'll be back in no time. It's my last deployment before I retire and neither my wife nor I can wait."

"I understand that, for sure. Let your sweetie know that if she needs some company while you're gone she's welcome to come over in her pj's and watch corny movies with me any time. I'll even provide the popcorn."

"Thanks, Solie. I appreciate that, ma'am. Take care."

The moment she closed the door, Burt wrapped her up in his arms and whispered, "I'm staying here today. You're not going to your office across town either. It's him, Solie. Coming in and out. Now we know why that key disappeared out of the spare key drawer."

And why the back door had been unlocked when she was sure she'd locked it. Hell, even Mac had caught it a time or two.

"But that key isn't missing. I just misplaced it or something."

"Think about it, Solie. The key that you don't use was

suddenly missing from its proper spot? You only noticed because you were looking for it to give to me. After we used *your* key off *your* key ring to make a copy for me, suddenly the missing key reappears out of nowhere? We brushed it off, but now we know that one of those times he showed up to bring you your mail, he snagged that fucking key. Then used his own copy to come inside and put the key back."

She knew Burt was right. Knew it down to her toes. But denial felt like a safer place, so that's where she decided to hang out just now.

"Uh, okay, Burt. So, why would he show himself a few houses down if he could have just come inside?"

A sweat-inducing image popped into her mind—her bedroom door sliding silently closed this morning. The following chill was so deep, it was as if someone had walked over her grave. What if…? No. No, it couldn't have been. She refused to believe it. Burt was just being paranoid.

"I can't speak to the man's motive, Solie. At all. Maybe the neighbors are right, maybe they're not. But we're not taking any chances. Now, get dressed and let's go see a movie."

"But you have work today. *I* have work today."

"Unless someone is going to die if you don't work today, you are taking the day off. And so am I."

"Fine. But if you're going to make me go see a movie, then I wanna see something with hot men and stuff that goes boom."

"You're on, woman." With a grin, Burt pulled out his mobile, made a quick call and just like that, he'd rescheduled a building walk-through and a design planning session. And none of Solie's clients worked on the weekends so she didn't have to call anyone.

Jogging pants exchanged for a cute skirt and sandals, hand-in-hand, they were out the door for a matinee. And Solie was so happy and comforted she stuffed the weird run-in with *that guy* into a mental sack with all the other shit that had been bugging her. In her head, she set it on fire and threw it off a cliff.

"I NEVER THOUGHT I'D LIKE A SEQUEL BETTER THAN THE original but that movie was just…" Two feet into the back den, Solie stopped short, whirled around to the man at her back and scowled. "Burton Khrys, why would you do that?"

"Do what?" he asked, helping her out of her sweater.

"That." She pointed to Mims who had her big furry butt up on one of the loveseats that faced the big bay window and looked out toward the Sound. The shepherd was eating dog food. Out of a can!

"You know she's not allowed on the furniture. And to give her wet food out of a can? That's not even the stuff we feed her."

Annoyed, Solie bore down on her poor dog. She almost felt bad when Mims cowered just a bit. She snatched the can of smelly cheap dog food away and headed to the kitchen to toss it in the trash.

A gentle but firm hand wrapped around her biceps and halted her steps.

"Solie, wait. Call 911. Now."

"What? Why?"

"You asked why I would feed the dog on the couch. But I've been with you since lunchtime yesterday. The only time I left you was to get Dunkin' Donuts super early this morning. When did you see me go buy this funky ass dog food and give it to the dog on the loveseat?"

Oooh, he had a point.

"Call the police, Solie. I'm going to have a look around."

"Okay." Her stomach dropped into her shoes. Oh God.

"No problem." This couldn't be happening. The neighbor had told her someone had been coming in and out while she was gone. She didn't want to believe it even though he described her ex. But then again, it could have been any other tall, bald, buff dude, right?

Okay, stop. That thought didn't make it any better.

She headed toward the stairs. She'd call 911, but after she changed into something a bit more comfortable.

She turned the corner to head upstairs…and ran smack into Marcais.

A scream ripped from her throat involuntarily as she scrambled backward.

"What the fuck are you doing in my house?"

She couldn't believe the baffled expression on his face, as if he was the surprised one. So he was off guard, eh? Good. The fucker.

When he didn't answer, Solie moved toward the phone across the living room. "I'm calling the police right now."

"Bitch, you pick up that phone and I swear…"

Solie's heart lodged in her throat when two hundred and fifty pounds of solid muscle stalked her way.

Then Burt was there, standing between her and Marcais.

"Oh, I've been waiting for this," Burt said with the most sinister grin she'd ever seen spread across his beautiful mouth. "Take one more step toward her. Give me an excuse to kick your ass. Any excuse will do."

Marcais might be brave enough to threaten a woman, but he wasn't stupid by any stretch of the imagination. But unfortunately for him, he wasn't that smart either.

He took one step toward Solie.

And in the next instant, he was flat on his back holding his jaw and his nuts.

Burton Khrys did not tolerate threats to a female. Period.

The police were on the way but unfortunately Marcais

had recovered his ability to breathe before they arrived. He scrambled to his feet, backed away, and used his coat sleeve to open the door. Solie just shook her head. What point was there to making sure he had no prints on the door knob when she was looking right at him? Amazing.

And after the police came and took their statements, Burt and Solie went on a little expedition in her house trying to figure out what the hell Marcais was doing up and down the stairs.

What they found had her sitting with tears in her eyes and her mouth wide open. One thing was for sure—she couldn't pretend all was well anymore. Couldn't bask in her own denial. The proof was in her hand.

Cameras. Wireless little cameras.

She'd been under surveillance and hadn't even known it.

The sheriff was already on his way to the base to make the arrest. What the hell else had Marcais done that she was unaware of?

Finally Burt pressed a shot of whisky into her left hand while he took her findings from her right hand and dropped them into a little baggie.

Burt lifted the glass that remained untouched and cool against her fingers. He tipped it up and she obediently drank it as he spoke.

"It's a good thing he's in jail or I'd kick his ass again. But now we know. And better to know what you're dealing with than not."

She emptied the glass and while her gut still burned from that first shot, Burt poured her another. She downed it without hesitation and then let her man take her to bed.

AND HE KNEW JUST WHAT SHE NEEDED. AS ANGRY AS SHE FELT

over this newest betrayal, what she needed was to feel cherished and loved. And that was something Burt could give her.

"Strip and then put this on," he said, handing her a robe identical to the one she'd worn at Twilight Teahouse on their lunchtime visit to the Japanese Baths. "The water is ready. So are the ropes. Are you?"

She looked up and Burton watched her expression morph from sadness and anger to resolve. "Oh God, yes. Always."

"Safe word?" he asked.

Without hesitation, she replied, "Kickass". His woman might be fragile. She might even be broken. But she was not down for the count by any stretch of the imagination.

LUSCIOUS

1

"*M*s. Ivers, your ten-thirty appointment is here."

"Thank you, Jolene. I see it on my calendar as a half-hour consultation, but I don't have any details. Who is it again?"

"It's a corporation based in Montana. I went ahead and booked it since you're licensed to do business there."

"That's fine. Do we have a specific name of who to expect?"

"Nope. It just says Big Sky Builders."

"Okay. Give me five minutes and then send them in. I'm headed to Seattle early, so if I haven't wrapped it up in exactly thirty minutes, save me."

With a familiar chuckle and a firm, "It's a deal, ma'am," from her assistant of ten years, Mac cleared her desk. She prided herself on keeping client's details confidential and made sure that no easily-identifiable information from her previous appointment was visible to whoever was getting ready to walk through her door.

She shutdown her desktop, packed her briefcase and set it near the door next to the coat rack. With a quick look around to make sure she was ready to leave as soon as the appointment was done, Mac smiled to herself.

She loved this space. It was a simple as that. There weren't many women in her field of expertise, and even fewer that did well enough in their own practice to have their own building, a staff of four architects, six engineers and surveyors.

Who cared that it wasn't a ginormous place? It was prime real estate built to her specifications. There were floor to ceiling windows, balanced by wood burning fireplaces in the private offices and common areas to keep the chill of the Pacific Northwest at bay. Thanks to her good friend, Burton Khrys, contractor extraordinaire, top of the line electronics were built into the very walls and gave a whole new meaning to the words "surround sound". Her smile grew exponentially as she thought on the Friday afternoons when high energy music pumped through the place and she sometimes caught her guys and gals dancing in the hallways.

Architectural engineering was a challenging career choice, but there was no rule that said it had to be a miserable one. The atmosphere was purposely upbeat and casual with a nice dose of "geek" thrown in, and it made Mac smile to know her team loved working here.

She switched on a quiet, classical tune with one of the small remotes on her desk. The smooth hum of string and quiet tinkling of piano filled the room without being overpowering. It wouldn't do for her potential client to have to battle with the stereo to be heard, and she found that music often put people at ease; cutting through the crap and posturing that was so common when they walked in and discovered that Mac was indeed, a female.

Next, she hefted her supposed-to-be-light-but-was-actually-heavy-as-hell laptop and hauled it over to the comfy chairs arranged at the round table reserved for consultations.

The thought of where she was going after this meeting had her practically skipping, and she'd just caught herself when a quiet knock sounded at her office door.

Get your head in the game, woman. Well, this game anyway. The other games are for later.

She almost giggled. Almost.

She smoothed down her skirt, sat and called out, "Come on in, please."

Jolene opened the door, stepped inside and introduced her potential client.

After Mac was able to pick her jaw up off the floor, she hopped out of her chair, flew over to the person who'd just entered, and then wrapped him in a fierce hug.

"Oh my god, Jay!" she said in a rush of breath. "It's so good to see you? How are you these days and what in the world brings you here?"

He hugged her back, and that tickle in her gut that she'd always experienced in his arms was as familiar to her as her favorite pair of kitten-heeled house shoes.

"I'm great, Mac. How are you?" he said, his voice a timbre that reminded her of that male actor who played Thorin Oakenshield on the Hobbit movies—deep and sexy as hell. Add a tastefully cut mop of thick, silky-looking, jet black waves on his head that set off jewel green eyes, and a physique to die for. He was the perfect bedtime companion with one exception—he wasn't her husband, Landon Ivers.

She stepped back and quickly said, "Jolene, this is Jay Frenz. We're old friends."

"It's nice to meet you, Mr. Frenz," Jolene said, her smile bright, but her eyes not missing a damn thing.

"Please call me Jay. It's nice to meet you as well. Mac used to talk about you all the time." Oh that smile was as deadly.

"Interesting. She never mentioned you at all."

Ouch.

"Excuse me, Mac. I'll let you two get to work." And with a glance down her nose, Jolene quietly left the room.

Mac and Jay's acquaintance had been of a personal nature, and she never, ever told her personal business at work. Especially if the Twilight Teahouse was involved in the story. So, yes, Jolene was correct—she'd never mentioned Jay *at work*. However, it wasn't like the other woman to say as much. They would be having a little talk about office etiquette later, for sure.

Mac motioned toward the waiting chairs. "So are you back in Seattle? How is it we didn't know you were back in town? Oh my god, it's so good to see you."

And she meant it.

"I wasn't sure you would think so," Jay said, easing himself down into the overstuffed chair. Legs crossed, the first thing Mac noticed was the exquisite cut of his trousers, silk socks and a pair of shoes that almost made her jealous. She was a bona fide shoe whore, and happy to admit it. Nothing rang her bell like a man in a nice pair of dress shoes. And Jay knew that about her.

"We parted on good terms, Jay. Why wouldn't I be glad to see you?"

"Well, you never know how things can change inside a person after a break up."

"Is that why you didn't give your name as the person needing a consultation?" she asked, not afraid to get right to the point.

"Actually, it is. But it's a legitimate business opportunity, Mac. I know you take your work seriously and I wouldn't try to play you that way."

"Good. I'm glad to hear it. Otherwise, I'd have to kick your ass."

His grin said he'd welcome such a thing, and lit up the

room as his gaze took her in from head to toe. "I expected nothing less."

Mac's head tilted to the side as a bundle of thoughts rolled through her mind. She was genuinely happy to see Jay. Same charm, same gorgeous body, same handsome face. And same million dollar smile and wardrobe to match. But her heart didn't turn over at the sight of him anymore. Sure, he made her mind play dirty fantasies, but what healthy woman with a strong appreciation for men didn't get a little tingly in the lady bits when she ogled a gorgeous specimen of a man? It didn't mean she wanted to fall into bed with him. In the jump-bones department, this was a sexy man, but she had no desire to literally hump Jay Frenz. Not anymore.

"Before we get down to business, are you available for dinner this evening, Ms. Ivers?"

"I'm sorry, Jay, but I'm not. I, uh, well, Landon and I are back together. Fully."

"Fully?" he queried. "As in, married again?"

She nodded and knew her happiness shone through. Just a thought of her husband lit up a sun within her soul. It was a glorious thing, precious and whole.

In short, she was one lucky bitch.

"Well, I didn't see that coming. I'm happy that all worked out, Mac. It was a very trying time, for sure," Jay said. His countenance was a little less bright than a few moments ago, but he appeared to be sincere.

And he was right. It had been a trying time.

Mac and Landon Ivers had been through, as in finished, done and over with. She had the divorce papers to prove it. At that time, Mac had thrown herself into work to try and pretend she wasn't falling apart inside. When that didn't work, she'd sought refuge in counseling with a master life coach instead.

A crap ton of sessions, as well as some time off for self-reflection, had put Mac on the right road. She was healthy in mind, body and spirit. And planned to stay that way.

Landon had noticed the change in her, saw that she'd bounced back from the devastation he'd wrought in both their lives. In his misery, she'd been a beacon. In fact, he'd noticed so keenly, he'd conned her into having dinner with him so he could ask point blank just what in the hell she'd done to get through their divorce with herself intact.

Landon had taken her words to heart, contacted the counselor and jumped in with both feet. The man had put himself through the paces, completed every session and all of the associated tasks, and got his shit together—which included getting rid of the submissive he'd had an affair with and wrought all the hell between them in the first place. In fact, he'd cut loose the mega-bitch and then removed himself completely from the BDSM scene for almost a year.

Then Landon Ivers, alpha maximus, had begged his wife to take him back.

And she had. Full out, no holds barred, no condemnation, and no bringing up his past foolishness.

And…no more Jay.

It had been almost two years since all that crazy had gone down. And Mac had no urge to revisit it. At all.

"Well, let's get down to business, shall we?" Mac asked. "We have exactly twenty four minutes left as I have another appointment directly after this."

"No problem, Mac. Here are the details on what we're trying to accomplish with this building project. If you think this is something you can design for us—"

"But why this firm? Surely there are architects in Montana, Jay."

"There are. It's a sustainability project and you're the best at designing these types of community buildings. Period."

He popped open his briefcase, slipped a few sheets of

paper onto the table and they got to work. At the top of the hour, they planned to meet again in a few days after she'd had a chance to go over the proposal and requirements with a couple of her staff.

A quiet knock on the door pulled them out of their conversation and Mac escorted Jay to the threshold of her private office.

With another quick hug and a promise to have Jolene call him to set up a follow up meeting, Mac closed the door and ran to her private restroom.

She was sure she'd never changed so quickly in her life. And just as she pulled on her boots, Jolene waltzed in. Without knocking.

Not bothering to look up, Mac grumbled, "Look woman, you've been with me for ten years. What in the hell was that all about?"

"I'm not sure, Mac. I just don't like him."

"Jo, I've known him forever."

"Yeah, but he's been out of the picture for two years."

Mac snapped her gaze up to meet Jolene's. The other woman simply grinned. That show of teeth was sharp enough to make the hairs on Mac's neck stand on end. Not in a frightful way, but in a way that spoke to her gut and said, "Jolene will skewer that man if he causes trouble."

"You didn't tell me all about him, that's true, Mac. But I know you were seeing a guy while you and Landon were apart. And from the description, that particular guy just walked out the door. And something just doesn't feel right, Mac. Why show up now? And that bullshit about you being the best. Period? Really?"

"Hey," Mac snapped. "I am the best, dearie. And don't you forget it."

With that, they both laughed.

"Just watch your back," Jolene insisted. "And don't forget your flogger."

"You are a bad old woman, Jo. You know that?"

"And?" With that, Jolene sauntered out the bathroom door and into Mac's office. She called over her shoulder. "Oh, and I cleared your calendar for the rest of the day. See you tomorrow."

"Cleared my calendar? Why? I'm just driving into Seattle for lunch, Jo." Mac heard the office door snap quietly closed. She shook her head with a chuckle and grumbled under hear breath about nosey assistants who had black belts in meddling.

MACKENZIE IVERS DROPPED OFF A CROCKPOT OF HOMEMADE steak chili to her workaholic best friend, Solie Shaw, and drove at breakneck speed to the Twilight Teahouse. Well, it would have been breakneck, but with the typical lunch time traffic heading into and out of Seattle, it was more like turtle speed.

Didn't change the fact that her heart was racing, even if the cars in front of her weren't.

It was rare to get away from the office in the middle of the day. But today was special—she was headed to lunch with the most wonderful man in the world, her husband, Landon. And the wondering why he'd asked her to meet him was killing her.

The man was as stubborn as herself and was head of the "I'm not telling you and you're going to like it because I said so" department.

To sum it up, Mac Ivers, architect to the rich and famous, was nervous and giddy as hell. And there were just enough butterflies dive-bombing her stomach to almost irritate her.

The only thing that kept her from getting completely pissed off at the surprise—Landon knew she hated surprises, damn it—was that he always made it worth her while.

Always.

Her face heated with a blush and she couldn't help but smile at herself.

She rolled down her window, swiped her access card and pulled into the underground parking at the most exclusive kink club in the area—The Twilight Teahouse. Once out of the car, she grabbed her play bag out of the trunk, unzipped it, and took a quick inventory of the contents—six different floggers, with suede, leather and rubber strips, several crops and canes in various thicknesses, length and flexibility, a few bundles of vivid blue and striking red bamboo rope, among other things. Mac even had several bars of dark chocolate and a couple of bottles of water, you know, just in case part of Landon's surprise included a bit of play.

While waiting in front of the mirrored doors of the elevator, she checked her outfit for the fifth time since she'd put the damn thing on. It was one of her favorites, and while Landon had seen it before, he never failed to express his appreciation for it. She sported black knee high boots with buckles up the side on classy five inch heels. A sleek black cat suit under a burgundy leather corset peeked out from beneath a matching leather bolero jacket. Over that was a custom tailored black leather trench coat. Solie called it her "Selene's-Underworld-Deathdealer-moonlighting-as-a-sexy-flogger-toting-Hollywood-starlet" outfit.

"Yep", she thought to herself, "I'll take that compliment."

Mac stepped inside the steel and glass lift and dropped her bag on the pristine carpeted floor with a soft thunk. Another swipe of her access card and push of a button and she was on her way to the first floor to check in.

For a moment her mind drifted back to her friend, Solie,

and then hung out there for a while. Solie was going through a really rough time right now. A nasty breakup of epic proportions had her wrapped up in misery, though she would surely be on the mend soon. Mac would see to it. Move heaven and earth if need be.

Mac, Landon and their good friend, Burton Khrys, were going to show Solie what she was totally *not* missing out on by leaving behind that douche-canoe she'd been tied up with. Moving on was the best thing the woman could have done for both her sanity and her heart.

Besides, if there was anything the Ivers' and Burt did well, it was take care of their friends in their time of need. Hell, it was their damn specialty, and they had a doozy of a post-breakup party planned for Solie.

A quiet ding announced her arrival at her destination. Stepping carefully out of the lift, she headed to the reception area. A quick glance toward the entrance to the dining room's waiting area confirmed something she already knew —this place was packed. In fact, no matter what time of day or night, if it was during business hours, Twilight Teahouse was never empty.

A perfect blend of a three Michelin star restaurant and a first-class, multi-storied kink-themed play space meant someone was always around.

Today, Mac expected a bit of both—good food and some equally good naughtiness.

"MacKenzie, dear!"

Mac turned and found herself enfolded in a friendly embrace by Madison Lee, the owner of this fine establish.

"Maddie, how are you, sweetie? I haven't seen you in a couple of weeks," Mac said with a genuine smile followed by a kiss on Madison's cheek.

"Kuri and I were away at a Leatherman thing in Chicago."

"Oooh, that sounds fantastic. Was it the yearly event? "

"International Mr. Leather? Nah. If that were the case, I would have spread the word to some of our patrons, to you and your crew to say the least. This was a small event, personal invitation. And to be honest, I've been so wrapped up in running this place, I took Kuri just to get her to stop talking about her to-do list in her sleep."

Kuri, a beautiful, caramel-skinned young lady, had come to stand next to her Mistress and blushed. She was dressed in full traditional Japanese garb—a brilliant purple and pink silk kimono covered with *sakura* blossoms. Her torso was wrapped with a cream and purple complimenting *obiage* and *obi*. She was a picture of perfection, from her coifed hair down to a sparkling white pair of tabi socks, minus the *geta*, or shoes, as no shoes were allowed past the reception areas of The Twilight Teahouse.

Kuri bowed politely, smiled and then stepped forward for a quick hug. "It's so good to see you Ms. MacKenzie."

"And you, Kuri. Though I must say that if your to-do list is that damn long that you dream about it, then poor Kinson must be running around with his hair on fire." Mac laughed out loud, shook her head and winked at Madison. Kinson was Madison's husband and Kuri's other Dominant. If Kuri's to-do list was a mile long, it was because she was attempting to take some of Kinson's tasks off of his own list. The man was a ridiculous, though soft-hearted, work-a-holic.

Mac knew exactly what Madison meant because her husband was the same way. There was always something to be prepped and cooked, baked or braised. Somewhere to go. Someone who needed to be tied up, spanked and the like.

As busy as they both were, it was all Mac could do to get the man to stop moving long enough to sleep at night, though his stamina did mean he was an energizer bunny in the sack—of which she had no complaints.

"So what in the world are you doing here in the middle of the day, woman?"

"I'm here to see my hubs. He in the kitchen?" Mac asked.

"Of course. I can't get him out of there. Actually, I'm wondering if there's something you can do about that?"

"Are you telling me that he still won't go near the play spaces?" Mac asked discreetly.

"Not even close," Madison Lee responded with a scowl.

.

2

A year ago, Mac and Landon had gone through a rough patch. Because of the specifics of that "patch" Landon was reluctant to play with anyone. And Mac didn't like that one bit. He was denying his nature. Denying who he really was inside. The old sayings claimed that time healed all wounds, but for her husband, he hadn't quite seemed to move on.

He was a Dominant. Period. Yet, he refused to do what he did best—tie up submissives in the prettiest decorative rope work.

When things were more "normal" in their relationship, Landon did the tying and Mac did the flogging. A perfect team...yet one of the players was now deliberately missing because he thought that was best for everyone.

Little did he know, Madison Lee had quietly shared a juicy secret with Mac—she'd just been contacted by one of the premier movie studios in the Los Angeles area. Incidentally, they were looking for someone knowledgeable with bondage. With the current kink craze, they were making a BDSM film and they didn't want it to be some horrid, hot mess like some others. They'd asked for permission to come get some first-hand knowledge, and there was no one in the area better suited for what they needed than Landon.

It was rare for a playwright, novelist, artist or movie director to ask for good, solid help with research from the kink community. Not to mention, the possibility of having one's name associated with a tastefully done, artistic work could really put a person, or establishment on the map. The opportunity was a once-in-a-lifetime kind of thing.

Twilight Teahouse didn't need such visibility, as it was already on the map. In fact, it *owned* the damn map. But a positive look at their little domain of kink couldn't hurt. And who knew where something like this could take Landon Ivers?

"I'll talk it over with him, I promise. Okay with you if I head into the kitchen to see him?"

"It's crazy back there right now." Madison Lee tapped a little device at her ear and spoke quickly to the staff on the other end. And just like that, someone was on the way to tell Landon that Mac was here. "Are you eating as well? If so, I can order your favorite dish for you. Kuri or one of the others can bring it to wherever you're going to be. We're packed today—"

"How is that different from any other day?" Mac laughed.

"Touché, my dear. You can have the private dining room if you like."

"I have no idea. Landon asked me to come, but he wouldn't tell me why."

Madison's deep blue eyes took on a sparkle of mischief and Mac wondered if she was in on whatever her husband had planned. The other woman continued in her typical quiet, yet confident, timbre. "He's on his way out now. He said to tell you that he did indeed order lunch, and if you would, please meet him on the fifth floor."

Mac's stomach did a freefall. "Oh my god, are you serious?" She practically forgot she was standing in a lobby full of people and started jumping up and down with excitement.

Anxious to know what the man was up to, she gave Madison another quick hug. The other woman whispered in her ear, "Kuri will bring your food up to the Hatshepsut room in an hour."

With that, Mac backed her way toward the elevator with the biggest, goofiest grin on her face.

The entire five-story club was private, except for the restaurant on the first floor. There, one could enjoy haute cuisine at the lunch and dinner spot on the public side, and a delectable dessert haven, with ankle stocks and spankings, on the private side.

All the other floors had their own special themes, with both enclosed and open spaces.

The second floor held a full-service spa, traditional Japanese baths and massage space with an open community feel, just like the family baths in the old country of Japan, but with mani-pedi heaven thrown in. Club members could even bring their young family members without any concern that they might see something they shouldn't. But that is where any youngster-friendly activity ended.

The Ice Palace up on the third level was Mediterranean in nature with gleaming white columns, white floors, white everything with strategically placed mirrors that made it all seem to glitter endlessly. The fourth floor held a private Japanese spa for couples and kink only. And the fifth floor was split into two themes, a hot Egyptian flavor on one side, and sultry Caribbean on the other.

Madison and Kinson Lee, the proprietor geniuses, had truly outdone themselves. Mac couldn't think of a single person she knew that belonged to the club who had much to complain about in regard to the luxurious accommodations.

. . .

A LYRICAL DING ANNOUNCED HER ARRIVAL. THE LIFT DOORS slid open and there stood six feet, four inches of hunka hunka burnin' love.

"What are you snickering at, woman?" Landon asked, taking her play bag from her fingers and pulling her into a hug with his free arm.

She shook her head and refused to tell him that an image of him doing the Elvis hip swivel had bounced right into her mind. Head pressed against his chest, his strong heartbeat was reassuring. God, there was nothing like being held by the love of her life.

She didn't love him because he was the hottest man in the world. Nor because he was a hell of a chef. Those things were nice, but not nearly enough to hold a relationship together. MacKenzie and Landon were bound together, through joy, tears, heartache, and reconciliation. Years of marriage, followed by divorce and remarriage. Ups and downs. Peaceful times and fighting times.

Bottom line, there was only one Landon Ivers in all the world. And she was on her way to being naughty with him in the middle of the day on a Tuesday afternoon.

LANDON'S TATAMI SLIPPERS QUIETLY SWOOSHED ACROSS THE tile as he led Mac to the shoe cubbies along the wall in the foyer. Kneeling, he unzipped the supple leather boots. Cool air was delicious against her calves as they were bared an inch at a time.

Once off, Landon put her shoes into a cubby, and then took a moment to rub her stocking-clad feet. The natural stress of wearing five-inch heels leached from her toes. Arches relaxed as she unashamedly sighed.

"Better?" he asked quietly.

At her nod, he let go of her happy feet and stood. Bag in hand again, fingers laced through hers and they were off down the hall. Shortly, then entered an open observation area full of overstuffed chairs and couches. Several piles of plush colorful pillows beckoned one to lounge in the midst of golden-colored X-style crosses and padded spanking benches. As always, the free-standing wall caught her eye and her gaze was drawn to the cuff hooks embedded between hieroglyphs that lined both sides of the ancient-looking adobe-styled structure.

Strangely enough, the plain black tee-shirt poured over Landon's ripped muscular chest and long legs encased in denim, looked as if they belonged among these trappings of ancient pharaohs.

Must be the man and not the clothes.

"Are you back there looking at my ass or are you admiring the hieroglyphs?" he asked in his oh-so-sexy Irish lilt. Hand securely holding hers, Landon glanced back at her as they moved through to the next part of the area.

"Hell yes to both of those questions," Mac responded without hesitation. After all, his ass was pretty damn spectacular. Must be all those squats he did when working out in the afternoons, of which she had no complaint. The wicked smile he sent over his shoulder put her gut into dance mode. And if she weren't mistaken, it was grooving to seventies disco music.

God, the man simply lit her fuse. All. The. Time!

At the door to a private space, Landon led her over the threshold and dropped her play bag at the entrance. He took a scrunchy from his pocket and pulled his jet-black waves into a thick tail.

Mac watched him settle into the only chair in the room. It was an Egyptian throne, placed between two huge replicas of hieroglyph-inscribed rose granite obelisks.

Behind him was a floor to ceiling mural of the walls of the Hathor Chapel from inside the Temple of Hatshepsut.

And in that moment, he was every bit her king.

Mac was an alpha to the bone. It was simply her personality and style. It allowed her to successfully run a thriving business in a field dominated by men, and deal with emergencies with ease. In her case, alpha didn't mean bitch...well, unless some bitchiness was required at the moment.

On the flip side of that coin, this man, her husband, brought out the submissive in her like literally no one else could. And when her man crossed his legs and let his vivid green gaze roam boldly from her head to her feet and back again, she automatically bowed her head with a blush.

"Today, it's you, me and some rope. Do you consent to this, MacKenzie Chalice Daniels-Ivers?"

Oh dear lord, he called her by her whole name! That was typically reserved for when she was in trouble, or when he planned something intense. Butterflies in her gut were a thing of the past as they morphed into pterodactyls. A shiver went through her whole body and settled down between the joints in her knees. A deep breath did nothing to calm her at all. But one thing was for sure—her nerves skipped around from sheer anticipation of some serious delight.

"Well?" he asked.

"Yes, of course I consent."

"Good. Go to your play bag and get all of the red bamboo rope."

How did he know she had that in there? Before she could ask, he said, "I put it in there two nights past in place of that rough jute stuff you had bundled up inside."

One brow winged its way up her forehead as his words

truly registered. And then her man gave her one of the most deliciously promising grins she'd seen on his face lately.

She smiled in return as understanding dawned that he'd planned this well in advance. Sure she'd seen the rope when she'd inspected her bag not fifteen minutes ago, but she always had some in there just in case. Easy knots for easy play was something she could handle. But all the ins and outs of rope and its intricate uses were Landon's domain. And it was a domain he ruled, completely.

Once she was across the room and standing over her bag, another command came.

"Put your locs up into a bun, high on top of your head. Then remove your clothes and leave them folded neatly where you stand. You may keep on the sexy ass panties that you were sashaying around the house in this morning though."

"Sashay?" she gawked.

"Absolutely. And it was a beautiful sight. Have a problem with the word, sashay?" he asked. He lowered his head and watched her through thick coal-black lashes. A smart ass comment was on the edge of her lips when he gave her *the look* and raised an imperious brow.

Mac blurted, "Nope. No problem at all."

Usually Landon liked to yank on her dreadlocs. Back to the task of putting up her hair, Mac was glad she always kept a few scrunchies on hand since he obviously had something else in mind today.

Squeee!

Hair up, skin bare and several bundles of rope in hard, Mac made her way back to her husband who sat regally on that golden throne.

Instructed to stand, elbows up and held at chest height, Mac placed her hands on her shoulders and stood absolutely still. A scrap of silk was secured over her eyes and her heart rate kicked up a notch or three.

There was nothing quite like the anticipation of being bound and at the delicious mercy of her husband. She trusted him not to ever hurt her, and to respect her limits. But she also trusted him to make her fly, aloft on the wings of sensuality.

Not to mention this was the first time he'd volunteered this kind of play with her or anyone else for almost two freaking years!

As he began to create a basic chest harness, the first pass of the rope over the bare skin just above her breasts sent a tremor through Mac's stomach. She made no attempt to demand the flying dinosaurs that danced around in there to behave. Instead she let them get a bit more rowdy until they reflected the excitement she felt in anticipation of what was to come.

Cinched tight in the back, he then brought the rope back around to the front, beneath her breasts this time. As the soft bamboo was put in place, Landon took every opportunity to touch her nipples—tugs, tweaks and the occasional lave of his tongue meant instantaneous and maintained arousal. With each tie, the folds of her sex swelled until they throbbed for release.

Mac floated away, her mind a haze of pleasure and anticipation of the end result of the rope session with her husband. Landon was one of the Pacific Northwest's top riggers and she knew when he was done, her body would be transformed into a work of art. Not that she didn't like her body minus being wrapped in rope, but the colors, designs and different knots that Landon pulled out of his head and wrapped around her muscles and limbs made her beyond beautiful.

He continued to twist and twine until the most gorgeous red harness covered her entire upper body, secured to her waist and hips. And last, arms were secured behind her back with rows of what Landon called overhand bow knots laid down her spine.

"Oh, I love this on you, baby." The hushed whisper in the wide open space seemed to vibrate in the very air. "You're a stunning woman. And in my rope, you're even more beautiful."

"I wanna see," she declared, wishing her hands were free so she could take off the blindfold.

"I think I can arrange that," Landon whispered, so close the heat of his big body caressed her breasts and belly. Planted a sweet kiss on her cheek and then moved away. She immediately missed his closeness but a moment later, the click of a shutter told her that she would indeed get to "see".

He reached out and brushed the back of his hand over her puckered nipples, then down the valley between her breasts. Fingers wrapped around the rope just above her pelvis and tugged. Mac shot up onto tip-toes.

An unexpected zing from her mons made her tremble. What in the...? Oh!

Landon let go of that bit of rope. Then gently yanked again.

Release.

Yank.

Up. Down. Up.

Dear god.

Sly man—he'd placed a fat square knot right over her clit!

The rasp of silky-smooth rope over her flesh combined with the firm tugs on her nipples caused blistering heat to spread outward in a slow, uneven burn until she squirmed against the well-placed knot.

"Oh god, please," she gasped at the sweet abrasion.

"Why, whatever do you mean, MacKenzie Ivers?" he

teased. "There's not supposed to be any sex between staff and patrons."

"Even if they're husband and wife?" He tugged again, and her eyes crossed.

"Well, maybe."

Thankful to be in a private space, Mac almost sighed with relief when her husband began to untwine her limbs.

She was damn near panting by the time the final stretch of rope hit the floor, and he carefully passed swift hands over her body. The move may have been to ensure she had full circulation, but he didn't miss a chance to touch her intimately, in every way she desired, as he went along.

By the time he was done, his breathing was short, and his gaze bright, and full of desire. He looked at her as if she were the only prize in the world, worth more than the gold found in the most opulent tombs of Egypt.

And just now, her king leaned her over the throne. The pop of the buttons on his jeans echoed in her ears and then he was filling her.

The heat of his cock pressed against soaked flesh, and in two strokes, he was buried deep inside.

No easy loving, or gentle touches. This was rough, hard...raunchy. And god, she loved it. Needed it. Craved it.

She wanted to be fucked. Hard.

As usual, her man sensed exactly what she needed and delivered. He slid out, gave her a moment to adjust, and then took her the way she needed. Strokes were sure, steady and deep. Nerve endings sizzled as his thick cock parted her sugared walls.

When he reached around to flick her engorged clit, wet and dewy from her arousal, she flew apart.

Unlike Humpty-Dumpty, she never wanted to be put back together, after spending time in this man's arms.

JAY FRENZ HAD LANDED AT THE AIRPORT THIS MORNING AND gone directly to MacKenzie's building just outside of the Seattle city proper. He replayed their meeting in his mind as he drove straight to the swanky boutique hotel he'd reserved for the next few days. It was a beautiful property that offered all the amenities a traveling businessman could want, but he didn't give a rat's ass right now.

Instead of removing his jacket, kicking off his shoes and considering room service, his briefcase went sailing as he grit his teeth. The thing bounced off the wall and landed on the floor with a thud. Jay barely resisted the urged to toss a chair after it.

Wrestling with his self-control, he stood in front of the mirrored dresser. What the hell was wrong with him? He was the most easy-going guy he knew, yet here he was practically seething. And for what?

In truth, he had no idea.

The one woman who'd always respected him had spent some time with him today. Jay was glad that MacKenzie was happy. Was even glad that she and Landon had worked out their differences. In fact, when Mac had released him from his collar and contract, they'd parted on good terms.

So why was he so fucking angry all of the sudden?

Jay shed his suit and jumped into a pair of sweats. A few minutes of stretching and he headed out for a much-needed run. The cool, crisp air of a Seattle Spring invigorated much more quickly than the tar flavored crap that passed for coffee in this town. As he turned up a steep hill behind Pike Place Market, he examined his conscience, looked for the truth about himself deep inside.

And found it.

The hole that had been left in his heart after breaking up

with Mac remained unfilled. It was his own fault, so he couldn't be pissed at anyone else.

Mac and Landon had been in the middle of a nasty divorce, and it was no surprise that MacKenzie let Jay go so she could focus on her circumstances. Yet, after leaving Seattle, Jay had never sought another D/s relationship. Actually, he'd not sought out *any* relationship, but had buried himself in work instead.

Now here he was, two years later, yearning for the one woman who'd always touched him on every level, even though their D/s play never included sex. Nothing was sexier to Jay than intellect, and Mac had that in spades. Mind, body and spirit, MacKenzie Ivers had it all. Was she perfect? There wasn't a single person on the planet that could claim that title, but she was pretty damn close.

And god, could that woman wield a riding crop like nobody's business.

Jay began to sweat from a combination of physical exertion and the sweet ache that settled into his balls anytime he reminisced about his time with Mac.

On his way back to the hotel room, rain had begun to fall, chilling him to the bone. Yet, even in the mist and gloom, his heart lightened as he realized the difference between what he needed and what he wanted.

Now all he had to do was figure out how to get it.

3

*W*hat was he doing up here? And just like the other seven times he'd asked himself that question since he'd hopped into the elevator, Landon still had no clue.

Madison Lee had been straight forward with him—typical for her no matter the situation. She'd told him that it was time he stop letting the past keep him from doing what he loved—tie up beautiful women in even more beautiful rope. He knew she was right. Also knew that Mac and Madison Lee had conspired to get his ass into the elevator and up to the Ice Palace on the third floor.

He could admit that rigging was under his skin. Had been for years and years, ever since he'd learned that there was such an outlet for his creative and kinky side. But a cunning sub in rope is what got him into a serious fix a couple of years ago.

Landon and Mac were both dominant personalities. Through mutual agreement, they'd both had submissives back then. Mac had a guy named Jay who'd enjoyed serving as her sub. If Landon recalled correctly, the man had especially enjoyed the exquisite sting of her expertly plied floggers, canes and paddles.

Landon's former submissive, Yazmin, had been in love with rope and serving him in whatever capacity he'd desired...or so he'd thought.

Their agreement had been simple—no sex with others. After all, BDSM wasn't always about fucking. Sometimes it was about the simple act of gaining their partners submission and giving that sub what they needed, whether that was impact play, psychological play, or Landon's area of expertise —bondage and rope suspension.

But Landon had broken the rules. He'd had his head so far up his own ass, had been so full of himself that his ego had caused him to break trust with Mac.

"Why doesn't she get home in time to give you what you need," he remembered Yazmin asking him. *"You're a busy man just like she's a busy woman. Why do her desires always come first? What about you?"*

He'd been such an idiot.

"If you were mine, I'd take such good care of you. You could tie me up every night and fuck me silly if you wanted to. I'd never be too tired."

Yeah. So much for the grass being greener in the neighboring pasture. In the end, he'd been pulled into a web of deceit. All the promises from Yazmin-the-submissive had come complete with an extra boxful of crazy topped with a tattered bow.

Before he knew it, Landon had found himself caught up in a full-blown affair, completely unaware that his little Yazmin had been taunting his wife about it every time their path's crossed.

And Mac, with her endless class, had handled it like a champ. Down to a painful divorce.

There was one thing he wouldn't do no matter what—get

so wrapped up in his own desires that he couldn't see past his dick.

Never again. *Ever.*

Getting his ego and his cock stroked had cost him his marriage, and by his choice, his rigging. He hadn't done any rope work, fancy or otherwise, on anyone other than his wife even though she'd encouraged him on multiple occasions to let the past go and get to tying people up already.

MacKenzie Ivers deserved everything he had to give, and nothing less. And if that meant that his wife would be the only recipient of his rope outlet, then so be it. Had his wife asked him to give up his love of rope? Nope. Not once. But she was his focus, and would remain so.

He might love rope, but he needed Mac more than he needed his next breath. Hell, Landon could turn his back on the entire world, as long as he had Mac in his corner.

But was he ready for this? Honestly, Landon wasn't sure, but the freefall of his gut—which had nothing to do with the speed of the lift—as he headed toward his destination made him wish he'd stayed downstairs in the restaurant's kitchen.

After all, he had a cake to bake for their friend, Solie. Yes, that was it. He had baking to do. Fuck this rope demo.

And as soon as he'd made up his mind to bow out, the sleek mirrored doors of the lift slid open with a quiet swish.

Too late now, he thought to himself as all eyes turned his way. Standing right in front of him was what must have been the entire movie team. A short, wiry man stepped forward with a welcoming smile and extended hand.

"Hi, I'm Harrison Smith, the director." His grip was firm, but not overly hard as he pumped Landon's hand up and down. The director thanked Landon for his time, and then turned and started rattling off names of screenplay writers, co-producers, artists and graphic designers. There was no way he would remember all their names, but each one sported a ready smile and seemed a friendly bunch that probably wouldn't care much.

In spite of his misgivings about the whole thing, he found himself getting excited about the prospect of twining supple material around limbs and manipulating the pose of whoever would be his rope bunny. He knew that what he created with rope was artistic. It fed something inside of him. Made him feel accomplished, talented. And in charge.

A low hum of vibration began to replace the apprehension that had been swirling around in his gut. And that hum was quickly becoming what he recognized as his planning energy. He'd automatically begun to visualize which ties, knots, patterns and positions, and the order in which he would need to tie them to create the design he'd just chosen in his head—a suspended phoenix bird.

Landon turned as Harrison pointed to the other side of the room to the woman who would be his rope bunny.

The entire room came to a standstill at Landon's, "You've got to be fucking kidding me!" followed by his sudden burst of laugher.

HEADED HIS WAY WITH HER PHONE PLASTERED TO HER EAR, WAS Yazmin Ross. Fake smile firmly in place, a damn-near maniacal glint in her eye told Landon that she hadn't changed a bit.

In that moment, scenes replayed in his head that he'd spent a lot of therapy time trying to move past. Not forget— he would never forget—but simply move to a space in his heart where they hurt less and less each day.

Images of him berating his woman rather than appreciating her. Of him not caring that MacKenzie Ivers worked sixty to seventy hours a week at her own business. He'd only cared that she wasn't always home when he wanted her there, wasn't always energetic enough after busting her ass at her firm to do all the little things that the mega-bitch in front of him had convinced him that he needed from his wife.

Yazmin had played him from the beginning of the fantasy she'd helped weave in his head, through to the end.

And the end had been nasty.

He'd lost the love of his life and discovered that the woman he'd thought he wanted was a mere facade, barely a sprinkle of what she'd claimed to be.

Beneath the sheep's clothing had been the queen of the wolves. And as she stood before him now, he could swear he saw fangs elongate in her lying mouth.

"Landon, please meet Yazmin Ross, the star of our movie. She volunteered to actually experience being tied up so that she could react appropriately in the role."

Yazmin reached out a hand and said, "Nice to meet you."

Da ferk? So she was choosing to pretend as if they didn't know each other, as if she'd never been bound by him? As if they had no history together?

Well whatever game she played, Landon wasn't signing up to be on the team.

He glanced down at Yazmin's outstretched hand, and then turned his attention to the director. "Will you please excuse me for a moment, Harrison?"

"Sure, no problem. We'll just set up over there and make sure you have plenty of room to work," he said, motioning over toward the area near the suspension rig.

With a polite nod, Landon left the room, headed back toward the elevator and rounded the corner just past the reception desk. He pulled out his phone and ducked into a little nook he knew was there for just such a purpose.

He hit the speed dial and the second his wife answered her private line, he quietly lost it.

"You're not going to fucking believe this shit!"

"Hold on a sec," she said. In the background he heard, "Hey, Jolene, will you please pick up line two and let Solie know that I'll call her right back? Thanks, hon." And then her voice filled the line and her concern bled through, letting him know he had her full attention. She asked, "What happened, sweetie? What's going on?"

"Yazmin is the goddamn rope bunny!" he fumed as quietly as he could, knowing that a room full of people was just around the corner.

"Yasmin? As in..."

"Yes, damn it. As in."

"Well, I didn't see that coming. But so what," Mac said.

"So what? So what?! What do you mean, so what? The last thing I want is to have anything to do with that bitch."

"Do you think Madison Lee knows she's the person you're to do the demo on?" Mac asked.

"I doubt it. She hasn't made it into the room yet. She's giving Kuri some instructions about some thing or another."

"Well, regardless, Landon, it's just rope. It's not a binding contract. Not a binding *anything*. I think you should do it. You're in a room full of people demonstrating the skills of a top rigger. What can she do in a room full of people?"

He listened, and as usual, his wife made sense. She was such a remarkable woman, his Mac. Most females would be fuming about having the author of the destruction of their relationship standing within a thousand paces. But not Mac. Instead, she encouraged him to look past his disdain for bitchzilla across the room, and consider where this could take him.

"I love you, MacKenzie Ivers," Landon said with a smile.

"You bet your gorgeous Irish ass you do. Dinner at six-thirty?

"You've got it. See you later."

He disconnected the call and considered his wife's advice...for all of five seconds.

Mind made up, a tightness in his chest eased that he hadn't noticed until the vice grip encircling his ribs began to let up.

Just as he made it back to the reception area on this floor, the person he needed most was mere steps away.

"Maddy, hold on a second," he called as he jogged over to the door that Madison Lee was just about to walk through. "Can I talk to you a second?"

A few moments later, with a genuine smile on his face and a spring in his step, he relished the gasps of surprise coming from the open doors behind him. Next came Yazmin's less-than-ladylike screech of denial as Madison Lee informed the movie crew that she would personally do the demonstration as Landon suddenly had something come up.

Landon hopped in the elevator, swiped his authorization card and grinned as the lift dropped down to the underground parking lot.

The rumble of the engine of his muscle car made that grin spread wider as he thought about where he was headed.

An hour later, his wife was laid back on her desk with her thighs on either side of his head as she stuffed her fist into her mouth to muffle a scream as she came. Twice.

MacKenzie had spent almost half an hour on the phone calming a pissed off Madison Lee.

"Woman, I don't know how you stay so calm," Madison had said. "I'd be spitting nails knowing that after ten years of marriage, the worm who'd squeezed herself into my relationship was back in town."

But Mac hadn't always been so calm and collected. She'd

gone through a period of time where she'd been in so much pain, she was sure her heart was going to fall out of her body through the hole in her chest. The Yazmin creature had been one source of that pain. But not the only source.

And though she'd forgiven him long ago, she could admit that Landon had done the most damage. Madison Lee had been right—after ten years of marriage, she'd found herself in quite an unpleasant pickle. Though no lies had been told between MacKenzie and her husband, trust had been broken. Broken into shards so numerous and sharp, she'd felt each and every one of them as though they'd cut through her very skin.

Standing in the strength that she'd learned from her own mother—the inner knowing and acknowledgement of her worth—she'd healed and learned how to live without dysfunction. Without regret. And, for a time, without Landon.

It hadn't been all sunshine and roses. Not by a long shot.

But since reconciling, Landon had gone well beyond proving how much he regretted his dumb ass decision, yet he was still inwardly paying for it. He refused to exercise his rope skills on anyone but Mac, and she knew it wasn't enough for him. Knew to the bottom of her soul that he needed to use his talent way more than he was at the moment. There had to be a way to get him out of his self-imposed punishment. She just had to figure out how.

Madison Lee had been quite clear why she'd been first, amazed, and then furious. Yazmin had been banned from Twilight Teahouse two years ago, yet today she'd waltzed her happy ass through those doors as part of the film entourage.

According to Madison Lee, she'd done a simple binding and suspension demo in Landon's place in as professional a manner as possible. She'd explained each knot and harness, as well as why one should always bind the arms last. Questions from the attendees were answered while Maddy made sure not to have Yazmin restricted or suspended too long.

Afterward, she'd taken the director, Harrison something-or-other, aside. Without elaborating on the circumstances, Madison had informed him in no uncertain terms, that Yazmin was not allowed to enter the facility again. Ever.

Mac had shaken her head and sighed as her good friend had shared that according to the director, Yazmin was the one who'd pushed for Twilight Teahouse to be the location for some of the movie scenes, as well as suggesting they "find" a top-notch rigger, knowing full well that Madison Lee would suggest Landon.

Hell, if Madison Lee had known ahead of time that Yazmin Ross was the one who'd instigated the entire encounter, she would have cut that particular horse off at the pass. After Madison Lee's firm, discreet, set-down, the director had thanked her for the informative demonstration. He'd then instructed the crew to quietly pack up, and they all left the premises with the entire group giving Yazmin the stink eye.

When Mac and Madison Lee had finally gotten off the phone, Mac was growling on the other woman's behalf, as well as her husband's.

After disconnecting the call, and completely unfit for company, she'd stepped out of her office for a refill of coffee that she really didn't need. But she had to do something, had to move, had to walk. Thankfully she had no clients coming by, and with one glance at Mac as she stormed past the front desk, Jolene quickly cancelled the conference calls for the afternoon. After a couple of laps around the inside of the building to check in with her staff on a couple of current projects, Mac was back in her office, and still fuming.

With a reprimand on the tip of her tongue for whoever

had opened her office door without knocking, Mac didn't even look up from her computer as she snapped.

"If you've been working in this office for any length of time, meaning more than two days, then you know never, ever to walk into my office when the door is closed."

When silence met her ears, she glanced up, gasped and then flew out of her chair.

"Oh my god, what in the world are you doing here at this time of day?"

"Took the rest of the day off," Landon said, just before he lowered his head, pressed his lips to hers, and then swept her off her feet. Literally.

Considering she was nowhere near a stick-figure of a woman, Mac appreciated her husband's physical strength. He was a gorgeous specimen of a man. God, she loved having a guy strong enough to pick her up and put her where he wanted her.

And right now, where he wanted her was in his lap on the loveseat in her office. Cradled in his arms, her body reacted to the bunch and release of his biceps. Without breaking the kiss, Landon held her securely as they reclined. One hand played with the hem of her skirt while his lips teased a moan from her throat as his tongue tangled sensuously with hers.

Arms twined around his neck, she opened enthusiastically for him. He tasted of some kind of tart fruit and a hint of cream. The man was simply delicious in every interpretation of the word. Handsome, brilliant, gorgeous. And a fabulous cook.

And right now, he teased and tempted her to want more of what only he could give.

"Mmm," he growled low in his throat. "I missed these this morning. How is that possible?"

She gasped as his fingers toyed with the top of her sheer thigh-high stockings and then stroked back and forth from thigh to almost-bare backside. Before she could answer his question, his lips left hers, nibbled along her jaw and down to a certain spot on her neck. And that tender bit of flesh made her pant and hang on the edge of orgasm whenever he marked her there.

And just as the thought passed through her head, his teeth gently clamped down and he sucked right where she wanted it most.

"Oh my god."

Back arched, hips twitched, and ass clenched as he nibbled. Temperature ratcheted up as she felt his growing erection nudge her bottom cheeks.

Fingers tightened in her hair as he bit down again, harder this time. Then came a brush against the underside of a sensitive breast. Eyes flew open then fluttered closed as she tried to catch suddenly out-of-control breathing.

Teeth again met the tendon between neck and shoulder. At Mac's squeak, she tensed. Holy crap, she'd forgotten about her staff!

"Landon, stop." She really didn't want him to, but if she didn't speak now, it would soon become impossible to form words. "Jolene is..."

"Gone to lunch," he whispered against the shell of her ear. "A few of your engineers are in their offices on the other side of the building. Nobody over here but us." In between kisses as he made his way to her throat and then back to her lips again. "And your door is locked. As long as you don't scream, we're good."

"Then don't *make* me scream," she demanded. Or at least she tried to sound demanding. It kind of came out all horny and desperate, but who was complaining?

"I canna make that promise, love. I'm tempted tae spank that beautiful arse of yours just tae watch ye squirm with pleasure. Lucky for you, the sound of the impact is too loud and someone would surely come a-runnin'."

She loved how his accent thickened when he was turned on, or riled up. Nothing said sexy quite like a black-haired Irishman, down to the red and gold clan crest inked onto his right shoulder, which she occasionally, and very purposely, licked.

REACHING DOWN, HE PULLED OFF ONE OF HER PUMPS. THE moment Mac heard the thud of the shoe as it hit the thick carpet, she positioned the other foot for easy access.

Next, hands traveled from calf, to knee to thigh. Then further beneath her flippy skirt until he reached her underwear. Or what there was of them.

"Oooh," he sighed into her mouth as he pressed kiss after kiss to her tingling lips. "Not much to these, is there, darlin'? Your entire arse cheek is hangin' out, yes?" Blunt nails rasped lightly over said arse, sending a wicked tremor up the nerves from her tailbone to mid-spine.

"Oh yes. Definitely yes," she gasped.

He gave a smack to the flesh and then rubbed away the slight sting. Mac moaned. So he did it again.

"Not enough noise to cause a ruckus, but enough of a smack for ye to remember I was here."

She'd always loved a little edge with her love play. And Landon knew his way around her body and could strum it like the finest instrument.

"Ah," he said, as if he'd had an epiphany. "I know just what ye need, darlin'. Stand up." He helped her off of the loveseat, then moved to pull one of the comfy chairs away from the table she used for consulting.

"Come to me and turn around to face the table."

She did as she was asked and then waited. There was the slight rustle of fabric as he sat down behind her, and then Mac felt her husband's gaze sear from head down to her now-bare feet, scorching nerve endings as it went.

By the time he spoke another word, she was a trembling, damn-near-on-fire piece of woman.

"MacKenzie Ivers, you're such a beauty. Now, drop the knickers. Leave the skirt."

Already wet, she imagined him grinning as she peeled the scrap of lace down her legs and off.

Then a firm touch eased from knees, up the front of her thighs, taking her skirt with it as it went. She tightened her butt cheeks in response to the zing that traveled across it when her man gently raked his nails across her that sensitive skin. Another light smack made her gut dance around beneath the skin.

"Relax," Landon demanded and smacked her ass again. "No butt clenching unless you're about to come."

"Keep that up and that's exactly what I'll be doing."

He chuckled, eased her around and then lifted her onto the conference table. Mac was sure she'd never see consulting at this table the same way again. Landon harrumphed and mumbled something about the angle not being quite right. Next thing she knew, the man had flipped her over to her back, then scooted her to the edge of the table until her ass was just barely on the highly polished wood.

Giving her no time to adjust to the literal flip of the script, Landon's knees hit the floor. A single warm digit eased into her moist heat, moved in and out in a strong rhythm as his tongue explored the folds of her sex.

Another finger joined in and his focus changed to the little bundle of nerves at her center. She wrapped her legs around his head and ground her hips frantically. She'd gone from curious to needy, wanton and unashamed in six seconds flat. And he had her exactly where he wanted her, of that there was no doubt.

"Yes. Oh my god, yes," she panted. Then lips and talented tongue worked over her clit. Mac arched against the table and moaned loudly before remembering to jam a fist in her mouth to stifle the sound. She buried the other hand in her own hair as if she were trying to keep her mind firmly anchored in her head.

But fate decreed that she would indeed lose her mind this afternoon, because when Landon hummed his appreciation at her open expression of pleasure, Mac's orgasm flew out of left field and smacked her in the head with its intensity.

"Oh! Oh my...ohmygod!"

She clamped her lips closed and bit down on the inside of her cheek to stifle her scream, but it did nothing to help her control the trembling of her thighs, or the clenching of her stomach muscles as Landon pushed her into, and through, her climax.

On the heels of the first mind-blowing orgasm, came a second.

By the time the lovers left Mac's office and headed home, she was a puddle of satisfied woman with knees that felt as if they were made of jelly.

And there was only one thing that would have made her happier—to dispel the ghosts in her husband's eyes. And today, that fucking phantom had come riding into The Twilight Teahouse.

One more visit from that particular Casper, and she might just have to play dirty. Because for Landon Ivers, she'd play as dirty as was required to protect him.

4

*T*he last few days had flown by, spent in meetings with Mac and her staff as they hashed out the details for the new project. The contract negotiations had gone well and with a few more tweaks to the requirements for the new eco-resort, the final pieces would be in place to wrap it up.

They'd gotten quite a lot of work done in a relatively short period, and Jay knew that it was almost time to return home.

Home. Huh. Thinking on his bare-bones place in Helena, Montana, the word "home" didn't come to mind. It was just a place to eat, work and sleep. Nothing more.

Tonight, he would celebrate a job well done, probably alone, and featuring more room service. But before he left town, a trip to Twilight Teahouse was on his to-do list, as well as a heart-to-heart with Mac.

After a quick shower and a bite of lunch—god bless spectacular room service—Jay powered up his laptop and began to work on what he hoped was the final iteration of requirements for the project Mac had agreed to work on with him.

The trill of his mobile device startled him. Jay jerked his gaze toward the plush drapes that opened to a balcony facing Puget Sound. Surprised to discover that the sun had long since set, he reached for the still-ringing device and the hotel menu at the same time.

Flipping to the wine selection page, he answered the phone. "This is Jay."

"Hello, Jay. It's so nice to talk to you. It's been a long time. Are you busy?"

"Who is this?" he asked. The voice sounded somewhat familiar, but he couldn't quite place it.

"My name is Ms. Ross. I thought I saw you in Seattle earlier today. You've been away awhile."

"Uh...okay? What can I do for you Ms. Ross?" Ms. Ross? Name sounded familiar

"I used to see you at Twilight Teahouse when I lived in Seattle. I was, um, involved with..." she trailed off.

Then the light bulb went on in his mind, and with it came a strong sense of unease.

"Hey, I remember you now. You were Landon Ivers' submissive for a time. How did you know I was here?"

"As I said, I thought I saw you today. I'm in town on business and could have sworn I saw you in the airport. Just thought I'd say hello and all. If you're going to be around, maybe we can do some pick up play or something."

It was bad enough he'd never heard tell of her in the two years since he'd been out of the scene, but for her to just happen to "see" him? Jay didn't think so. Not to mention he'd been nowhere near the airport today. He had, however, been over at Mac's office.

The hair on the back of Jay's neck stood on end. What the hell was this woman up to?

And if she thought he didn't know who the fuck she was, this chick was mistaken. This woman was the one who'd hurt Mac so deeply. And Jay didn't betray his friends. Period.

"So how are things? What brings you to town?" Ms. Ross asked.

Being a fairly private person, Jay simply said, "Just business. And you?"

"The same. I landed a part in a movie about BDSM and the film crew is here doing some research. We'll be headed home to Los Angeles in a few days. By the way, how is that beautiful MacKenzie Ivers? Have you seen her since you've been in town? I'd like to say hello to her. I hope she's forgiven me for all the...you know."

The woman's words trailed off as if she'd forgotten what she was saying rather than out of any embarrassment for the *"you know"*.

"No, I haven't seen her on a personal level. She's back together with her husband."

No response. Jay's brow dove down into a fierce frown as the immediate silence on the other end of the line told him everything he needed to know. The lightbulb that had snapped on inside his head flared even brighter as the silence continued. Blood pounded in his ears and the calm, controlled face he showed to the world morphed into a mask of anger as the fury he kept tightly leashed slipped free for a moment.

"You knew didn't you? You knew they were remarried!"

"So what," she snapped. All semblance of class and seduction disappeared in a blink and this female tiger was now showing her claws. "Doesn't mean I'm not interested in gaining MacKenzie's forgiveness."

But there was no sincerity in either word or tone. All Jay heard was anger, sarcasm and downright nastiness. And this kind of "nasty" was *not* on his to-do list.

"Are you fucking kidding me?" Jay knew this woman had

no intention of playing nicely with others, whether she was in town on business for only a few days or not. "Mac is an honorable woman, you idiot. She doesn't deserve your bull-shit. Never did." Jay bit his lip as he cut himself off mid-rant and slammed the phone down on the top of the solid wood chest of drawers.

He didn't even flinch at the unmistakable crack of glass. Hands balled into tight fists, he literally snarled as he raked his fingers through his hair and pulled. After a ten-count and a few deep breaths, he picked up the phone, almost amazed that the call was still connected.

"Listen, Ms. Ross," said with a disdain he didn't bother to conceal. "There's a reason she let me go in the first place—her husband. She is devoted to him, no matter what. And he, to her. So whatever the hell you're planning—"

"Shut. Up." The malevolent energy of the voice fairly crackled the air around him. "If you listen to what I have to say, you'll get what you want and I'll get what I want. One way or another, I'm going to have it. The question is, do you have what it takes to get what you really want?"

He didn't have to think long or hard. There wasn't another woman in the world like MacKenzie Ivers. "Fuck. You."

The line disconnected without so much as a good bye, fuck off, dog kiss my ass, or anything else. Fine with him.

A few moments later, he picked up the phone again and dialed.

JAY WAS RELIEVED WHEN SHE ANSWERED ON THE FIRST RING and he wasted no time telling her what Yazmin Ross had done only moments before.

"This Yazmin bitch is nuts. I had to tell you what she's up

to. I still can't believe she tried to...I mean, hell, what was she even thinking? She doesn't even know me, yet she called me and tried to go on a fishing expedition for information on you and Landon.

"Mac, I came here because you're the best person for the job, and your friend, Burton Khrys, is the best one to execute the construction of it. Neither I, nor my client in Montana, have the expertise and I respect your professional opinion. So here I am, in Seattle. I'm not trying to get over on you or anything. I hope you know that."

Jay shook his head and huffed out an exasperated breath. "As for Ms. Ross, well, I guess it's good to know we're not running low on crazy."

Mac burst out laughing.

When her laughter waned, Jay asked, "Mac, can we be frank?"

"Always, handsome." He blushed and then lay his heart out on a platter for her.

"I know you ended our relationship so you could concentrate on getting yourself together during your divorce. I respect you for that. But we were play partners before you and Landon fell apart. Now that you're back together, are you two still part of the lifestyle?"

"We are, but we're taking it slow."

"I miss you, Mac."

He heard the smile in her voice as she wistfully said, "I miss you, too."

The knot he hadn't realized was lodged in his chest began to unravel just a bit. He took a breath and tread out into the deepest ocean of his longing and hoped she would meet him there. "Believe it or not, I miss Landon as well. He always made me feel welcome. I won't lie about how I feel about you. I love you as much today as I did two years ago. At the risk of sounding cliché, I must also admit that I love so much that all I want is your happiness, even if that means we'll never be involved again. And while this may sound self-deprecating, if there's any room in your life for me, I'll take you any way I can get you."

It didn't matter that they'd never had sex—it had been negotiated and agreed upon before they'd ever played together. It didn't change the fact that this woman was everything he'd ever wanted. The perfect mix of dominant and submissive—dominant to Jay and submissive to her husband. The woman's expertise with floggers and body work had Jay practically shaking with need at the memories of her hands on his body. The way she used to get into his head. Gave him what was needed just when he'd needed it...and sometimes when he hadn't *known* what that need was, she'd still managed to read him and deliver.

Not to mention, the woman was fucking hot.

Caramel skin glowed with vitality. Dark brown lashes framed even darker eyes that twinkled with happiness and a hint of mischief. Super-small, finely cultivated deadlocks, shiny with health, hung down her back to tease the curve of her spine. Flawless skin and high cheekbones were enhanced by nothing. Usually, the only cosmetics on her lovely face was a bit of eyeliner and a light sheen of gloss. She was, in truth, a natural beauty to Jay.

Average height for a woman, Mac carried more-than-average curves with style and grace. A self-declared shoe whore, the woman's collection of super-high heels was second to none. And when she wore a pair of stiletto or platform boots, she owned them. Hell, owned *him*, body and soul.

"Jay, I hadn't expected this. Any of it. Not from Yazmin. And not from you."

"It's okay if you don't—"

"No, Jay, that's not where I'm going with this. Let me finish, handsome."

He almost smiled, because even though they were on the phone, he knew exactly what she was doing—waiting a moment to be sure she had his attention. It amazed him how well he knew her, and how he still reacted to the no-nonsense, but not quite bitchy, tone of voice—Mac saved the "bitchy" for when it was truly needed. No other woman made him want to kneel at her feet, give her the world.

"And stop holding your breath, Jay."

It was Jay's turn to laugh out loud. Guess he wasn't the only one who still remembered.

JOLENE STRODE INTO MAC'S OFFICE AND PUSHED A PIECE OF paper directly under her nose. Mac read it quickly, looked up and tilted her head in question.

"That's all he said, Mac. You were in a meeting so I told him I'd bring it in personally as soon as you were done."

The request was short, and as far from sweet as East was from West. She read it again and frowned. The words, "get over here, Mac, right now," had her hauling ass.

Her gut danced around beneath the skin with the feeling of impending doom...and Mac did doom as often as she did drama...which was never, if she could help it. Forty minutes later, she parked her car in the nearest spot outside and flew toward Twilight Teahouse with her heart racing as if she'd run a quarter mile in her heels.

She rounded the corner at the back of the steel and glass building and doom morphed into pure alarm. Rushing past a police cruiser that flashed blue and red lights, tension filled the space between her shoulder blades. Men in blue spoke with a fuming Madison Lee and a perplexed, angry Landon.

"What. The. Hell?" she whispered to herself.

A very disgruntled Yazmin Ross sat in the back of the police car.

Though she desperately wanted to ask what the hell was going, Mac stepped through the typically-closed double security doors and into the posh establishment. Just as she hit the first hallway to head to Madison Lee's office, a door opened off to her right. A single-file line of the entire grim-faced Twilight Teahouse staff streamed out of the private conference room used for their business meetings.

As they walked past in complete silence, a grim picture filled her mind of a scene from a movie about a young wizarding school that had been taken over by some pretty mean bastards. In that scene, no one smiled. No one had spoken. With forbidding faces, they'd marched along as if headed to their deaths.

In the halls of Twilight, if a pin had dropped, she doubted it would make any noise just now.

The attendants were all dressed in crisp and colorful traditional Japanese attire—the women in kimono and obi and the men in *haori* tops and *hakama* pants. Today's theme appeared to be the Spring season, with each person sporting some light, soft version of blue, pink, yellow or creamy white.

The kitchen staff that worked under Landon in his role as head chef, wore typical sparkling white chef coats with appliqued bamboo leaves done in dark blue. Loose black pants were covered with half-aprons, and on their heads were blue and white checkered cotton headbands with the Twilight Teahouse symbol embroidered in the center.

Kuri came up in the line. A baby-pink kimono with bright red *sakura* cherry blossom petals along the hem, graced her lithe body. Long, jet black hair was twisted up into an elegant knot on top of her head in a geisha-like style. As usual, Kuri was the picture of elegance, though her usual bubbly countenance was missing today. The other woman put out an arm and gently tugged Mac so that they ended up walking together. Kuri kept her focus straight ahead so Mac kept her questions to herself as they all moved, some turning directions or getting into the elevator to go about their duties.

Kuri and Mac ended up in the executive wing, a two-story affair that was connected to the five-storied main building. At its center was an atrium alive with plants and trees under a frosted glass skylight. The round space was circled with shoji doors that let into several offices. Kuri escorted her to Landon's office, gave a polite bow and departed without a word. Mac settled in to wait and every minute felt like an eternity as the nervous twitch in her gut morphed into a higher state of alarm with each tick of the clock.

Checked her watch. It had been five minutes.

Shit! I swear I've been in here for an hour!

Up out of the chair set aside for visitors, Mac paced. Checked her watch again—seven minutes.

"Fuck a duck!" she fumed aloud.

Finally, the door opened. Mac's relief became a mix of confusion and bone-chilling fear when Madison Lee entered alone.

"I want to tell you what happened before Landon gets in here. He's almost done giving his statement to the police."

Mac opened her mouth to voice one of a million questions that bounced around in her brain.

"Nope. Just listen, MacKenzie. Everything is fine, but I'm doing some interference here. And no, Landon doesn't know I'm in here. But woman to woman, I know how I'd feel if this happened to me, so I'm totally sticking my nose where it doesn't belong, so if you feel the need to cut it off after I'm done, then so be it."

Mac took her seat again, crossed her legs and waited.

When Madison Lee finished talking, the woman slipped back out of the room. And Mac had to admit, even if only to herself, Maddy had been correct—a little bit of female intervention had indeed been needed. Otherwise, she might have castrated her husband rather than applaud him.

ONE OF THE SERVING STAFF STEPPED INTO LANDON'S OFFICE with a tray of refreshments for MacKenzie. A note in Landon's handwriting had been slipped beneath the small glass of ice-cold tea.

"Sorry for the wait. Be there shortly."

Much more relaxed since Madison Lee had given her the skinny, Mac enjoyed the beverage and sat back. She'd just powered up her electronic reader to spend the time enjoying a novel when the door opened again.

Her husband stepped in and she flew into his arms.

Without hesitation, he shared Yazmin's latest nutball antics. All the while, he kept his hands on her. Buried his hands in her hair. Held her close. Ran his fingers down her spine and gave a grunt of appreciation when he felt the sexy corset she wore beneath her silk bolero jacket. When she wasn't wrapped in a tight hug, he caressed her arms, her waist, and the underside of her breasts.

Mac began to melt.

Amazing how stress and fear turned into the need to touch and taste, to chase the demons away. Now that she knew this man was all right, heat began to infuse her core, as it always did when she was the center of his particular attention.

"How did she manage to even get in here, Lan?"

"Beats me. Looked like she waltzed in through the doors

on the rear street where my crew takes out the kitchen trash. But Madison Lee is beyond pissed. She's the one who called the police and reported a stalker."

"Holy shit! Seriously?"

"Yep."

"Well, I heard Yazmin was all up on you, handsome." She let the sultry smile on her face belie any anger in her words. Landon's deep rumble of a laugh made her tremble.

"She tried to, but Maddy pretty much appeared out of nowhere. She didn't interrupt, though. Instead, she acted as witness and left it to me to handle it. I made it clear that I was not interested in revisiting old friends, reconciling with her, or being in her presence for any reason. I told her that we all knew about her clandestine phone call to Jay, trying to get information on you and me. In short, I told her to go the fuck away and stop chasing me."

"Did you actually say that? Really?" Mac's expression was one of amazement. Not because she didn't believe her husband, but because he was usually so careful with a woman's feelings, and tried not to purposely cause pain with his words.

"I did say exactly that. Word for word, in fact. I was especially eloquent with the four-lettered ones. I also made sure to repeat it to the police. It's in the official report, I'm sure. And Maddy was able to make a statement that she'd just told Yazmin's film director and crew that the woman had been banned from the premises two years ago, for life."

"Well considering how her lips were plastered to the side of your neck, I guess she wasn't buying the fact that you're happily married. Again."

"Woman, as fucked up as our last go-round was regarding Yazmin, I never ever lied to you. Either of you. And I don't plan to start now. I am saying, for the last time, that I am not interested in her."

"You do know that I'm aware of that, right?" Mac asked, walking around the desk and sitting down in her husband's lap. Strong thighs flexed beneath her butt as she rocked back and forth playfully.

"Yes, I know, but I wanted to say it anyway. The aggression was hers and I was truly trying to get out of there without totally destroying her with words I could never take back. I don't want that kind of karma following me around. And neither do you."

He was definitely right on that point.

"Point taken," she said. "Now kiss me, you gorgeous Celt."

"Nope. No kisses just now. We need to go. I made a reservation for us in the Japanese baths in five minutes. It'll take that long to get to the elevators on the other side of the building. After the news about the police and the bullshit made the rounds, they were willing to squeeze us in."

"Second floor or fourth floor," Mac queried. The second floor held a bath space where families of members of the club could come and enjoy a spa day as well as a true Japanese community bath. The fourth floor held the same concept, but for couples and kink, only.

"Second or fourth? Fourth, of course. Who do you think you're dealing with, lass?" Emerald eyes sparkled with mischief and Mac almost backed up a step with the sudden urge to run so he would give chase, catch and ravish her. She felt like a stick of dynamite just waiting for the match to strike. Gah!

"Dinner afterward?" Mac knew her expression was hopeful as she felt her face light up with expectancy. At Landon's nod, her tummy did a little dance and her happiness kicked up a notch. Sure, Mac was an excellent cook, but her fare was reserved for family and friends. Landon, on the other hand, was one of the best sushi chefs in the state, let alone Seattle proper. Most people found it amazing that as a young man, he'd made his way from Ireland to Japan to train under one of the most strict, but equally respected *itamae,* a true sushi master. The ten years he'd spent as an apprentice was considered a short amount of time.

But the boy was skilled, and that was just the way of it.

After "doing his time" he'd come to the Pacific Northwest and began to make a name for himself. Now, with twenty years of experience under his belt, the man was a wonder in the kitchen, whether he was preparing fresh fish or whipping up delicious *wagashi* desserts. Either way, Twilight Teahouse was lucky to have him.

And so was MacKenzie.

"I'm so ready for a trip upstairs." Mac sighed with longing and relief. "It was a long, but thankfully productive day." She'd gotten the deal close to finalized with Jay, and sent a preliminary copy of the contract over to legal for a head start on the review process.

Her heart did a sad little dip at the thought of Jay jetting off to Montana again. Rather than following that rabbit down a hole she really shouldn't go, Mac snapped her thoughts back to the present. "Burt and Solie should be here by the time we make it back downstairs. I'm sure I'll be starving by then."

"That's tomorrow night, darlin'. Tonight it's just you and me."

She had no complaints on that score. At all.

"And speaking of tomorrow, Solie is going to love the cake I made for her. It's a seven layer death by chocolate, get over your dick wad ex-boyfriend and celebrate the awesome new guy, kind of cake."

"God, I love you, Landon Ivers."

"Damn right you do, MacKenzie Ivers."

Hand in hand, they walked through the executive wing, back to the main building and to the main bank of elevators on the first floor. Landon pulled out his access card and swiped it over the reader. In moments, they stepped across a threshold and were flying upward.

The doors swished open to reveal, as with every floor, a huge immaculate tiled foyer with a wall lined with shoe cubbies just past the reception desk.

A traditional Japanese bath meant scrubbing down in the shower, soaking in a deep tub for relaxation, followed by deep tissue massage. Foregoing the water part of the experience, Landon raised his wife's wrist for a kiss and headed straight to their private room. One step into the room, he turned and pulled her into his arms.

Her breasts were firm beneath her corset and her strong arms held him as tight as he did her. Then, Mac sighed and relaxed into the caress. Allowed herself to be held, loved.

Landon pressed a kiss to the side of her neck. "So, since I didn't get to tie anyone up the other day..."

Mac braced her hands against his chest and pushed back so she could look up into his face. With a raised brow, she gave him her best I-told-you-so look. "That was your choice, Lan. I told you to go ahead and do it." Then she laughed at his disgruntled expression.

"But I didn't want Yazmin. Didn't want to put my hands on her. Not even a little. I want you. Period. Now, strip lovely."

"Strip? Why is it your turn to *not* strip?"

"Because I'm the Dom."

"Well so am I," Mac countered.

"True, but since we only submit to one another, that means I get to pull the man card."

"That's not even bullshit. I'm calling horseshit on that!"

"Call it whatever you like. It can be your turn next time, woman."

They both knew good and well that she didn't truly want

to dominate her man, yet Landon humored her. And she loved him even more for it.

Besides, how many couples argued over who got to *give* the massage rather than receive it?

Clothes off, folded and placed on the wide cushion of a thickly padded chair, Mac climbed up on the massage table. She laid back and sighed with contentment as warmth leeched into her bones from the heated blanket beneath her body.

———

EASING THE LIGHTLY SCENTED OIL OVER HER SKIN, LANDON eased strong fingers into the tight band of muscled knots on her left shoulder and mid-back. "I think you need a new toy. You need an outlet for your alpha bitch side."

When Mac didn't respond, Landon continued. "I know you believe I need to play with someone else in order to satisfy my kinky rope fetish, but honestly Mac, you're all I need. Now and forever. My concern is that you have no submissive, and I am not so egotistical anymore that I believe you can go without, while I'm entitled to do whatever I want. I'm so done with that shit, woman. I can't express how done. So, what are we going to do about your needs, darlin'?"

Well, he had her there. She did miss having a submissive. She was a dominant personality, for sure, but she didn't now, nor would she ever, want Landon to submit to her. He wasn't wired that way. And honestly, she didn't want him wired any other way than how he was—dominant to the bone.

Before, they'd each had their own sub, but now her brain lit up like a Christmas tree as an idea came to her. "Lan, what if we play with a submissive together rather than the way we did it before?"

He hadn't considered that, and rather than answer right

away, he wanted to think on the pros and cons. Landon could admit he was just a tad bit nervous about introducing anyone into their relationship dynamic and wasn't the least bit interested in a full-time submissive. But that didn't necessarily apply to Mac.

"Mac, this isn't about just what I want or need. Remember that as we hash this out."

She nodded as brows dove into a frown. Landon could almost hear the wheels in her head turning, searching for a solution.

Suddenly, their gazes swung to one another. "Kuri!" they declared in unison.

Madison Lee and Kinson's submissive was a live in, twenty-four seven sub who happened to love kink. Maddy was the rigger in their family, but she didn't get around to it much these days. The growth and popularity of Twilight Teahouse sucked up more and more of her time. Kinson was the impact player, but he spent more time overseas for work than he did at home. Which meant an occasionally neglected Kuri.

"Do you think Kuri would be interested?" Mac asked excitedly.

"Maybe. The last time she got tied up and suspended, it wasn't by Maddy."

"Really? Who?"

"Burt." Burton Khrys wasn't only their good friend, and a hell of a building contractor. He was also a fully recognized Master in the BDSM community, as well as boyfriend to Mac's best bud, Solie. "Maddy actually called him to come into the city in between projects just to see to Kuri's needs because Mad had been up to her eyeballs in planning the expansion to the upper floors. Still doesn't' change the fact that she's owned and collared by someone else."

True.

"What if we ask Madison Lee and Kinson to recommend someone who has some time to play with us at Twilight a couple of times a month or so? For example, someone who is interested in rope and a little impact play, but isn't looking for anything permanent?" Mac asked.

Hmm. That might work. Someone that they could play with, minus the attachment? It would give him more rope time, and her more impact play time, yet allow them to do so together.

"Maybe someone who literally just wants to do some pick-up play every now and then? And, of course, you have me all the rest of the time, and I have you...sort of," Mac suggested with a bit of snark in those last six words. Landon smacked her bare ass and she grinned. They both knew that the last thing Landon was going to do was take a flogging from anyone, including her. But fuck her silly? Yeah, he could do that. All day long. Actually, all night, too.

"So, who?" Mac wondered aloud.

"Well," Landon said as he knuckled a particularly tense spot beneath her scapula, "there's Jay. You've always been half in love with him." When she started to protest, Landon cut her off. "There's nothing wrong with being attracted to him, Mac. It would have never worked between you in the first place if you hadn't liked the guy. Besides, what if he's that missing bit that we've been looking for? It would be remiss if we didn't at least think on it, and if we agree, talk to him about it. Besides, I don't think it's a total coincidence that he happens to be in town at the same time Yazmin popped up."

"What do you mean?"

"Mac, think about it. We've got the epitome of nutball who pops up at the same time as the one man who always treated you with respect and care. And he's the one who didn't show up with the intent to wrest you away from me. I respect him for that. We've had perfect examples of the good, the bad and the ugly all within a matter of days."

She remained quiet, but he could tell she was mulling it over. After a few moments of silence, Landon asked," So tell me what you think?"

Mac thought of the man who'd just popped back into her life. Her lips spread into a huge grin. Just couldn't help it. Jay might be easy going and quiet, but he was a still-waters-run-deep kind of guy with a spine of steel and a sense of humor that never ceased to cause her to double over.

If she were honest, she'd always had a soft spot in her heart for Jay, and had always been honest in regard to her attraction to him. Time away from the man had done nothing to dim the little flame that always flickered with life and passion when in his presence. Did she prefer him instead of her husband? Not at all. They were so very different...but each brought something different to the table. And damn did she love that particular feast.

Landon kneaded the tense muscles around the edges of Mac's trapezius muscles. The action pulled a moan of pleasure from deep in her chest.

"Mmm, that feels wonderful. You're good with your hands, but just be aware that part of that moan is because your big cock is getting hard right in the crease of my ass."

He chose that moment to flex said cock. Mac squealed. Landon chuckled.

"Big tease," she accused, but knew he would deliver. Always had. Always would.

---

5

*M*ac considered procrastinating about calling Jay, but changed her mind.

Jay picked up immediately and for the next twenty minutes, she was sure she'd successfully flipped him right-side up as she shared the conversation between Landon and herself about finding a third—specifically a *not-female* third. A thrilled, yet cautious, Jay agreed to a dinner at the one place he'd been longing to re-visit.

Not ten minutes after disconnecting the call with Jay, she'd received another phone call. Now, Mac sat at her desk, stunned.

"This must be the result of some seriously good karma," she said to herself, still unable to close her mouth that had fallen open.

Madison Lee had just rocked her world. Harrison, the director of the movie crew that had come to Twilight for the rope demo, had called Madison Lee. It had started out as a simple apology for the ridiculous situation they'd found themselves in through Yazmin's underhanded bullshit. But the conversation turned into a friendly, more comfortable exchange with Harrison finally asking, "What can I do for you, Madison Lee?"

Maddy's response had been instantaneous and before that phone call was done, she'd negotiated a special short film, featuring Landon and his rope. Harrison had even agreed that if Landon preferred to have his rope bunny be a man instead of a woman, he had no issues with that.

In Mac's eye, she saw a fit, gorgeous and gloriously naked Jay as the base for a beautiful design done in nothing but rope. It would remove the 'female' issue for Landon so he could simply be creative with his bondage, minus any worry about crazy bitches. And it would give Mac an outlet for her own needs while giving Jay something he needed equally as much.

A win-win-win if there ever was one.

But would Jay agree?

God, she hoped so because just the thought of what she, Landon and Jay could be together literally had her heart racing and a grin spreading across her lips. She put a little skip to her step as she rose from her desk and headed home to get ready for a dinner date that she was sure would change their lives from this very night, into the foreseeable future.

6

*J*ust off the main dining area was a lavish room reserved for the head chef, the owners and executives of Twilight Teahouse and special guests.

Jay was running late and Landon was in charge of the kitchen for another hour. Even still, dinner was a lovely affair.

With walls of cream silk, and sconces shaped like Japanese lanterns, the room was awash in a muted, inviting hue. In the middle of the tatami floor was a low polished wooden table surrounded by big fluffy cushions.

Tonight, her husband had personally served her, rather than have one of the attendants wait on her. Each time he'd stepped into the room, she fell just a little bit more in love with him, if that were possible.

He'd created and delivered all of her favorite nom noms— fresh Maguro tuna sashimi, such a deep red it made her think of the candy on candied apples. Creamy-fleshed salmon topped with minced chives, sweet Hawaiian ono with some kind of miso sauce, and fresh greens with ginger dressing finished her off.

After practically inhaling the delicious fare, along with a pot of aromatic jasmine tea, Mac could only nod and rub her belly when Landon reminded her to leave room for dessert. Surely she was waddling as she headed into the club to find Solie and Burton.

Spotting them in the dessert room, Mac plopped down on the loveseat directly in front of them with the world's biggest grin spread across her lips. Tonight she would play mediator and help them negotiate their new D/s relationship. They'd all been friends for years, but until recently, both Solie and Burton had been in relationships with other people.

Solie had gone through hell with a douche-canoe sociopath named Marcais, who'd left her psychologically broken and torn. Burton believed wholeheartedly in caring for those he considered his. He put a lot of time and energy into his relationships, whether they were of a sexual nature or not. As such, he was very selective about who he gave all that energy to. He didn't believe in casual anything. With Solie, Mac and very few others, Burton cared in action, not just word. The man had stepped in to help Solie heal by simply being the good friend to her that he always was. And along the way, the two had fallen in love.

Tonight was the official beginning of their relationship. Mac couldn't be more thrilled. Solie was, like herself, the alpha bitch submissive of the Universe. Burton was the yin to that woman's yang, dominant through and through, and as gorgeous as the day was long.

The two knew each other so well, the negotiations went smooth as ice as they both laid out what they would and wouldn't tolerate in this new facet of an old friendship. As soon as limits were set, Landon walked over to their table with a smiling Jay in tow.

"Look who I found," Landon said, nodding his head

towards Jay while carrying the biggest cake Mac had ever seen.

Jay leaned over and gave Mac a peck on the cheek, then shook hands with everyone else at the table. Both Solie and Burt remembered him and voiced their genuine pleasure at seeing him again.

Mac's heart leapt up into her throat as it began to sink in that Solie and Burt might not be the only ones beginning a new "thing". She was beyond nervous. And it was totally a good thing!

The whole crew offered congratulations to Solie as an oversized piece of seven layer chocolate decadence was placed in front of her, along with a steaming pot of lightly minted tea to wash it down.

After a few bites of sinful deliciousness, Mac sat down her fork and looked at her best friend. "So what's your poison tonight, Sols?"

With a tired sigh, Solie simply replied, "Nothing."

It was not the answer Mac wanted to hear. It had been a *loooong* while since Solie indulged her love of impact play and it was time to step out into the deep. Mac took both her hands while Burton sat back and let the moment happen.

"Solie, listen, you can't be so hard on yourself. There's no way you could have known what Marcais was. Sociopaths are experts at concealing the truth. Pros at charming people out of anything and everything. For them there's no empathy. It's about winning."

But when Solie explained all of the different red flags that Marcais had waved in her face, she couldn't help but empathize with the other woman. Sociopaths moved in fast. Pushed the relationships quickly for a reason—while Marcais had laid on the charm and manipulated Solie, he'd gotten her addicted to his special kind of attention.

She'd been hip deep into him before she knew what hit

her. In the end, she'd come to her senses and left the bastard...but not before he'd infected her, broken her heart, and put her in a position where woman after woman had been contacting Solie about his particular assholery.

"I see what you mean about the red flags, but knowing it wasn't personal should make that particular pill a bit easier to swallow, right?" Landon asked as Mac and Jay both nodded in agreement.

"True, but it's still a bitter pill, you guys. Cod liver oil mixed with crushed aspirin bitter. I mean, dayum."

Burton rose to his imposing height and held out his hand to her. "Well, if you'd like some medicine that's a tad bit sweeter, come on up to the third floor. I think I have something you might appreciate."

"Should I be scared?" Solie asked.

"It's me we're talking about here, Solie," Burton said in mock outrage.

"Yep, scared. Definitely scared," she said, voice deadpan with mock fear.

Mac glanced over at Burt and winked, knowing what he had in store. When Solie asked what the two of them were up to, Mac simply waved and blew a kiss as Burton gave Solie some instructions and then headed out of the room.

Once they were gone, Landon said, "The Ice Palace, eh? I must admit I love that particular themed floor." He then turned to Jay. "Ever been up there?"

"I don't think so. Last time I played here, Mac and I were in the Caribbean. It was...pretty hot." He winked.

Mac blushed. But not because her husband and former dude were talking about bondage-themed play spaces together. It was because of the wicked looks both men gave her.

SHE HAD A GOOD IDEA OF HOW THIS WAS GOING TO GO DOWN, but rather than setting expectations in her head, Mac decided to expect absolutely nothing, one way or the other.

"After I act as protector for Solie during her scene with Burton, where would you like to meet up?" Mac asked her husband.

"I reserved the Bamboo Room for us. Work for you?"

"It certainly does," Mac said as she leaned down to give Landon a sweet peck on the lips. "I may be awhile."

"That's fine. It'll give Jay and me a chance to talk alone."

Jay nodded his agreement. The energy rolling off of the man was almost palpable in its intensity. He was a jumbled mix of high vibration that made Mac suck in a breath when his gaze landed on her.

Arms crossed over her chest as she settled her weight on one hip, Mac glared at the two men grinning like lunatics.

"I'm not sure I want you two to talk alone. You'll conspire on how to manage me and I call bullshit before you even get started down that path, Landon Cleary Ivers."

"Did she just use your whole name, man?" Jay asked, eyes wide. But the laughter in his eyes told her that these two were going to be trouble with a capital "T".

Her hands were now on her hips, eyes shot daggers and left toe tap-tap-tapped an irritated cadence on the glossy wood floor.

Without looking away from Mac, Landon replied, "Yep. She sure did. But that doesna change a thing. Off you go, Mac. You don't want tae be late, now do ye?"

"Interesting," Jay said, glancing at Landon with a newfound curiosity reflected in his beautiful jades. "I don't think I've ever heard your accent so thick."

"Seems tae happen when a certain female riles me up, or makes me horny."

Jay nodded, lifted his glass of steaming jasmine tea and sipped. He didn't say another word.

Mac, on the other hand, had plenty to say. In fact, she opened her mouth to tell her husband exactly what she thought of his "riles me up" statement when Landon said, "Ye need a bit o' punishment this evenin', Mrs. Ivers?"

Nostrils flared with her irritation, but she clamped her lips shut and grumbled that she was going to be late for Solie's scene.

Screw them anyway. Who needed to hear what they had to say to one another? In the end, she would have her say or there were going to be two very unhappy men leaving Twilight Teahouse tonight, damn it.

Damn men. Always trying to run things.

One side of her mouth tilted up into a saucy grin as she turned on a sharp heel. Whistling a raunchy tune she'd learned from her husband, she swiped her access card and hopped into the elevator on the way to the Ice Palace.

*J*ay set his cup down on the beautiful mosaic tiled table they occupied. "So tell me about this Ice Palace theme? Am I going to want to visit that particular floor?"

"You'll totally want to visit. Hell, I believe you'll want to take up residence there."

Landon explained that the spot was endless white—white walls, white tiled floors and one-way glass. Secrets were safe within; even with all the lights on in the darkness of night, no one could see inside from the street.

Mirrored pillars topped with marble and crystal sculptures reflected light in a mix of rainbow-prism arcs and edges. Muted brilliance filled the room until you swore you were inside a sparkling masterpiece of ice, minus the bone-chilling cold.

Like all of the other themed floors, the Ice Palace had several stations with spanking benches and massage tables. The private areas appeared to be wide open but could be closed off with shoji screens. Some had sliding glass doors embedded in the walls so that when they were open, it looked like there's no way to have any privacy. But there were doors that slid closed, with luxurious drapes that could be drawn closed.

Pretty classy.

"It's like tooling through a crystal palace in a science fiction movie, minus any scaly green women".

Glad that Jay had taken the lead in breaking the ice, Landon was ready to get down to business.

"When MacKenzie left, she was wearing her 'I'm worried but I'm not going to say I'm worried' face." Landon forked up a bite of chocolate decadence.

"Ah, I see. I don't think I've ever seen that look. But it would make sense why not. Anytime we were together she was in complete control. Always exuded that crackling Dom energy. Fucking brought me to my knees."

Landon looked thoughtfully at the man sitting across from him. Sure, he'd spent time with Jay back in the day, but it was usually a polite dinner with friends or a social event. The other man used to belong to Mac, so Landon had always kept his distance to allow his wife to handle that relationship as she saw fit.

That, however, had changed.

"So Mac talked to you about what we're proposing, yes?"

"Yes, she did. We didn't discuss the details, but I assume that's about to happen right now."

"You'd be right. You were Mac's, but Mac is mine. So I'm acting as her protector. You and I will come to an agreement, and Mac will be informed of what that agreement will be."

Jay cocked his head, confusion clouding his expression.

Guess I need to be clearer.

"I am Mac's dominant. Before, what went on between the two of you was always shared with me. I just kept out of it because it was her thing. This is no longer *her* thing. It's *our* thing. And any of *our* business will have my hand in it in some way."

The *"Ah, I see"* expression on Jay's handsome face showed no hesitance or concern. On the contrary, the man seemed to really get it. To Landon's surprise, it was a huge relief to have no hard feelings right off the bat. After all, this whole arrangement would depend on Jay's consent. No consent meant no triad.

He let his words sink in, then continued. "She loves you, Jay."

"Excuse me?"

Landon almost laughed at the completely gob smacked expression on his guest's face at hearing the extent of Mac's feelings. Obviously the woman had been remiss in telling Jay exactly where he rated with her. Landon would have to make sure Mac remedied that particular situation.

"I'm not such a selfish dick that I would keep something like this from you. Consider this, Jay. I didn't even love Yazmin, yet I let her take from me the most important thing I had between me and my wife—my integrity, my honor. It won't happen again. So I have to be honest, even if I'm not thrilled about the topic. Mac does indeed love you, man. Heart and soul."

"I love her right back. But as I told her, I love her enough to back the hell up if that's what's needed for her to be happy."

"I think you would make her happy."

"I don't follow."

"You can give her something that I can't." Landon paused and let the words sink in. After a few moments, he put Jay out of his curiosity-induced misery. "Your submission. And what I'm about to say next, I haven't even shared with Mac. But if she wants it, I will go along with opening up our marriage to you, and only you. That includes sex."

Jay's jaw dropped before he fell into a fit of coughing.

"Sorry, didn't mean to make you inhale your tea. Need another cup?"

Jay shook his head vigorously and tried to catch his breath between juicy-sounding hacks. Man damn near drowned himself in jasmine green. "Holy shit, Landon. I...just give me a minute."

"I HAVE NO INTENTION OF DOMINATING YOU, JAY, BUT THERE will be times when I'm in charge. You'll be Mac's and mine. You'll have our protection and anything you need from us. But when it comes to a D/s dynamic, you're primarily hers."

"But how would that work if we're all together?"

"Let's just let it flow. I'm her Dom, she's your Dom. Just let it play out.

"AND WHAT ABOUT YOU, LANDON?"

"I don't consider myself bisexual, if that's what you're asking. But I'm comfortable enough in my skin that if we're both with Mac, and we end up touching each other, I'm not going to freak out."

"No matter, Mac is always the focus for me."

"Good, as she's my focus as well. But understand one thing, if you hurt her, I will skin your ass, tie you up and hoist you up in one of the foyers of Twilight Teahouse. And yes, Madison Lee will allow it."

"Holy shit."

"Holy shit? Yeah, I'd like to think so." Landon flashed his most evil grin. If he'd been a vampire or something, he was sure he'd be flashing fang right now. Because when it came to Mac and pain, he'd be damn sure to exact retribution. No holds bar. "But before we get that far, we need to negotiate limits and such. If you're interested, that is."

"I'm interested. Totally and absolutely. As for limits, I don't have any new ones since, you know...before. They're all in writing. I'd be fine with just using those with the understanding that I may want to revisit them every now and again."

"Thank god," Landon mumbled, grateful for no complications on either end. "We just need to make sure that Mac is fine with sex, and I can't imagine she'd have any issue."

Relief flowed over both their faces followed by deep breaths, almost in tandem, as one of the staff dropped off a warm flask of sake, and they continued. Jay's hard limits were already negotiated in writing. To Landon's surprise and utter delight, the man had even suggested doing some counseling together to ensure their triad was functional rather than dysfunctional.

With that done, they raised a small cup and toasted to Mac with a quiet but lusty, *"Kanpai!"*

Landon's gaze remained glued to Jay's handsome face—yes, he could admit the man was good looking—keenly aware of the emotions that washed through the other man. If he was reading him correctly, Landon needed to get this deal done for Jay's peace of mind. If his shell-shocked-but-happy-yet-anxious expression was any indication, he was waiting for the other shoe to drop.

Thankfully, there was no shoe.

"Now," Landon said as he stood. "Let's go get our woman." He extended his hand to their new 'third', shook it firmly and watched Jay smile, *truly* smile, for the first time tonight.

AT THE APPOINTED TIME, MAC SAT IN THE BAMBOO ROOM

alone. She literally twiddled her thumbs while tapping the toe of a high-heeled boot with an annoyed cadence. Funny thing was…she wasn't annoyed. She was nervous.

It was a giddy kind of feeling rather than one of concern. She knew that Jay would accept their offer. Knew it down to her toes. But it didn't change the fact that this was something new, fantastic and wonderful.

It was like a kid waiting to open presents at Christmas. A kid who kept checking the clock to see if it was time to get up yet so she could rush downstairs and start ripping open the various goodies awaiting her.

And this room contained zilch to keep her mind occupied as she waited for her two pieces of yum to arrive. There was absolutely nothing in here but a huge beanbag-like chair literally big enough for five people. The floor and walls were finely pressed bamboo, and the door was made of hundreds of super-thin bamboo reeds lashed together. Hence the name, the Bamboo Room.

Eyes closed, she imagined Landon and Jay standing before her, both tall, dark and handsome. Both with green eyes that seemed to peer right through her, body and soul. Where Landon's upper body was wide and muscular, Jay's was sleek with a runner's build. Both had hair, black as sin and both had eyes of jade and emerald. And both loved her to no end.

And Mac was a trembling mess by the time her men joined her.

She looked up and saw both of them had hands extended to help her up off the oversized oval beanbag sac that could serve as a couch or a bed.

She stood and accepted a small cup of sake as Landon explained.

"We've had a thorough conversation about how we think

this will work. And in celebration of Jay joining our little posse, we brought you a bit o' sake to toast with.

Mac just stood there, looking back and forth between them.

When she didn't take the little ceramic cup, Landon looked down at the sake in his hand and back at his wife's face.

"Mac, you okay with this?"

"I…" She reached out and retrieved the little porcelain cup with the potent clear brew from his hands. "Yes. I'm okay with it. I'm just…overwhelmed."

Jay's face tightened.

"It's a good thing, both of you. I'm not overwhelmed like I want to run away from home or something. I'm just…I never thought this would play out this way. And I'm happy as shit."

One of her men smiled as if he expected nothing less. The other sighed with relief, then burst out laughing as if he were the happiest man on Earth. Which made her even giddier.

"Toast?" Landon asked.

"Absolutely," Mac replied and raised her glass and waited for Landon to pour a bit for himself and Jay.

All three cheered, "Kanpai!" and downed their sake in one swift shot.

"And now, to truly celebrate, I think a bit of naughty is in order. No holds barred, Mac. No limits on affection."

Her eyes widened and her mouth fell open. Sure the two of them had discussed the "all in" solution he felt would serve them all best. But again, she'd never hoped for such a thing. Letting Jay go had been a difficult, but necessary, choice. He'd been nothing but good to her, understanding, caring. Oh, the man was just as alpha as Landon, but his needs were different, more subtle. He could be a real handful, but it had always been a challenge that she'd savored and cherished.

She'd been satisfied with their previous arrangement because it was best at the time.

But now that Jay was here and back in her life, their lives, losing him wasn't something she wanted to experience again.

However, there was more to this than what she wanted. She wasn't a one-some. She was part of a couple-turning-triad. So, it was her turn to ask Landon if he was sure just one more time.

Her husband's answer was to step to her without hesitation and pull her into his arms. "Woman, I am in this for the win. And to be honest, you could do worse than having two men who love you more than all the world."

With that, he lowered his head and kissed her silly. Not giving her a chance to do anything but feel, Landon began and held the power of that kiss even as he began to set up what would follow.

It began with a simple order to Jay to remove her boots as Landon continued to hold her tight, plunder her mouth and taste her deeply. He kissed her until she was almost out of breath. When he released her, she had no time to pant as he took her mouth again, and again.

Feet bare, she giggled as Jay massaged her toes. Her chuckle became a moan as he moved his fingers into her arch and pressed gently before applying the same delicious pressure from calves to thighs to the under-curve of her backside.

Jay's touch was familiar and comfortable, like her favorite pair of slippers or the silk robe she always wore around the house—soft and comfortable.

But not enough.

Between the kisses and touches, and the realization that these two men were both hers, Mac was soon flying towards a need so great it made her scalp tingle.

She threw her head back and cried out when Landon's teeth nipped the tendon that connected neck to shoulder.

"More! Please!"

"Well, Jay," Landon growled with that little touch of evil that always raised the hairs on the back of her neck. "You heard the lady. More."

Clothes went flying until they painted the room in a myriad of fabrics and colors. Shoes thudded as they were kicked off, and even a few rips were heard here and there.

Yes!

She was wet and ready and so eager she was almost angry with it. Her world was on fire and these were the two men who could see to putting that damn thing out!

And they were ready to oblige her. Who said quickies were only for morning time? Nobody, that's who!

Jay lay on the big cushiony oval and Mac assumed her favorite position—on her knees, ass up, head down...right over his face.

Jay lapped at her tender folds, while Landon wasted no time feeding his generous cock deep into her ready channel. In not time, she needed to come badly, yet her men pushed her up, up and up only to let her hang there to contemplate life or some shit.

Just as she was about to threaten castration, Jay suckled her clit with a fierce rhythm. Landon pistoned into her sex and slipped just the tip of a single digit into her rear passage.

"Oh my god!" Mac fell from the precipice, tumbled head over heels with an orgasm so powerful, she didn't think she would ever touch bottom.

Breathing like a winded racehorse, Mac stilled to let her heart and lungs catch up to her endorphin-laced brain.

God bless sex hormones, husbands and mates, she thought happily.

"Don't leave him in agony, Mac. Help Jay come." Landon's

words reached her from far, far away. When they finally registered, she instantly obeyed as Jay got to his knees in front of her. Still in a haze of completion, she heard herself moan as the tang of his unique flavor registered in her brain seconds after it touched her tongue.

The scent of their skin, sweat, and the remnants of expensive cologne, filled her nostrils and settled deep inside.

She swirled her tongue around the tip, then let Landon's rhythm move her back and forth to take Jay deeper down her throat. The man's head was thrown back, teeth bared like some wild thing racing for release.

The next time she looked up, her lovers' gazes were locked on one another, as if some secret understanding passed between then.

And as one, they flew apart at the seams, called her name as one released down her throat, and the other deep in her womb.

Spent and satisfied then fell over together. Mac leaned down, grabbed the light cotton throw laid across the bottom of the bed and settled it over them all. With a satisfied sigh, they lay in a sweaty cuddle puddle on the huge oval cushion.

Mac yawned and snuggled in, so relaxed and happy, even a new pair of kick ass suede stilettos with the red soles couldn't compare. Landon's hard muscular thighs, slick with sweat, pressed against hers. Perfectly formed pecs were heavenly against her upper spine. Strong arms encompassed her body, held her close. Safe. Secure.

She reached out, pulled a languid Jay into her body and curled herself around him.

Was there anything more decadent than laying spoon fashion with a strong man at her back, while another equally strong male trusted her enough to expose himself completely and let her cover *his* back as his dominant?

Not likely.

After several moments of companionable silence, questions began to tumble through Mac's mind.

"Jay, when will we see you again? Have you considered moving back here?" Mac asked on a sleepy yawn as she snuggled in.

"Actually, I have. I never sold my house here. Always held out hope that one day I'd make it back to Seattle. But now I can't think of a better reason to move back to town than the woman laying right here in my arms.

Mac ducked her head and blinked back tears, grateful to her men who'd made all of this possible.

Then she bolted upright, dragging the throw with her to cover her bare breasts.

"But what about your client in Montana? What about your work? I don't expect you to…"

Jay sat up, smoothed an errant loc behind her ear and rocked her world. Again.

"I can work anywhere, Mac. As for Montana, I'll see that project through, wrap it up and then skip town. So, yes, I'm moving back here."

Landon laughed as Mac squealed, then threw her arms, legs and everything in between against Jay as she took him back down to the sheets.

After round two, she lay there between two luscious men. MacKenzie Ivers considered all that she'd been through over the last two years, even the rough cut of the last few days, and wondered at how things had worked out in the end.

She decided on a simple truth—she was, indeed, one hell of a lucky woman.

SUCCULENT

1

*E*ven though the television was turned down low, Madison Lee's ears perked up at the sound of the voice she'd recognize anywhere after so many years.

Without looking up from the memo she penned, her fingers closed around the remote on her desk. With a quick flick of the wrist, the volume increased.

She still didn't look toward the screen. Not yet.

Deep breath in, Maddy, then let it out slow. Just breathe.

After a few quick ins and outs, she gave up on the whole "calming breath" thing and lifted her gaze toward the set. And there he was—Kinson Lee, hipster, yogi extraordinaire…and missing husband.

Well, he wasn't really missing, but he was away so much that he was becoming more of a figment of her imagination than a spouse.

The man was the epitome of style with a bit of gives-a-damn thrown in. Kinson was the type of man who might wear a designer suit with a pair of sandals. He walked to the beat of his own drum, and the fact that he didn't give a rat's rear end about what conventional yoga should or shouldn't be, came through when he was teaching.

In this particular news spotlight, they highlighted the work he was doing overseas and showed him teaching a packed class. Gorgeous tanned skin glowed with health. Honeyed hazel eyes sparkled with a hint of mischief. Much more muscular than any yoga dude she'd ever seen on TV, Kinson looked more like a professional athlete, all toned, lean and buffed.

Madison cocked her head to the side with a thought. "Well, I guess he is a professional athlete if yoga is considered a sport," she said to the empty space of her office. The man was gorgeous with a neatly trimmed beard and reddish-gold hair, cut in the latest style.

A strong jaw and high cheekbones were the foundation for a man who was all kinds of good looking. The sight of him never failed to make her body and mind stand up and take notice.

And after the week she'd been having, she could really use a husband just now.

Guess her best friends would have to do.

Her personal phone vibrated from its perch on her desk. She snatched it up. "Well, think of the devil," Madison said, her words full of genuine joy.

"Think of the devil? I thought the saying was 'speak of the devil'?" asked MacKenzie Ivers.

"Well, I wasn't talking at the time, so it didn't quite seem to fit. You know me, I'll *make* it fit when necessary."

"You're so bad," Mac giggled.

"Could I run this place if I weren't at least a little bit naughty?"

"Nope."

"So what's up, darlin'?" Madison asked her best friend.

"Landon said he'll do the documentary on bondage and

rope for that Hollywood producer who called you. Jay is in as well."

"Really?" It was the best news Madison had heard all day. Her life was ideal, yes, but being lonely while married didn't really pep up a girl.

Clicking off the television didn't banish her husband's image from her mind, but it would be a start. God, she missed him, but she had shit to do. Moping would have to wait. Pulling her Superman cape around her heart, she pushed the gloom away and focused on her conversation with MacKenzie. "So, how are you guys settling in?"

"Fantastic! I was able to talk Jay into keeping his house in Montana. He can rent it out as a vacation house or something, and it would give us a place to go to get away sometimes. And Landon talked him into skipping out on buying a house here and moving in with us."

"Seriously?" Holy hell, that was huge. Landon Ivers and Mac had gone through a serious rough patch. The result had been a divorce, followed by reconciliation, but Landon hadn't jumped back into the lifestyle, even with Mac prodding him to do so. Well, the man had finally stopped punishing himself for his role in the crash of their relationship and was back into his rigging. The man was a master with rope, after all.

Jay had been Mac's submissive until all hell had broken loose with Landon's major fubar. But he was back now and the three were an official triad.

It was a beautiful thing. They cared so much for one another.

"Maddy?"

"I'm here."

"Well, you went quiet all of a sudden. You okay?"

"Sure," she said, giving her most practiced, perfect answer. Even her inflection said, "I'm happy!"

"And you're lying to me, Madison Lee. What's going on? When is Kinson home again?"

"Should be next week."

"But you don't think he'll make it, right?"

This woman knew her so well.

"I don't know, Mac. And I don't have time to worry about it."

"Well, I love you, woman. Feel free to come and hang out with us when you're lonely. It's not good the way you and Kuri sit up in that big house, moping."

"MacKenzie Ivers, I do not mope."

"Uh huh. Offer's still open."

"Thank you, love. You guys headed this way soon?"

"Yep. We'll see you Friday. Dinner as usual, and dessert in the Hatshepsut chapel."

"Oooh, that sounds decadent," Madison wolf whistled.

"Jay is flying in on Thursday night and you know how he loves that particular space. So we'll accommodate him. Besides, I can be nice since he's only here a couple of times a month while he's getting things settled in Montana. I can't wait until he's here permanently."

God, the woman sounded completely thrilled. MacKenzie had what every woman secretly wished for—a husband she could submit to in the bedroom...and a third who submitted to *her*. "And after he's here permanently, you'll still accommodate him."

Mac laughed and said, "Well, you know I'll occasionally have to remind him who's the Dom in the relationship."

"You mean the delicious way that Landon occasionally reminds you?"

"Of course! See you later, doll. Love you bunches."

"Back at you, MacKenzie."

With an inward sigh, Madison admitted to herself that she was bordering on pure jealousy, plain and simple.

Landon and MacKenzie had something she wanted for herself.

Sigh.

But one had to be around to have a triad. And Kinson just…wasn't. As a result, Madison was unhappy, and Kinson's submissive, Kuri, was unhappy. The only one happy in this situation was Kinson fucking Lee.

Madison hung up the phone and pretended her heart wasn't breaking into a bazillion pieces.

KINSON LEE WALKED OUT OF THE MEETING SPACE WITH A smile as wide as the waterway next to the boardwalk he strode down. An accomplished and sought after yogi, he wasn't surprised his class had gone well, but it made him feel good none the less.

This was his third instructional conference, in three countries in as many weeks. He loved teaching people how to live a healthier lifestyle. Right now he wished he could talk to his best friend about his success, but she was a million miles away holding down the fort at home. Madison Lee was his life, his love, and thankfully, a very strong support system.

Without that woman, there was no way in hell he could do this kind of work.

She was smart, strong, and brave. And sexy as hell.

When she was horny, his woman's green eyes glittered with a feral need that melted his bones and brought out the tiger in him. He was a natural leader, but so was Madison Lee—funny that he, as well as all of their employees, sometimes called her by her entire name.

And he couldn't wait to get home at the end of the week.

Kinson thought about the way her favorite black corset

looked against her smooth skin and was instantly hard. His next thought was of how she stripped for him, eased his stress by putting her hands in all the right places. And her favorite position? On her knees.

Delicious.

He hadn't bothered to change clothes and headed directly to the elevator, ignoring the looks he received as he went. By the looks on their faces, he could tell exactly what the people on the mezzanine thought of him. Half the women were in awe, the other half were in lust, and the men were equal parts astonished and annoyed.

He looked down and bit back a grin at his obvious hard-on from thinking about this woman.

They must be looking at the yoga pants.

He pulled his phone out of the little pocket on the side of his gear bag and hit the speed dial.

Madison Lee picked up on the second ring.

"Hey, beautiful. You have people eyeballing my cock in the hotel lobby."

"Excuse me?" Madison Lee growled.

Whoa. He hadn't expected that kind of response.

"I was thinking about you and my cock went haywire. What did you think I was talking about?"

"Oh. Nothing," she replied with a tightness in her tone that made Kinson wonder exactly what was going on at home.

"Kuri giving you problems?"

"Nope. Kuri is perfect, as always."

"Then what's wrong?"

"What's wrong?" she snapped. "What isn't wrong? The business is taking up all of my time because my partner is never here."

Oh man, here we go. He almost rolled his eyes, but his

woman's points were valid. He was pretty much an absent partner. But still...

"Madison Lee, we agreed on this before I ever started this part of our business."

"I know we agreed that you would do your yoga thing and travel the world." She paused and Kinson waited for the other shoe to drop. He didn't have to wait long. "But we never agreed that would mean I was a single woman pretending to be married."

"Okay, this isn't like you. What's really going on?"

She took a deep breath and filled him in.

"Yazmin Ross was arrested on the grounds today." Kinson's eyebrows flew upward at that bit of news. That bitch had been the cause of all the trouble between their good friends, Landon and MacKenzie Ivers. After being banned from Twilight Teahouse forever, Yazmin supposedly moved to Los Angeles to pursue an acting career—which was perfect considering she was excellent at playing a human being when she was really a barracuda.

"And Landon and Mac have picked up a third in their relationship."

Wow! He was missing all the cool stuff.

"And Solie just found out that her ex had been sneaking in and out of her house and planting cameras and shit. Burton had to kick his ass."

Holy fuck.

Madison explained that even though the business was running smoothly, it was still a huge responsibility. All this crap went down while she'd been in the middle of arranging interviews to bring on more staff—some for the executive wing, some for the restaurant, and some for the dungeons.

And with him being on the other side of the world, there wasn't a damn thing he could do to help her with any of it. So he let her vent.

"And Burt and Solie just became an official couple."

Again, a piece of unexpected information, but at least this bit was good news.

"And we are getting requests to do more in the local community."

The elevator dinged. He stepped inside, phone still pressed to his ear as he punched the button for his floor. The ground fell away as the sleek steel and glass lift whisked him up above the lush, plant-filled atrium.

She rattled off the list of events, new hires, expansions to their buildings and endless issues. Usually he was the one with a list a mile long, but to Kinson's surprise, Madison Lee's to-do's outpaced his by a good stretch.

A quick glance at his watch and he winced. Given the time difference between Sweden and Seattle, his wife should have been in bed hours ago. Guilt niggled at his conscience that he'd called her without thinking, but it would have been worse not to have learned what the hell was going on at home.

"Maddy, I'll be home soon. I promise. Get some sleep. I'll be home soon. I love you."

Her response was a sigh followed by, "Yep."

Kinson's gut clenched and it had nothing to do with what his woman said. It was what she *didn't* say.

Madison Lee's patience was nearing an end. And that was an end he never wanted to see.

Exuberance at the yoga session he'd just conducted became nothing more than ash on his tongue. The hall had been filled to capacity with one hundred and four students all seeking the balance, health and stress relief of his craft. Yoga could be a life changer for others as it had been for him. Yoga had literally saved his life and transformed him.

Gone were the days of his inability to manage his physical stress. His to-do list no longer ruled his life.

No, it doesn't rule your life, because now your list rules your wife's and submissive's lives.

Ouch. Damn conscience wasn't going to give him a break today.

Well, he might be thrilled about how well his practice was doing—considering all he did was what he loved—but his super-supportive wife wasn't sharing in that joy. Not anymore.

God, how many times had they had that same conversation, with her expressing how much her load had grown? Telling him that she missed him, not just because Twilight Teahouse and Kuri required all of her time, but simply because time with him was important to the health of their relationship?

And how many times had he ignored her, thinking that she was just being needy, even though she was one of the strongest, most independent women he'd ever known?

Idiot.

Well, today, something different had laced her tone. Her words were short, clipped and brought to mind a certain...finality.

And Kinson didn't like it one bit.

2

A week later, Kinson dragged himself toward baggage claim, along with the other suitcase-toting zombies. After an excruciatingly long redeye flight home from Stockholm, through New York, he was so tired, muscles trembled and eyeballs ached. Hell, even his hair hurt.

Though he existed in a fatigue-induced fog, he wasn't too far gone to realize after an hour and a half of sitting with no one but his luggage for company, that something was amiss.

Calls to Madison Lee's mobile went straight to voice mail. Kuri's number got him nowhere. Even the landline at their house went unanswered.

What. The. Fuck?

Now, he navigated the slick streets of his own city in a rental car. His first impulse upon finding no one at the airport to meet him was anger.

It wasn't an emotion he allowed himself very often. He'd spent so many years walking through life, turned up like a simmering cauldron. These days he tried, and often succeeded, at keeping his energetic vibration on an even keel.

Just not today.

Today, pissed off became disappointment, and disappointment became bewilderment. But then like a runaway brace of horses, his last few conversations with his wife plowed into his brain.

"Will we see you before your birthday?"

He cocked his head to the side, mentally flipped through his schedule and winced. His birthday was six months away, but he was so booked up between now and then that Madison's question actually had merit.

That is not a good thing, Kinson Lee. Not a good thing at all.

And when he'd asked her about how things were going at their teahouse, her answers weren't passive aggressive...but she hadn't actually answered the questions either. And on one of his calls home, he'd mentioned that he was going to try to get back to Seattle earlier than originally planned.

Madison hadn't been thrilled in the least. In fact, she'd sounded downright bored when she'd responded. He'd thought she was just tired...but now he wasn't so sure.

"I'm sure you sent me your itinerary, but I don't really read them anymore."

It hadn't crossed his mind at the time to ask her why not.

When the lightbulb finally turned completely up in his mind, Kinson was tempted to find the nearest tree and introduce his forehead to it. Repeatedly.

Well, that does seem an appropriate way to deal with hard-headed men.

Why?

Because there was a reason he'd found it necessary to find his own way home after years of having his loving wife pick him up at the airport like clockwork.

Guess that fucking clock is broken.

Madison hadn't actually believed he would show up, which made him think back on previous trips.

Hell, he wasn't sure how many last minute schedule

changes there'd been, or how many unplanned extensions that resulted in his being away from home longer than originally planned.

The fog was thick and made it difficult to see the rain slick road as he'd made his way into Seattle proper. When the mist lifted it would be a hell of a sunrise, and the thought made him smile as he used his access card on the digital lock.

Shoulders tight with tension and eyes gritty from lack of sleep, Kinson walked into Twilight Teahouse and breathed a sigh of relief. He was home and there was no place like it.

Through the rear entrance and into the main hall, he was a bit surprised to see that the staff was bustling about already.

Though she'd ignored all of his calls so far, Kinson knew his wife was here. But rather than go looking for her, he headed straight to the kitchen in search of the one person that could give him what he needed—Landon Ivers.

Landon, a literal tall, dark and handsome, green eyed Irishman, happened to be married to one of their closest friends, MacKenzie Ivers. He was also head chef at Twilight Teahouse.

Kinson stepped into the Landon's domain and almost ran smack into the man.

"Kinson! What are you doing here?"

What was he doing here? Seriously? He owned this place with Madison. But Landon's bright smile and honest expression said the man wasn't trying to be an ass. He'd honestly, truly wondered what brought Kinson here.

He dropped his bag on the floor to one side of the doorway and extended his arm to the man he considered a friend...that he hadn't seen in a long time.

"Haven't seen you in ages. Missed you around here, man," Landon said, just before Kinson found himself yanked into a bear hug.

Considering no one was at the airport to pick you up, be thankful someone is glad to see you.

Landon turned to the kitchen staff who were busy going about their tasks and called out, "Hey, look who's here!" They all waved and called out a greeting followed by...applause?

He waved them on, but the clapping went on for a few more moments.

Oh god, just open up the floor and kill me now.

Finally, after a few more, "Welcome backs," the staff went on to their duties and Kinson's neck and cheeks were on fire. He'd seen and done some kinky things over the years and had been sure, until this very moment that he was incapable of blushing, but this? To have his own staff acting as if he'd been away for years? Yeah, this was embarrassing.

Kinson cleared his throat. "So what's going on?" he asked Landon. "It's rather early for you guys to be running about, isn't it?"

"Madison Lee didn't tell you? Aw, man." Landon put a hand on his hip and looked down at the floor with a very *not-*subtle shake of his head. "I told her to give you a heads up, but she said you weren't going to be back here in time anyway."

Not good.

"In time for what?"

"We're opening the club to the public in celebration of *Hinamatsuri*. You know, Girl's Day. She's already over in the executive wing, working."

Girl's Day? Crap, was that today?

While Twilight Teahouse was a Japanese teahouse downstairs, upstairs were several stories of kink friendly, multi-themed, sleekly designed adult playhouse.

In their early days, Kinson and Madison had spent some time in the Land of the Rising Sun. The place, the people and their strong family-centric culture had made an impression on them. This place had been modeled after a genuine Japanese tea house for a reason. Neither Kinson nor Madison were Japanese, and their staff was every culture under the rainbow, including *nihonjin*.

They followed Japanese tradition in their dress and protocol, and had just started opening up this very private and exclusive club to the public during certain holidays and celebrations.

And this was their first Girl's Day.

Today, the place would be decked out, including a huge six-tiered, red silk covered platform that displayed a set of ornamental porcelain dolls. These dolls represented the Emperor, Empress, attendants, and musicians in traditional court dress worn from around the year seven-hundred fifty to the eleven hundreds. Overseas, this celebration rolled around every March to pray for the safety of girl children.

Damn, he was really going to be in the dog house. Actually, maybe not considering he managed to make it before the event started, right?

Yeah. Right.

"I need your help, Lan."

"Sure, whatever you need."

"I'd like to take my wife some breakfast. Actually, I'll need three, one for Madison, one for Kuri and myself. I came straight from the airport and neither of them know I'm here yet."

"I think I can help you with that," Landon said with a wicked twinkle in his eye. How about some—"

"Whatever you think Madison Lee would like. How long?"

"I can have it ready in fifteen minutes, complete with her favorite *genmaicha* tea."

"Perfect. I'm going to run upstairs to the Japanese baths and take a shower. See you in fifteen."

Kinson picked up his overnight bag and turned to exit the kitchens. A firm hand came down on his shoulder.

"Wait a second, Kin. I think you'll need this."

He breathed a sigh of relief when Landon pressed a cup of hot, strong coffee into his free hand.

With a nod of thanks, he forced his over-tired body to move faster than it wanted to. Once out of the kitchens, he headed straight to the staff elevator, sipping as he went. The black brew hit his nervous system with more of a quiet poof than its typical bang.

He downed it in several large gulps and smiled as he thought of surprising his wife with the beautiful breakfast he knew Landon was putting together right this minute.

Kinson thought about the place he and Madison had built together. It was a brilliant endeavor. They owned all five floors of the club, and two floors of the connecting building where the executive and headquarter offices were.

In this building, the first floor had a very popular public-accessible sushi restaurant on one side, and a private kink-friendly dessert bar on the other. The second floor held a full-service spa, traditional Japanese baths and massage space with an open community feel, just like the family baths in the old country of Japan, but with mani-pedi heaven thrown in. Club members could even bring their young family members without any concern that they might see something they shouldn't. But that is where any youngster-friendly activity ended.

The Ice Palace up on the third level was Mediterranean in nature with gleaming white columns, white floors, white everything, including strategically placed mirrors that made it all seem to glitter endlessly. The fourth floor held a private Japanese spa for couples and kink only, and the fifth floor was split into two themes, a hot Egyptian flavor on one side, and sultry Caribbean on the other.

Kinson considered going to the second floor because it was closer, but changed his mind. Instead, he stripped down in the private baths on the fourth floor where he hit the shower and shivered all the way through it with the water purposely set as cold as he could stand it.

Somewhat refreshed, he shook like a leaf as he slipped into a warm fluffy robe.

Maybe I overdid it on the cold water. Damn.

Past the oversized, comfy loveseats that all the bathing suites had, his teeth chattered as his gaze zeroed in on the massage table in the middle of the room. He hopped up onto it and turned up the heat on the electric blanket spread over the thing.

A quick glance at his watch said he still had seven minutes. He couldn't wait to see the look on Madison's face when he walked into her office.

Yep. Today was going to be a good day after all.

MADISON LEE SAT IN HER OFFICE WITH HER FEET UP ON HER desk and crossed at the ankles. It was rare that she wore shoes in here. Usually she, along with the rest of the staff, wore *tatami* slippers inside, opting to leave street shoes in the cubbies designated for them. But today, after getting dressed in her big empty house, she'd examined herself in the mirror and felt...empty.

Her shapely curves were just as she liked them. Her hair was shiny and healthy.

Her skin wasn't flawless, but nothing a bit of makeup couldn't cure. She wasn't a gym rat, but she was healthy in body and spirit.

Yet she didn't feel as sexy as she looked. At all.

So after walking in through the rear employee's entrance,

Madison Lee had removed her rain boots, stuffed them in a cubby, and then pulled a pair of five-inch, black suede fuck-me pumps out of the duffel she always carried to work.

She looked down at those shoes now and felt her lips spread in a sad smile. Yes, the shoes were definitely gorgeous. Her gaze slipped down to the custom-made ruby and gold bracelet her husband had given her years before.

She closed her eyes and could swear she heard his voice even now as he'd boldly stated his dare.

Kinson had crossed his arms over his wide muscular chest and given her the smirk from hell—the one that never ceased to make her go all wiggly in the tummy. He'd dipped his head to better pierce her with his gaze and drawled, "Go skydiving with me and you get rubies."

She'd called his bluff. The opulent, royal looking piece of pizazz on her wrist was the result. And a similar dare got her a pair of matching earrings, a pendant and rings. And when the ruby set was complete, Kinson had introduced one fling after another until she'd collected sapphires, topaz, peridot and whatever other gems her little heart desired. The memories of how she'd collected such a lovely horde over the years used to bring with it an energy that zipped up her spine.

Why? Because Kinson hadn't thought she was materialistic. No. It was his way of keeping the zing in their relationship. He'd always introduced something exciting and new until Madison Lee had enough memories for a lifetime...or she'd thought so once.

But that was then, and this was now.

The thoughts tumbled through her head as she rose to refill her coffee cup at the wet bar in her office. Pouring the last of the strong brew into her cup, she put on another pot and strode back to her desk.

So where had the spark gone? How had she gotten to this place within herself?

Madison Lee was married to the most gorgeous yoga instructor in the Northern Hemisphere. They were successful beyond her wildest dreams, had two awesome businesses, and even better friends.

Yet smiling was something she seldom did these days.

Yeah, kind of like sleep, right?

Madison Lee couldn't argue with her conscience as she blew out a genuine, tired huff with a jaw-cracking yawn on its heels.

A glance down at the jewelry she used to never take off brought the tumbling thoughts to a halt. The realization that she'd gone from wearing these very meaningful gifts on a daily basis, to occasionally forgetting them sitting on top of her dresser, brought it all home in her head.

She was miserable.

The head chef of Twilight Teahouse, and her good friend, Landon Ivers, had come and gone, leaving behind a gorgeous spread of breakfast.

When Landon informed her that Kinson had special ordered her breakfast and then run upstairs for a quick shower, Madison had almost felt guilty that she'd forgotten to go pick her husband up from the airport.

But after an hour and no Kinson, she found that she wasn't even worried. He was obviously somewhere doing something else, with someone other than her.

The story of my life.

Luckily, the breakfast had been delicious. If Madison Lee didn't trust Landon implicitly, she would have called him a liar when he'd brought her the laden trays claiming that Kinson had had a hand in it.

Kuri had come into her office and enjoyed the sumptuous fare with her. Poor thing. She was so unhappy, it showed even when she tried to bluff her way through her misery with light conversation and not-quite-bright-enough smiles.

Madison hadn't bothered to show up at the airport this morning because she honestly hadn't believed he would be there. She'd headed out to that damn airport too many times over the past couple of years only to learn that Kinson had changed his itinerary and forgotten to tell her.

It was the nature of his yoga practice when he was out of town for him to find himself swamped with requests. People tried to catch him while he was around, and she understood that.

But none of those people were his *wife*. When had she become less important than total strangers?

She'd been holding up this particular fort for so long that she wasn't sure how she'd act knowing her husband was around here getting into things.

She'd transitioned from 'the co-owner, co-runner-of-things' to the head bitch in charge.

Did she love Twilight Teahouse? Hell yes. She just wished she didn't have to love it alone…

LIDS SO HEAVY THEY FELT AS IF THEY WERE GLUED SHUT AND secured with a five-pound barbell, Kinson groaned, rolled over…and landed on his ass on the floor.

"Fuck!" He scrambled up off the plush gray carpet and slammed back down as he tried to free his legs from the blanket that…

Blanket?

When he'd sat down on the massage table after his bath, he'd been wearing the same thick white spa robe, but no blanket.

A quick glance around told him that someone had come in to see about him. Dirty clothes had been folded and placed inside a little plastic bag, and the fresh clothes he'd had in his duffel were pressed and laid out over the back of a loveseat.

The coffee cup he'd brought upstairs, courtesy of Landon, was gone. It didn't sit well that he'd been so out of it that he hadn't heard or sensed anyone enter or leave.

A smile a spread across his face when the truth blossomed in his mind—his wife was the culprit!

Maybe he'd imagined her irritation with him? Perhaps the resignation he'd heard in her voice before was all in his head and she wasn't quite *"done"* with him yet. It was obvious that Madison was so happy he was home that she couldn't wait ten minutes for him to shower. She'd come all the way up here to make sure he was all good.

Kinson picked up his phone off the side table.

"Fuck!"

He tossed the phone into his bag and jumped into the clothes that had been left for him. Not bothering to get his shoes from the cubby, he shuffled into the small washroom at as swift a clip as his tatami slippers would allow. Moments later, with hair combed and teeth brushed, he headed to the elevator that would take him back to the ground floor. From there he could cut across the building to the executive wing where the corporate offices were.

He only hoped that Madison Lee would leave his balls intact when he finally got down there.

Because it hadn't been ten minutes.

It had been *two fucking hours*!

3

*K*inson walked into his wife's office and closed the door. He slammed to a halt, head tilted a hard left.

She'd cut her glossy coal-black curls into a bob that barely brushed her shoulders. In all the years he'd known Madison, he'd never seen her super-curly locks shorter than mid-back. To his surprise, he liked the glamorous hairdo.

She was as lovely as ever. Sitting behind the custom executive desk surrounded by highly polished wood, steel and glass furniture, bookshelves, and a slew of awards hanging on the walls, that queenly aura swirled around her.

Her skin glowed with health and, as usual, she wore a minimal amount of makeup. That would change when she dressed in her Japanese traditional regalia for the event today, but she would be just as gorgeous. He started to ask where her change of clothes was, but caught of flash of color in his periphery. A quick turn and he saw a spring-themed kimono hanging on the back of her door.

"Hey, Maddy."

Her response? A very flat, "Thanks for breakfast. Kuri and I enjoyed it."

No "hi" or "how are you". Hell, she didn't even look up at him.

"Madison?"

"Yes?" Still no eye contact. Instead, her nails tap-tap-tapped on her keyboard. She appeared completely engrossed in whatever she was doing on her computer, but the stiff set of her shoulders told him there was more going on here than met the eye.

Annoyed at being ignored, Kinson, as tired as he was, still tried to keep his temper in check. Instead of leaving her to her devices, as he was tempted to, he dropped his bag on the floor next to the door and stalked forward.

She stopped typing long enough to snatch up a pen and write something on a scratch pad. He reached for the pen, and then her hand.

She looked up then, and what he saw in her closed expression broke his heart. He knew in the moment that she had not been the one to have his clothes pressed and laid out for him. Nor had she gathered up his dirty stuff, or taken care of his coffee cup.

Kuri, I owe you one.

If he were honest, he owed both Madison and Kuri more than just one. He owed them everything. If not for Madison's ability and dedication, there was no way in hell he could globe trot doing yoga. And Kuri was the delicious satisfaction to his need as a Dominant. Kinson was an impact player in the BDSM lifestyle. While his specialty was being able to give everything from sensual pleasure to pain with floggers, canes, crops and the like, Madison was the rigger—an expert in tying rope for decoration or bondage.

His woman was nobody's submissive, but she'd recognized the Dominant needs in Kinson before they ever got married. In fact, Maddy was the one who'd encouraged him to consider having a submissive of his own.

Given that they were two ridiculously busy entrepreneurs, Kuri had become a lifesaver. She took care of the house, worked here at Twilight Teahouse with a handsome salary, and was also Kinson's personal submissive.

"I didn't expect you to make it. Sorry for not getting you at the airport, but I didn't want to drive way over there before the event just to find you'd forgotten to tell me not to bother."

Ouch.

Well, she had him there. Idiot extraordinaire.

Wow, I made a rhyme.

Typically he'd be impressed with himself, but not today. Today, he felt like a total and complete jerk of a heel.

"I don't blame you, honey. I made it here on my own so no worries, okay?"

She raised an imperious brow that said, "I don't need your permission not to worry."

Double ouch.

But classy chick that she was, she didn't give voice to her opinion.

"I'm so sorry I haven't been here for you, Madison. I won't blame you if you haven't noticed that I'm actually home early. I just needed to get here, so here I am."

"Uh-huh."

She reached for her pen with her free hand as if she intended to go on working.

Not gonna happen, hon.

Taking both her hands, he swirled her chair around and pulled her gently to her feet. "Holy shit, those are some sexy shoes. Unexpected, considering we never wear shoes in here, but glad you did. They're stunning."

She didn't answer, just smiled a bit as if she were waiting for him to take the compliment back or something.

"I missed you, baby. Missed you like crazy. And I'm so very sorry for..."

"Wait, Kinson. I really want to talk about this, but we have less than two hours until the opening for the *Hinamatsuri* celebration and I have three hours of work to do."

"Okay, let me help."

The dismissive glance accompanied by her raised "are you serious" eyebrow rubbed him the wrong way.

"I still remember what needs doing, Madison. I may be a yogi now, but we ran this place together forever. Give me a list of stuff and I'm on it."

"Fine." She typed up a quick list and then hit the intercom on her desk phone. "Dani, please bring me the list I just sent to the printer by your desk. Thanks."

Seconds later, their secretary came in, dropped off the sheet of paper and was back out the door. Madison pressed the piece of paper into Kinson's hands and said, "And there's an outfit hanging in your office if you want to wear it. If not, no worries."

He pulled her into a hug and was thankful when she hugged him back. "I'm on it. And don't worry. I've got this."

"Uh, thanks." She stepped away, sat back at her desk and got right back to work.

He grabbed his bag and headed for the door. "Oh, and I love the haircut. I look forward to playing in that. Later."

Her lips formed a surprised "oh". Her expression —priceless.

Kinson watched his wife's blush spread from her cheeks and dip down along her neck. It was the prettiest thing he'd seen in at least a year.

Which was terrible, in and of itself.

4

*M*adison sat in her office, somewhat stunned. The Kinson who'd just walked out of her office like a boss was one she hadn't seen in a while. And she *liked* this old version of him.

These days, when he returned from one of his events, he walked in, told her a bunch of stories about his travels, then went home to sleep and plan the next trip. In between arriving home and leaving again, he practiced his yoga and accompanied her to an occasional dinner with friends. That was it, no more, no less. It was like living with a visiting relative or something.

And she fucking hated it.

But today, he'd thrown her for a loop. She couldn't remember the last time Kinson Lee had asked her how he could help her. Usually, he assumed she had it all handled, which most times she did, but at a cost he couldn't begin to calculate.

The man had walked into her office...and *apologized* to her?

She had to acknowledge that his consideration caused the

smallest spark to ignite in her gut as she sat and thought on the events of the past couple of hours.

She and Kuri had both been resigned, unsurprised and kind of numb to the fact that Kinson had arranged breakfast and then didn't show up to share it with them. Madison felt sorrier for Kuri than she felt for herself. Kuri was a beautiful young woman, inside and out. She had a quiet grace that made Madison think of the young ladies who graced the halls of princes and princesses as their attendants—poised, soft spoken, yet capable in their own way.

So not only had she been stewing over how Kinson shirked his home-bound duties toward herself, but she was beyond resentful of what Kuri was dealing with. After all, she hadn't signed up for this crap. Kuri had agreed to serve as a submissive for Kinson, not an attendant for Madison.

As much as she wanted to put a metal bucket over his head and whack it continually like a gong until he understood how she felt, compassion had flooded her heart when she and Kuri had headed upstairs to find him laid out on top of a massage table in their private bathing room. Of course, she hadn't bothered to reveal that little bit of information when she'd practically run him out of here a few moments ago.

Anyway, he'd been asleep on his side with no pillow, head canted at a weird angle. For a moment she'd wondered if he would wake with a headache from having his neck contorted like that.

Between the two of them, they'd taken care of his clean and soiled clothing, as well as a cold coffee cup in record time. The entire time, Madison had glanced at Kinson's face, boyish in sleep and scrubbed clean. Freshly washed hair all over his head and mouth wide open, the man had been snoring like a freight train.

The two women had worked with nothing but expressions of stone, faces devoid of emotion or care. After pulling his clean clothes out of his gear bag, a sheaf of papers had fluttered to the carpet. She'd knelt to pick them up, took a quick glance and felt her heart quicken at what she'd just learned.

In that moment, Madison Lee had taken stock of herself, of her heart.

Had she really lost all care for her husband? Was she really so resentful that she felt nothing about the fact that he'd worn himself so thin that he hadn't twitched a single muscle as she and Kuri had come and gone?

Did it really mean nothing that the documents she'd accidentally seen proved that he'd changed his itinerary and cancelled the next four yoga conventions so he could get home to her and stay there?

Well...did it?

By sheer force of will, Madison pushed all of her concerns to the back of her mind and refocused on the event at Twilight Teahouse rather than her marriage. She really wanted to keep thinking about her husband rather than the duties she needed to perform for their place of business right now. But she couldn't. But she really wanted to. But...

God, it was like having to continuously re-latch a shutter that kept blowing open in a storm.

Ugh.

A press of the intercom button on her phone was followed by a quick, "Dani, I'm getting dressed for *Hinamatsuri* now. I don't wish to be disturbed."

"Yes, ma'am."

"Thanks."

Out of her chair, she kicked off her high heels and headed toward the gorgeous outfit hanging on the back of the closed door. The morning fog was finally beginning to burn off and the muted glow was giving way to a bright sparkle of sunlight off the Sound. That same natural light streamed in through the large windows and brought out the true colors of the kimono she would wear today.

Removing the protective plastic, Madison ran her hands over a purple and pink silk kimono that was a gorgeous exercise in Japanese couture so beautiful, a sigh of appreciation left her lips.

With the push of a button, all of the blinds closed, leaving her office in shadow. When she'd gotten in it had been pitch black outside. Even now it was still quite early but even with the blinds closed, there was still a pleasant glow off the glass and steel building so her office was pleasantly dim rather than midnight dark.

With a tired sigh that had more to do with where her mind was rather than any kind of physical issue, Madison yanked her royal blue shift over her head and off.

Then she just...stood there.

Eyes closed, the image of her husband, who was out taking care of her to-do list, filled her head. In nothing but her bra and panties, she stood in the middle of that floor, stocking-clad toes wriggling in the plush carpet, and thought on the man who'd caused hope to spring up in her chest. Hope that he was truly serious about being here, being with her.

She plopped down in her executive office chair, the leather still warm from her body heat, and let her mind go where it willed.

Kinson. Kinson Lee. Yogi extraordinaire...who had taken a red-eye home, rented a car and drove straight here from the airport, sent her breakfast, and canceled his upcoming yoga retreats where he'd been scheduled to teach.

Totally capable of running her life and her business on her own, it didn't change the fact that she needed him as her partner, not just in her bed...though the bed would be nice.

God, when was the last time she'd truly enjoyed a raunchy, messy, all-over-the-house romping good time with her man?

And he was so drool-worthy when he'd stuck his head into her office just a little while ago. Even with the dark circles under his eyes and the exhaustion rolling off of his body, he was still the epitome of delicious.

But there was more to Kinson than looks. The man was steadfast and capable. When he was paying a-fucking-tention, he was as giving a lover as she could have ever asked for. And he could handle her bullheaded tendencies with a loving stubbornness of his own. In fact, he was probably the only person she knew that could successfully get her to rest or do anything else, for that matter.

"Madison, sit your butt down somewhere before I turn it another color. Work will be there tomorrow. It's not going anywhere."

How many times had he told her that over the years? Well, not lately, but still. Her skin heated at the thought of his wonderfully-delivered spankings—just enough sting on this side of pleasure that she couldn't really call it a punishment. As tension coiled between her shoulder blades, Madison lifted her hips and eased her underwear down and off. A chuckle escaped when she caught them on the tip of her shoe and kicked them across the room.

Her hand eased beneath the cup of her lacy demi-bra to palm a full breast. Madison moaned at the contact, even as her head filled with images of her husband, naked, ready and willing.

When his hands were on her skin, it felt nothing like when she touched herself. His touch was electric. Alive. Made her blood flash beneath the skin.

She twisted and rolled a nipple until it was a ripe berry between the fingertips. The other hand dipped low and teased the plump lips of her sex until the flesh tingled, eager for more.

Kinson's name escaped her lips as her spine began a slow undulation that soon became an eager grind of her hips as her fingers pressed into the honey that began to gather at her entrance.

Her legs were spread wide now, one over each chair arm. She wished she had a battery operated boyfriend right now. Obviously she was coiled up tight and needed the release.

The soft click of the door closing followed by the deep rumble of male appreciation had her jumping out of her skin.

"Damn, that's a sexy sight."

"Kinson! I told Dani I was not to be disturbed."

"And I see why."

Skin went up in flames with a furious blush that felt as if it burned from neck to knees. Geesh.

"After all these years I'd think you were over being embarrassed in front of me," he said, head lowered just enough so that he looked at her through his lashes.

"What are you doing here?" Her hands seemed stuck to her body as her heart pumped furiously, air soughed in and out of her lungs and she tried to catch her breath. Damn adrenaline rush.

His gaze followed from the fingers around her breast, down to the trimmed mound of her sex where her hand pressed against the folds. And when that gaze met hers again, it made her think of the red-hot coals of a hardwood fire that scorched anything that came in contact with it.

Finally, he spoke. "Everything is ready. I came to get dressed." That was when she noticed the clothing bag folded over one arm. And it was such a nice arm, too. All muscular and veiny and tan and just…gah!

He pinned her with a look so blatantly hungry, a frisson of alarm shot up her spine. Animalistic was the only word that popped into her head. Would his light amber eyes start to glow like one of the television werewolves any minute now?

"What's wrong with your office for getting dressed?" She panted, a hand at her throat now in a futile attempt to stop the galloping of her heart. He'd pretty much scared the shit out of her, but that wasn't the only reason the damn organ practically beat out of her chest.

And embarrassment had nothing to do with it. It was all about the whole stalking-toward-her-with-pure-male-intent thing.

"My office doesn't have a view nearly as succulent as this," he rumbled, the words like rolling thunder in his chest, and deeper than she'd heard in quite a while.

He swiped a cherry out of the bowl of fruit left over from breakfast. God, she'd completely forgotten about them. She watched him sink his teeth into the firm flesh, watched as his tongue made the short journey from left to right to gather up the juice.

And her eyes were glued to the little pink organ as if she were in a trance that she didn't want to shake herself out of.

HE SPIT THE CHERRY PIT INTO THE LITTLE WIRE MESH trashcan near her desk, and then he was on her.

Wardrobe bag forgotten in a crumpled heap on the floor, Kinson dropped to his knees in front of his wife's chair and pulled her close. The clean scent of her pussy wafted up between them and he considered their position—naughty as hell, no panties, her legs draped over the arms of her chair, spread wide and him kneeling between.

Sexual energy arced between them in a wild stream of passion. Touching her skin was like holding a live wire, she was so amped up. But just underneath that scalp-tingling hum was a thread of uncertainty. Just a hint, but it was there all the same.

Rather than easing away, he pressed closer, wrapped her up in himself. "God, you feel so good in my arms. I've missed this, Maddy. Missed you so fucking much."

Tall enough that he could still kiss her, even though he was on his knees, he reached up and pressed his fingers into the always-tense spot on her shoulder. She gave a moan of pleasure that pulled at the pit of his stomach. Fingers around the back of her neck, he pulled her forward and down just a bit.

At her gasp, he took her mouth, claimed her with his kiss. Branded her with his tongue. Groaned deep in his throat as her arms wrapped around his neck and she held on for dear life. He felt out of control, like a tsunami, a ginormous tide that rolled in and swept over everything in its path.

Claiming as it went. Cutting a new path as it moved.

The kiss was wild, abandoned. Perfect.

When Madison broke the contact and let her head fall back, Kinson knew exactly what she needed. Kissing a path down the side of her neck, he nibbled as he went, but was careful not to mark her as he usually did considering their establishment would shortly have some unusual visitors—a slew of parents and children.

He slipped the strap of her bra down her shoulder so he could suck the sensitive spot there. Luckily, it would be hidden by her kimono so he did not hold back. He sucked until she squirmed in her limited mobility, until the spot was a dark deep red, indicative of the grape colored bruise it would be come morning.

"Mmm, Kin. That feels so good."

Time to up the ante.

Removing her hands from his neck, he placed them above

her head and instructed her to cross them at the elbows. The position was twofold—to support her head and neck, and to keep her hands where he wanted them. Since he didn't have rope or anything to tie her, his verbal commands would have to do.

"Keep your arms there, Madison. Don't move them for any reason."

A quickly masked mutinous expression had him expecting her to snap her eyes open and snarl, "You're not the boss of me anymore!" But she simply smiled and complied.

This woman was everything to him. Before he'd made his way back to her office, he'd already made up his mind that he needed to woo her all over again. Now all he had to do was convince her that he was serious about it. Earlier she'd insisted that they talk about things later. Kinson decided that later was now...only he would do a different kind of talking.

He would talk with his touch. Use his love language to spell out exactly how much she meant to him.

A deep breath in through her nose and out through her mouth on a sensuous sigh said she was too far gone for teasing anyway. Thank God, because the sight of her teasing her own breasts, with her slender fingers buried in her pussy, had sent him up in flames in zero-point-two seconds.

But part of being a decent Dominant was being able to anticipate and read his woman's needs. And right now, she needed to feel cherished.

And she needed to come, considering she'd probably been halfway there when he'd interrupted. So he dove straight for her sweet pussy and feasted like the starving man he was.

"Holy shit," she gasped, fisted hands flexed and then flexed again as she fought to keep her hands where he'd put them.

Madison struggled to resist burying her hands in the

thick silken strands on his head to hold him firm against her ready sex. Rolling her hips up to meet his questing mouth, she sought more. *Needed* more.

Two long fingers slipped into her dewy gate, sought that spot, and found it unerringly. The tips tapped, rubbed and teased while his thumb circled her clit. Oooh, it was divine.

Thumbs spread her labia and her clit became the focus of some very talented manipulation. He sucked, swirled, and tapped his tongue against that bundle of nerves until it was strung so tight that her thighs began to tremble. Madison's body hummed, literally.

"I need you, Madison." The words were an urgent gush of heated air against the damp folds of her ready sex. The sex had always been good between them, but this desperate need was the Kinson of old. He wasn't just slaking his lust because he'd been away. This man was giving her pleasure because he wanted to. Had to.

A long lick up the seam of her sex sent her thoughts careening out of control. His words brought them back…barely.

"Let me date you, baby? Win you?" It wasn't quite a question, but he was giving up the high ground here, which was more than he typically ceded. "Take you to coffee. Do some of the things we used to do together."

Oh, yes. She remembered how this simple act used to hold so much more meaning. And she wanted it to again.

"I love you, Madison Victoria Lee. And I'll do what I need to in order to keep you."

In that moment, Madison felt as if he'd been re-imprinted on her soul…but she was nobody's fool. As much as she wanted to give him what he asked for, he'd left her high and dry for weeks, months at a time, and returned home as if everything should be just fine.

This time, he was going to work for it. And Madison Lee

had a feeling she was going to enjoy being the focus of this particular alpha.

"I want an answer, Madison. After you come."

Her back arched as she tried her best to bite back the scream building in her throat. She was close. So very close. It was like riding the rapids and watching the water disappear only to realize that she neared the edge of a waterfall. And it was coming up fast.

"Come on, baby. Your pretty pussy is milking my fingers. Let it go and give me what I want."

Like a bowstring stretched taut and then plucked by an experienced archer, her orgasm released and flew into the wind like an arrow.

Mouth still latched to her throbbing core, Kinson reached up and stifled her cries with the very fingers that had been buried in her sex only moments before.

"Taste yourself, baby. You're so good, I could eat you all day." The erotic words and the persistence of his tongue tossed her headlong into another orgasm hard, her muscles clenched. Juice trickled down past her rear passage to puddle beneath her.

The man had her panting around his fingers still between her lips, in a potent rhythm.

Pant.

Suck.

"Oh my God."

Pant.

Nibble.

Suck.

Oooh, she'd totally missed this.

He left her sitting in her chair, eyes closed, as he moved in utter silence about the room. Moments later, a warm towel was pressed between her legs where he alternated licking with gentle swipes of the cloth.

She almost laughed, but she didn't quite have the breath for it yet.

They would never get out of here if he kept laving her flesh after each pass of the towel.

Kinson's words rang in her head—*"I could eat you all day."*

Madison shivered, knowing that if they didn't have a celebration to host, her husband just might try such a thing in his current mood. Finally, he stopped nibbling on her soaked flesh and finished cleaning her up. It was clear that he was pleased with himself when he stood and his clear amber gaze was streaked with a hint of green—which only happened during times of strong emotion.

And he had a right to stroke his own feathers. After all, he'd just rocked her world in a way that he hadn't in a while. But it wasn't just that he'd made her come. His energy was different. He *felt* different to her just now—sincere and earnest and hungry…and hers.

Madison knew he wouldn't ask her again to give him a chance to mend their marriage. She knew that his offer stood, but the ball was in her court.

So what was she going to do, serve it back to him or forfeit the game?

A smile spread across her lips as she said, "I would very much like to date you, Kinson Lee."

Her stomach did a little twirly thing that made her think of giddy school girls and first dates.

Oh, and orgasms. Lots and lots of orgasms.

"Good. Now, let's go have a good Girl's Day and greet our community. Later, we'll negotiate what this dating thing looks like."

She nodded and stood on wobbly knees. Kinson made her sit back down, then knelt and removed her shoes. "Tabi socks?" he asked.

At her nod, he turned and grabbed a pair off the book-shelf near her desk where she kept her regalia.

Thigh high stockings removed with practiced ease, he slipped the socks on her feet, then helped her to stand.

Oh yes, that was better. Heels and two volcanic orgasms weren't the greatest combination.

They talked about mundane, but pleasant, everyday topics as they dressed, her in her kimono, *obiage* and *obi,* and him in his *haori* kimono jacket and *hakama* pants.

Thirty minutes later, a quiet chime sounded.

Madison hit the intercom on her phone.

"Yes?"

"It's time, ma'am."

"We're on our way. Thanks, Dani."

Arm in arm, Madison and Kinson Lee walked into their destiny. Again.

THE TWILIGHT TEAHOUSE WAS PACKED. IT WASN'T AN UNUSUAL occurrence, but the clientele was definitely different than the norm. All of the dungeons and kinky spaces were closed until later tonight, after the public had gone home and those who were members of this exclusive club would come out to play.

To Madison's delight, all of their closest friends, Solie, Burton and MacKenzie, had all come into Seattle proper a bit early. The first thing they'd done was group hug Kinson. Madison's inner witch had poked at her and insisted that she let her out to play when it became apparent that Kinson had been a bit uncomfortable with all the attention. Instead, she'd simply said, "See? I'm not the only one who has missed you, mister." Her husband had had the decency to blush.

Then it was game on.

The guys went out back and dragged in bundles and bundles of spring flowers, individually wrapped with colorful tissue paper and secured with little bows. As their guests came in, they handed them out to *all* of the little girls, not just the ones in traditional garb. And Madison would never forget all the bright smiles, giggles and glowing faces.

Today, people from all over the Seattle area had converged with their little ones in tow, some to celebrate Girl's Day, and others just to see what the hubbub was all about.

On the first floor, the restaurant that was always open to the public, served a special brunch to all who'd come to visit. Landon and his staff had outdone themselves. The decor was bright and airy, and Madison was still trying to figure out where the hell they'd gotten hold of the real cherry trees full of sakura blossoms whose containers were strategically placed all over the dining area.

The other side of the floor, a private "dessert heaven" had been transformed as well. That space had none of the spanking benches, St. Andrew's crosses, walls of shackles, suspension rigs or cozy furniture where spectators typically relaxed with their dessert while watching the scenes of their choice. Instead, it was filled with *hina* dolls and various other displays, while out in the parking lot were rotating *taiko* drum groups, musicians and dancers.

Madison, Kinson and the rest of those designated as "tour guides" happily took pictures of, and with, the people who'd showed up to enjoy the event. And for those who wanted something to really remember the day, a professional photographer had a booth set up for the occasion.

Kuri and the other attendants handed out girl-sized oriental parasols and even showed the children how to work them properly. It was already a free event and the mothers and fathers hadn't expected the additional gifts.

Madison had caught her husband's eye several times and all she could do was shake her head at how he'd thrown himself into the occasion. He hummed with energy, didn't stand still as long as there was something that needed to be done. If he felt the effects of his long red-eye flight all the way from Stockholm, Sweden this morning, it wasn't evident at all.

The day passed in a blur. Once the last visitor had cleared out, cleaning commenced, followed by checking and double-checking that all was ready for the dungeon to open. Thankfully, someone else was on duty tonight and Madison was able to drag her tired ass home.

Needless to say, the first Girl's Day celebration at Twilight Teahouse had been a resounding success. So happy that it had gone well, she didn't even mind that Kinson passed out on the couch as soon as they got home.

5

*K*inson rolled over and once again found himself tumbling onto the carpet.

Palms pressed against his sockets, he rubbed as if to dislodge the sand that someone had poured behind his lids. Heavy and grainy-feeling, he forced his eyes open and squinted against the bright laser beam—oh, not a laser beam, just sunlight—that flowed in through the wide open drapes. Typically, he loved the big bay windows in their living room but today, not so much.

The last thing he remembered was clicking on the television last night and sitting down on the sofa to check the weather for the coming day.

After that, nothing.

He lifted his head and looked down his body. A quick assessment told him that he'd at least been conscious enough last night to remove his *haori* before he passed out cold from sheer exhaustion.

Eyes closed once more, Kinson tried to gather his scattered wits. Perhaps a bit of meditation would do it? Instead, his brain zeroed in on the silence that surrounded him. No one moved about. No hint of Madison or Kuri's voices. No television or quiet tapping of a keyboard. Just…nothing.

He could have sworn he'd heard Kuri's voice and a simple, "You fell asleep on the couch," just before he toppled to the floor. Perhaps he'd dreamed it because she definitely wasn't here now.

But had he also dreamed the short, pale yellow robe pulled around her petite, but lush frame, with the hem swaying as she walked from the living room into the kitchen? At all of five-foot-nothing, her beautiful golden skin, almond shaped eyes and fall of thick bone-straight hair always drew him in, though there was no sex between them as Dominant and submissive.

And how long did he lay there before successfully coaxing his heavy body to heave itself up off the floor?

Long live jetlag. Ugh.

He rose to his feet and stretched. His nostrils flared at the enticing aroma of coffee, smoked meat and some kind of baked good. Still dead tired and stomach rumbling, he called out.

"Kuri, come here please."

A few moments passed and no Kuri. Strange. She'd never just flat out blown him off or ignored a request from him. In all the time she'd been his submissive, he could count the number of times she'd disobeyed, and each time she'd had a reasonable explanation that had caused him to change his mind about punishing her for it…though she did love the spankings anyway.

A short trip down the wide hallway and around the corner and he discovered that Madison wasn't in their bedroom. He hit the button on the console mounted on the wall and engaged the house-wide intercom.

"Madison?"

No reply.

"Kuri?"

Nothing.

"Well, shit."

He stalked to the kitchen. It was empty, but he'd been right about the breakfast goodies. The oven warmer had been left on so the food was still hot, and the coffee maker was timed to stay on for another hour.

Kinson chuckled at finding the largest mug they owned sitting on the counter with sugar and cream already in it. He practically moaned at the scent of the steam rising from the cup as he filled it.

He sipped and sighed. God, that was good. He could probably use a few more hours of sleep but when the clock in the foyer struck ten, he hit the shower instead.

Get moving, man. You have a woman to woo.

An hour and a half later, Kinson watched his two lunch guests approach. He'd already ordered their favorite beverages, which sat iced cold and ready on the table. Uncommonly warm for this early in the spring season, he'd opted to sit outside.

Clear blue skies, with the occasional cloud floating by, reflected off the water of the Sound and made it appear a sparkling blue. They were really having a nice run on good weather. Kinson took it as a sign.

Landon picked up his mug of ale and took a long drink. Wiping the condensation from the glass off of his hands, he set the glass and napkin aside. Kinson's interest peaked when the other man pinned him with a glare he was sure he'd never seen before.

Lots of never seen's and never heard's lately, eh, rock brain?

"Okay, so what's up?" Landon asked.

"What's up? Can't I just have lunch with my two best friends?" Kinson replied dryly.

"Come on, man," Burt said. "We're your best friends, and we haven't seen you in almost four months."

"I've been home several times in the last four months, I'll have you know."

"Yeah, long enough to fuck your wife and head back to the airport," Landon said without hesitation.

Kinson was almost offended, but he couldn't be. Not really. These two men were never ones to mince words or play nice when ugly was what he needed to hear.

"Fine. I've been beyond absent. I didn't realize what a hole I'd dug myself into because I was too busy looking at the success of my yoga practice. But there's got to be a way to balance it all out. I love yoga, but I love my wife more, so I need to do something awesome for her. Something she really wants."

"What she wants is you, man," Burton said.

"I got that. Loud and clear. But I want to do something special."

"Special, as in surprise?"

"Yep."

The two men looked at each other, then back to Kinson. After a moment of silence, Landon said, "Man, you know Maddy doesn't like surprises. But if you're willing to put your balls on a platter to win her over, who am I to stop you? In fact, I say bravo."

"So you guys will help me?"

Burt winked and said, "Sure. I even have an idea of what might work."

Burton filled both Landon and Kinson in on what he'd learned from his woman, Solie, about a very special charity event. It turned out that Solie's cousin, Desreé Shaw, had just inherited a literal fortune. Along with her inheritance came a few high profile board positions, including a seat on the committee for a charity of Hollywood celebrity, Tamela Harvin.

Tamela's group, "Helping Hands, Caring Hearts", often took on personal requests that others would not. According to Desreé, Miss Harvin had just briefed her committee on a new community project. They'd loved the idea so much that the board of directors had quickly approved it. Madison Lee was big on giving back to the local community in ways that would make a real difference, and this venture seemed right up their alley.

After getting all the particulars, which included a conference call with Solie for a few minutes, Kinson was sure this would do the trick.

WITH LUNCH DONE, KINSON DIDN'T WAIT TO GET BACK TO THE office to get moving on his new win-my-wife-over project. As soon as he was in his car, he hit the hands-free and got busy. Half an hour later, in the executive wing of Twilight Teahouse, he dropped a half-dozen chocolate covered strawberries on his wife's keyboard along with a message, and then went straight to his office and closed the door.

He sat down at his desk, then got right back up again. He'd once again forgotten that while his wife had a personal assistant in Dani, he had a secretary of his own.

He stepped up to the wide white and gray granite reception desk that he'd just walked past moments ago. Mauren's fingers flew over the keyboard and her brows were furrowed in concentration. The woman was obviously busy, so Kinson waited before interrupting. Finally, she looked up.

"How can I help you, sir?"

"I need you to get Tamela Harvin on the line."

"Tamela Harvin? Isn't she famous?"

"She is. She also heads a charity organization called

'Helping Hands, Caring Hearts.' I've already spoken to her staff and she knows what we need. Unfortunately, she was in a meeting when I called earlier. Here's the number. Get her on the line and then send the call straight back to me. And don't tell Madison. It's a surprise."

"Yes, sir. Give me ten minutes."

"Will do. And thanks."

He got about six steps away when Mauren called out to him.

"Excuse me, sir. Uh, well..." she paused as her cheeks flushed a pretty pink. "I just want to say that it's good to have you back."

Kinson nodded. "Good to be back."

"Yeah?" she asked, eyes bright and smile genuine. "Sometimes we wondered if maybe this place was too much for you. I don't mean to pry or anything—"

"It's okay. I wasn't away because I don't like Twilight, I just got caught up in my own thing. And now, I need to fix that. So remember, no telling Madison. As a matter of fact, if you can keep it quiet, I'll let you help me pull one over on her."

"Oh, that sounds splendid, sir. I'm definitely in. As for getting your person on the phone, let's make that five minutes instead of ten."

HE WOULD NEVER SEE THE BLACK EXECUTIVE CHAIR IN HIS wife's office the same again. As he walked into her room, his mind immediately played images of when he'd gone down on her, savored her succulent flesh as if she were his favorite dessert.

Perhaps she would be up for a replay? The smirk dropped off of his face when his wife looked up. Beneath her eyes, the skin was puffy and smudged a purplish-blue. The space between her brows was furrowed as she returned her stare to her computer screen. Temples as puffy as the bags under her eyes, one hand slipped up to press gently at the side of her head.

Kinson immediately recognized the signs—she was exhausted and sported the headache from hell. And he was immediately pissed that she sat there forcing herself to work when it was obvious that she was wearing herself into the ground. A quick glance at his watch had him snarling her name.

"Madison Lee, what time did you get here?"

"Don't 'Madison Lee' me as if I'm in trouble," she snapped.

"Madison, it's almost eight o'clock at night and you're dog tired. And I can tell you have a headache just from the set of your shoulders."

She didn't respond, which was smart of her. His wife had never lied to him and Kinson knew that if she attempted to deny any of what he'd just said, that's exactly what she'd be doing.

He stepped up behind her, put his hands to her shoulder muscles and gently pressed. The deep moan of relief vibrated through her body. "So what time did you get here? You didn't answer my question."

His thumb found a particularly nasty knot. "I got here early," she hissed around the pain.

Early, eh? He figured as much considering her and Kuri had been long gone by the time he'd fallen off the couch. And speaking of Kuri...

"Where is Kuri? Did she do the early bird thing with you?" he asked.

Madison's words formed around a jaw-cracking yawn. "She's in the main building serving as hostess in the restaurant. And yes, we birds do tend to stick together, early or otherwise."

Ignoring her snark, he asked, "She's running the house? I had no idea that she'd learned that part of the business so well as to do that."

"Yep. She's good at it, too. Sometimes she's dungeon master on the upper floors, believe it or not." Then came another huge yawn that she couldn't quite hide, even though she'd covered her face with her hands. "Tonight she's staying over at Mac and Landon's. They're doing dinner and movie night. Solie and Burt will be there, too."

Kinson frowned. He hadn't seen or talked with Kuri since he'd returned days ago, but he had a feeling he knew exactly why Kuri was making herself scarce. And he didn't blame her.

She was a beautiful woman, Kuri. Both inside and out. A warm giving soul, she found pleasure in serving others. If Madison was disappointed in Kinson's lack of attention, Kuri's avoidance of him said she was just as upset.

Just then, the intercom buzzed and Dani's voice flowed into the room through the speaker on the desk. "Kuri is here."

"Send her in," Madison responded.

And a moment later, Kinson's amber gaze locked with Kuri's coal-black one. Suddenly, he was tempted to go and find his thickest winter coat and bundle up to stave off the arctic frost rolling off of the woman.

She stopped short and said, "Oh! I'm so sorry, Madison. I didn't mean to disturb you."

Kinson smiled. "You're not disturbing us, Kuri. Come on in."

"No, that's okay. I'll come back later." And just like that, she was gone.

There wasn't anything he could do about it right now, but

he needed to speak with her soon. One, he owed her an apology, and two, he hoped to come up with a balance that would work for all of them.

He waggled his eyebrows and said, "So, if Kuri is elsewhere this evening, we'll have the house to ourselves tonight?"

He immediately knew it was the wrong thing to say. Madison and Kuri usually had the huge house to themselves because of his constant absences. The last thing Maddy wanted was to be reminded of that. And that was the problem with words—once they left your mouth, they were impossible to take back.

He almost shook his head at himself—he'd been doing that a lot lately as the depth of his wife's pain was made more and more apparent. What the fuck had he been thinking? In truth, he hadn't. And now that he saw firsthand how his selfishness affected those he loved, it was almost like coming awake from a dream only to realize that you'd had no idea you'd been asleep in the first place.

The silence between them was deafening, but rather than continue to prove he had foot-in-mouth disease, he moved on to a subject that he knew quite well.

"You've been here all day and no doubt skipped dinner. How about a little pampering?"

"And if I say no?" she challenged. Her bit of snark fell short considering she was yawning. Again. Kind of hard to come off as a badass when you could barely keep your eyes open.

"You don't get to say no. You're tired as hell and you're getting some pampering. It's long overdue and I accept responsibility for that. So grab your shit and let's go."

"In case you hadn't noticed, I happen to run this place. I can't just leave."

"Says who? Being the boss means you delegate." He

reached across her desk and hit the speaker. A second later, Madison's personal assistant came into the room.

"Dani, who's on tap as dungeon master tonight?" Kinson asked. When Dani looked to Madison for permission, Kinson ground his back teeth, took a breath, and then promptly lost it.

"*I* am talking to you. And when *I'm* talking to you, you will not look to Madison for permission. Now, answer my very simple question or bring me someone who can."

Ouch. He hadn't meant to skin the woman with his tongue like that, but he had a lot of lost ground to make up for and his patience was wearing thin. It wasn't Dani's fault but right now, he needed results and he would do what was necessary to get them.

Without looking to his wife, Kinson leaned back against the solid executive desk, arms folded over his chest and legs crossed at the ankle. He hoped he looked unmovable because right now, that's how he felt. He needed something, damn it, and this bitch was going to get it for him.

So he stood and waited.

Madison's quiet but firm voice filled the suddenly silent space.

"You heard him, Dani."

With a nod, Dani replied with a simple, "I'll go get the schedule."

After Dani left the room, Kinson glanced over his shoulder at Madison Lee. "Where's Mauren?"

"It's late, remember? She went home already."

Damn. Kinson hadn't realized that he'd been so focused on his wife's surprise that the time had flown by. Guess it was everybody's day to be super-busy. But while he acknowledged it, he also pinched himself. His focus is what got him into this ditch with his wife that he was currently trying to dig himself out of.

Shaking himself out of his stupor, he said, "Well, I like Mauren better."

"And you're just saying that because she's all biddable and shit." Madison laughed, Kinson joined in. After all, his wife was right. He never would have been able to get things in motion with Tamela Harvin by involving Dani. The woman would have asked too many questions, and worse, probably gone straight to Madison and spilled all the beans. He'd purposely steered clear, and was glad that he had.

Dani poked her head in just as the thought cleared Kinson's head.

Speak of the devil.

Twenty minutes later, one of their subordinates already scheduled to manage the place until closing had been contacted and happily agreed to cover for Madison. A couple more quick calls and both dinner and a bath were handled.

Hand in hand, they headed out of her office and straight to the elevator. As they zipped toward the fourth floor, Madison bit her lip to keep from grinning. She was crazy if she thought he hadn't noticed.

"Don't get plucky, woman, or I'll have to take you in hand."

"Finally," she sighed happily.

And Kinson vowed to hear that particular sound from her a lot more often.

6

*K*inson peeked his head in her door and said, "Come on. I have a surprise for you."

Madison Lee gave him the side eye. The man knew she didn't particularly like surprises. Well...except for the one he'd arranged for her when they'd gone up to the private baths. Club members could reserve a private room to have a massage by a certified therapist, or a traditional scrub before soaking in the deep pool-like tubs. However, Kinson and Madison had a completely private space assigned solely to themselves.

And it was a good thing. Her sighs of appreciation had quickly become grunts and groans of both pain and relief as a masseuse worked over muscles she hadn't realized were sore. A full body scrub preceded a soak and, to her utter delight, dinner in the water, courtesy of someone's ingenious idea of floating serving trays!

Madison knew that Landon's crew of über chefs had put the yummies together, but her husband was the one who told them what those yummies should be. Her most favorite food in the whole wide world—sweet and succulent lobster—had been steamed to perfection and paired with maguro tuna and sprinkled with sesame seeds and seasonings. Along with that had been some *nigiri*, a type of sushi consisting of seafood over pressed seasoned rice. In that case, the seafood was king crab meat.

By the time they'd headed home and got tucked into bed, she'd been little more than a limp, soggy, and wonderfully stuffed noodle.

And here Kinson stood with more surprises? Quickly saving her file, Madison locked her computer screen, rose to her feet and took the hand he held out to her. Once at the bank of elevators on the teahouse side of the building, they stepped across the threshold together. A few moments later, the lift glided to an easy stop on the fifth floor.

The moment the frosted glass doors slid open, she looped an arm around Kinson's as they stepped out together.

"Before you say anything, there is no one at the reception desk on purpose. I don't want anyone in trouble over my little stunt today."

Her ears heard what he'd just said, but the rest of her attention zeroed in on something else. Madison's head tilted a hard left as she took in the scene just past the reception area.

This was the Caribbean and Yucatan-themed side of this floor. The tatami mats that covered every inch of the huge space were their natural green shade to resemble the grass of the jungles. Floor to ceiling murals were painted in a 3D style that brought to vivid life the jungles and ancient temple walls of civilizations long past.

Directly in her path, though some feet away, was the perfect replica of a Mayan seat of power. It was similar to the Throne of Hatshepsut on the Egyptian side of this same floor, only up on a dais. But today, over the delicate tatami mats, was something she'd never seen in this building before—a length of red carpet. It stretched over the grass-green reed floors, clear up to the stone-and-gold throne and made the place look more like the entrance to a Hollywood affair.

About halfway up the carpet, there was a narrower path to one of the private rooms off to the right. On either side of the "walkway," several blue square mats had been placed side by side.

Arm in arm, she walked the red carpet with her husband. Madison Lee's imagination ran wild with wonder at who else was going to be walking this particular road, and just what were they going to be doing on the soft mats near the dais.

More than once, she almost balked.

You used to trust him, through and through. Meet the man halfway, Madison Lee.

Why did her conscience have to keep giving its forty-two cents? Who cared that it was right?

You care.

"Oh shut up," she snarled under her breath while ignoring the "I know what you're thinking" look from Kinson as he gave her some side-eye of his own.

When they reached the throne, Kinson released her arm and motioned for her to sit.

She didn't move.

A breath of time passed. And then another.

"Madison Victoria Lee. Have. A. Seat."

She hiked a brow at the quiet, but no-nonsense tone he seldom used with her. It may have been awhile since she'd engaged the man in this way, but she hadn't forgotten that he could take her in hand.

God, he had such nice hands, too.

A dreamy sigh of reminiscence almost slipped out. Instead, she lifted her head, gave him a bratty grin and stalked the last few steps. With a fluid grace from years of hosting this classy establishment, she eased her body down, crossed her legs and waited.

A flutter of anticipation danced across her gut as Kinson gave her a devilish wink and a smile of his own.

What in the hell was he up to? And would she like it?

Of course you will, you goof. He may have been in his own little yoga world lately, but you remember what it's like to have all his good taste and manliness focused fully on you.

Damn. She sure seemed to be talking to herself a lot lately. And yes, she did indeed remember because she had recent memories to draw on. Kinson had been wholly engaged since returning home from Stockholm. In short, he'd been wearing her out in a good way, both emotionally and physically. The man was present in all areas of their lives. And damn, Madison knew she'd missed him, but she hadn't realized just what a big hole he'd left in her world until he'd come home and began to fill it again.

She knew what it was costing him to step back from his practice for a while, but she also knew what it had cost her to have him absent.

Madison's gaze followed him three steps to the left. He stood as if he were an attendant at her own personal court.

What was it doing to him to woo her all over again? To let go of something he truly loved? Even neglecting Kuri, his submissive, because he needed to dedicate time to his marriage? She'd never been needy. Ever. But right now, she really did need him. There was no embarrassment for that... but she did feel bad that he wasn't off doing what he loved. Would he come to resent her for it?

"Kinson," she hesitated, shaking her head as her throat clogged with tears that she refused to let fall. "Kinny, I—"

"Madison, stop worrying."

"But..."

"Just sit back and enjoy what I have for you." His words were firm, yet full of care.

"But you aren't able to engage your dominant nature because of me and…"

"Woman, are you nuts?"

She blinked at the question and thought, *"Jury's out."*

"No guilt, Madison Lee. No guilt that I'm here and not off somewhere else. What I love is right here. Understand?"

She nodded, holding her sobs at bay by sheer will and stubbornness alone.

She sucked in a shaky breath and Kinson's brows crashed together in the center of his forehead as he took in the misery on her face.

"Baby? You okay?" He stepped toward her.

God, please don't let him touch me right now. If he touches me, holds me…I'll lose it.

She nodded quickly and attempted a quivering smile while waving him away.

She knew he wanted to rush forward and take her into his arms. Instead, he respected her wishes and slammed to a halt. It made her want to bawl even more knowing that he stood there, fighting against his instinct to fix her unhappiness.

"Maddy, you know that my dominance is part of me, just like yours is part of you. Being an alpha doesn't mean I become weak by keeping my woman happy. It's my responsibility to see to my family. I was being a crap-tastic Dom by *not* being there for you. We have some good memories together, you and I. And now, it's time to make some new ones. Okay?"

Respect. Love. Desire. It was all there in his gaze as the man's sincere smile lit up the room. He was filled with an energy she hadn't noticed before…or maybe she'd seen it and chosen to simply shut down and refused to feel his amazing vibration. Right now, he fairly crackled with such an aura of love that it reached out to her and unfurled the forty pound medicine ball of regret lodged in her guts.

After a deep breath or five, Madison wrapped her composure around herself and allowed happiness to reign rather than uncertainty and pain.

"Okay, handsome, what's going on?"

"You are being recognized by Helping Hands, Caring Hearts for participating in their newest charity endeavor. The project is backed by Tamela Harvin."

"Tamela Harv...wait. What?" Eyes wide, she stammered, certain she hadn't just heard what she thought she had. "Excuse me?"

"I thought it was something you could really get behind, so I got us involved. They're looking for a way to help out men who have lost their wives to tragedy and suddenly they're single dads with small children. These men are now both mom and dad. And while there are plenty of programs to help women who find themselves alone with little ones, there are far fewer for men."

"So what does it entail?"

"They're putting together an adult calendar and you're going to pick who from Twilight Teahouse is going to be featured as Mister or Miss March."

Madison Lee's mouth fell open. And when nothing came out, Kinson called out.

"Model number one, come on out, please." He turned and whispered conspiratorially, "Oh, and by the way, Maddy, our theme is erotic yoga."

Now her eyes joined her mouth—wide open.

This was going to be soooo good!

THE PURPOSE OF THE CARPET BECAME CLEAR THE MOMENT THE private room's *shoji* screens parted and the first model sashayed into the play space. With the ribbon of red protecting the delicate tatami floors, this chick walked with sexy determination. Flawless caramel skin and a lush fit body, she wore nothing but some well-placed royal blue rope, a pair of sexy barely-there underwear and black suede pumps that made Madison Lee gasp in appreciation of such style.

Her gait was fluid, legs long and smooth, and expression determined. Even the hair, secured in a glossy after-five bun artfully arranged on top of her head, screamed *purpose* as the dark-haired beauty stopped just short of the throne.

Wow. What a stunner.

"Good day. My name is Julie and I'm going to audition with the Vinyasa style of yoga." Kinson turned and explained to Madison that Vinyasa was a fluid, less traditional style that involved a lack of specific poses and often included music to keep things lively. At her nod of understanding, Kinson pulled a little remote out of his back pocket and a jazzy, yet mellow tune filled the space. On cue, Julie dropped dramatically into her first pose. The routine was crisp yet erotic, and Madison wondered how the woman managed to pull off such a feat.

And then came a common move called Downward Dog. Madison Lee's womb jumped when her imagination decided to flood her head with images of herself down on her knees like that...naked, panting and soaked between her thighs. So far gone, she writhed as she succumbed to the fever in her blood and begged Kinson to take her. And her husband kneeled right behind her in the same sorry shape.

Imaginary Kinson's magnificent chest was covered with sweat. It trailed across perfectly sculpted pecs and made little rivulets through the dusting of reddish-blonde hair that narrowed into an arrow at his groin. The flesh of her back-side jiggled on impact as he worked himself into the silken heat of her channel with a frenzy that she never tired of.

"Maddy?"

"Huh?" She looked up and found her husband's honey-brown gaze plastered on her, but her rebellious eyes wouldn't stay on his face. No, they had to dip down to where she'd just been staring.

Kinson followed her line of sight, looked back up into her eyes and grinned as evilly as a Sith in Star Wars.

"Are you watching the audition, Maddy?" The words were a sexy rumble in his chest that made things on her body slicken and swell.

"Of course I'm watching," she snapped, more annoyed that she'd been caught ogling her husband's magnificent ass when she should have been watching the female in front of them who performed perfect yoga pose after perfect pose. Cheeks flamed and Maddy cursed under her breath that it seemed impossible to get away with much with her very observant husband.

One part of her thrilled with the hots for her man, and the other part was annoyed that he *knew* she had the hots right this moment.

Madison forced herself to pay closer attention. After all, it wouldn't do to arrange a photoshoot for the charity event with someone who wasn't at all suitable.

Damn it.

The music faded out and Kinson's sure voice quietly said, "Thank you. Great, great audition routine." His praise was professional and not-at-all pervy as he gave suggestions on how the nearly-naked woman might improve her forms. The man even got down on one of the mats in his street clothes to demonstrate some of his ideas.

The spark of instant-horny simmered down in her belly

as Madison watched. In a word or three, her husband knew his stuff and she was impressed as hell.

Sure, he was a well-sought-after yogi, but Maddy had lost interest in that particular skill a *loooong* time ago. To see him in action reminded her of exactly what he was capable of. Strong and flexible, he folded his body in ways that brought all kinds of naughty thoughts crashing right back into her brain.

Julie left the space the same way she'd come in—swaying hips, high heels and a lot of beautiful bare sin...uh, skin.

Kinson called out, "Next model, please."

Another gorgeous female entered the space in bare feet with brightly painted shimmery blue toenails. Her long red hair was pulled back into a simple ponytail that played off of a black sheer baby doll outfit that made Madison Lee do a double take. The long-sleeved lace dress was expertly cut and fell just to the top of her thighs. It covered her completely, yet beautifully silhouetted her body.

And what a body it was. Lush breasts, hips and thighs with curves galore were highlighted by the glow of health and the sparkle in her lovely gem-green eyes.

Whoever said yoga chicks were skinny stick figures that wore workout clothes twenty-four/seven and smelled like wheatgrass had obviously never met these women.

She introduced herself as Laurel and at her signal, Kinson hit the remote again. This time the music was hip and funky, rather than jazzy. Madison wondered when was the last time they'd gone dancing...or anywhere, for that matter. It was so tempting to dwell on the fact that Kinson hadn't done much of anything with her in entirely too long. Instead, Madison looked around at all the evidence of her husband's love.

He'd prepared all of this without her knowledge. The charity event. The models. The music. The play space. The throne. All of it.

Sheer joy pumped through her, lighting her up from the inside out. The music and model in front of her added to her "happy" and Madison Lee found herself tapping her toe a time or two as Laurel performed. When the woman finished her last move and the music shut off, Madison Lee clapped. Kinson turned and laid that heart stopping grin on her and joined in the applause as the model blushed furiously and smiled her delight.

For the next hour, Madison enjoyed the show of all ten models, but she'd realized a few important things long before the last one left the floor.

One, her sex had twitched through the whole damn audition, and while she'd never been much of a voyeur, she was a bit taken aback at the level of need building in her body due to a few models posing nearly-naked at her feet.

It's not the models and you know it.

Well, that was her story and she was sticking to it, damn it.

Stubborn.

And?

Second, each woman who'd auditioned was spectacular, unique, and gorgeous. They were all beyond qualified to walk into a photoshoot for the calendar event and do a superb demonstration of yoga with a side of kink.

And third, the sight, sound and scent of Mr. Kinson Lee still lit her fucking fuse!

"Kinson, can I have a word with you, please? In private?"

He put down the notebook that he'd been taking notes in and gave her a simple, "Of course." To the ladies all lined up perfectly in front of Maddy, he said, "You were all wonderful. We'll contact your agents within the next ten days, or if you've instructed us to, we'll call you directly. Thanks so much, and please enjoy lunch on us downstairs in the Twilight Teahouse restaurant."

As soon as they'd changed clothes, Kinson escorted them all to the elevator and then returned to Madison. She watched his long-legged gait as he walked that spectacular red carpet toward where she sat waiting.

Kinson took Madison Lee's hand and walked her into the room where the models had dressed.

It had a perfect view of the Sound through a bank of floor-to-ceiling one-way glass windows that allowed patrons to see out without concern of anyone seeing in. Another wall made of one huge mirror was flanked by two others with bright white paint edged with bronze hieroglyphs.

Madison sat on a big two-person chair with big fluffy cushions. Tucking her feet underneath her, she waited as Kinson slid the *shoji* screens closed to give them some privacy.

His long stride brought him to her side quickly. Rather than sitting next to her, he reached down and plucked her right off the cushions. The deep timbre of his chuckle at her squeak of surprise made her already nervous tummy wiggle at double time.

"So, what's up, lovely?" he asked even as he dipped his head and buried his nose at the point on her neck where he knew she dabbed the smallest hint of perfume in the mornings. "Mmm. Coco by Chanel, right?"

"Uh...yes. That's...uh-huh."

Stammering and sweating, she went still when he asked, "What's wrong? Didn't you like the presentation?"

Damn. She hadn't considered that he might automatically think she had a problem with his actions. What had she been thinking when she'd dared to say the five words that every man hated to hear—the dreaded, "May I talk to you, please?"

Wasting no time, she spilled her concern.

"I absolutely loved the whole thing. I'm still amazed that you're doing this for me. For us. And I understand exactly what's going on here, and it's huge. You know this kind of stuff is near and dear to my heart, and it's even more amazing that you're basically doing all the work while letting me get the credit."

"I hope you don't have a problem with that, Maddy."

"Hell no, I don't have a problem with it. Not trying to rub salt in that particular wound, but you kind of owe me right now, and this idea of yours totally works."

He laughed and her skin heated more, though how it was possible to get any hotter, she had no idea. In this case, Kinson had done everything right. The old saying that a way to a woman's heart is between her ears was true, and her man had nailed it.

Nailed.

Her sex throbbed at the thought.

He wrapped her up in his big, strong arms and held her close. "I do indeed owe you, and I'm willing to pay whatever price you want to write on that particular I.O.U."

"The models were all lovely, Kin, really they were…"

"But?"

"Well, what I'd really love is for *you* to represent Mr. March for the charity calendar. Besides being gorgeous as sin, who knows yoga better than you? And the erotic part? Yeah, you've got that down, too."

"Me? Model?" He sounded so borderline incredulous that Madison bit back a giggle. Good thing her back was pressed against his chest so he didn't see the big grin on her face at his amazed tone. "And I can see you laughing at me, you know."

Her gaze snapped up and her mouth dropped open. She'd completely forgotten they sat in front of a mirror…and they happened to be facing one that stretched from floor to ceiling.

He might be looking at the goofy grin on her face, but her

eyes were drawn to the spot just below her hip where his hands played expertly over her body.

KINSON WAS REELING. THE LAST THING HE'D EXPECTED WAS for Madison to ask *him* to be the model for the calendar project. Then he realized that wasn't it at all—the real shocker was Madison getting super-aroused and ogling his ass. Guess the request that he be the model slipped down a notch to the second-to-last thing he'd seen coming.

"So," she gasped as he lowered his head to nibble her ear, "how about it?"

The answer was easy—yes. So he said, "I'll model for you."

"And you'll let me have a bit of creative license," she declared.

Uh oh.

"I felt you go all stiff just now, Kin. Don't you trust me?"

"Absolutely, but when it comes to creative license, you and I have a difference of opinion."

Like the time she'd caught him wiped out and snoring after a long day and put his hair in a bunch of little red pigtails. He'd chased her around the house for that one and tackled her in a heap of arms, legs and laughter on the back lawn. Or when she'd asked to practice a new rope knot on him, tied him up as a prank and tried to play spank the Dominant. Thankfully she'd underestimated the tightness of the knots and he'd managed to get free and turn the tables, and her ass, upside down.

He snorted at the memories.

"Oh god, what are you thinking, Kinson Lee?"

No way in hell was he going to remind her. Instead, he said, "I'm not sure about the creative license part, but I will agree to be your calendar man."

And now that it was settled, he could concentrate on other things. Like the heat of his wife's beautiful ass burning into his groin as she sat on his lap. The hitch in her breathing every time he shifted the focus of his fingers from the underside of her breasts to the sensitive spot just below her lowest rib on the left.

Lowering his head, he trapped a lobe between his teeth and watched her closely in the mirror. Her eyes slipped closed and the smoky makeup she'd applied to her lids drew his eye. It was artfully perfect, just like the rest of her.

"I love this outfit, Mad. What's underneath?" He licked up her neck, a wet, open mouthed caress that made him shudder as the scent and taste of her skin filled his nose and mouth.

"I…" She gasped, swallowed and then tried again. "I come with edible wrappings."

She nibbled on the very corner of her bottom lip and gifted him with a half-smile that told him all he needed to know—she was happy and aroused. Honestly, even as horny as he was, he would have settled for her joy alone, but the slight push back against his body followed by a fluid undulation of her spine said Madison Lee was also turned on. As in, *far* gone. For him.

After all the absences, broken promises and lack of attention, this woman was still willing not only to stay married to him, but to give her body to him. Sex was the most intimate act between a man and a woman, an act he'd taken for granted time and time again.

Yet she only had eyes for him.

And then she said the words that he'd most longed to hear.

"By the way, handsome, I love you. And I forgive you. I don't want you to give up your yoga practice all together. We just need to find some balance is all."

Humbled, Kinson bit down on his lip, but for an entirely

different reason than Madison Lee. Sure, they'd had a few sexual interludes since he'd managed to make it home, but this felt different, more defining than any previous moments.

His woman's trust, forgiveness and total acceptance threatened to bring him to his knees. Though he was a man typically ruled by logic, he found that a mass of emotion formed as a lump in his throat. And for the first time in too many years to count, Kinson Lee teetered on the verge of tears.

Just then, Madison lifted her arms and wrapped them behind his neck. The position caused her beautiful breasts to lift in bountiful display. Wanting to please this wonderful female as she so patently deserved, Kinson pushed passed the tightness in his chest and returned his concentration to his wife.

He'd taken in her ensemble earlier, but now he paid closer attention. She sported a heavily beaded corset with so many clear, gold and silver cut crystals sewn into the fabric that it sparkled like diamonds, even under the muted lighting. Underneath was a cream silk blouse that covered her arms down to her wrists.

It was an amazing combination that showed off killer curves while actually showing nothing at all.

Fucking sexy.

A black finely knit skirt with an oriental pattern looked as if it had been painted over her hips. Sheer stockings covered long legs, and her shoes—good lord, those shoes— winter white leather pumps with heels covered in shiny silver screamed, "Give it to me."

Suddenly, the image of a disheveled Madison Lee filled his head. He wanted to bury his hands in the silky dark curls of her sexy new haircut and angle her head the way he wanted.

So he did.

Madison wasn't a submissive by any stretch…except in one place—the bedroom. And this particular spot would do nicely.

It brought to mind a song where a sultry singer declared that she and her lover were in the back of a car on their way to an evening outing, but they were so hot for each other that even though it took forty-five minutes to get all dressed up, they weren't going to make it to their destination.

Kinson's expression claimed he was totally calm, but inside he fought the impulse to literally take her in hand. They would get there, but first, there were negotiations to be made.

"Consent, Madison."

"To what," she damn-near purred as he continued to play with her warm skin.

"A bit of power exchange, and perhaps some sensual impact play."

Their gazes clashed in the polished glass. Kinson felt his already jacked up energy flash up a notch or two. The swift intake of Madison's breath and the shocked expression on her lovely face told him that she'd felt it as well, but he didn't attempt to take it any further. In fact, he ceased moving all together, and Madison's longing in her eyes morphed to surprise that he would stop now. But unless she consented, stop is exactly what he would do. Wife or not, her consent was essential.

Finally, she spoke. "I consent, baby."

"To?"

"Well, you know I'm not big on pain, but there are certain levels of it that I enjoy. You know what they are, so I trust you."

"And?" he pushed.

"I consent to whatever you want to do right now."

She lowered her gaze to the floor, then raised it back up

to the mirror. Excitement was evident there, but so was curiosity and just a tad bit of fear.

"Good. Stand up. Lose the skirt."

With easy grace, she stood and shimmied out of her skirt. Kinson moaned because she did indeed sport edible wrappings. The woman wore no underwear beneath her skirt, and her juicy flesh was accessible for whatever kind of nibbling he wanted to do.

But first...

"Come here. Stand in front of me and turn around to face the mirror again."

The moment she did, his hands went to work on the lacings that bound her succulent body into the crystal-covered corset. It was truly a thing of beauty, just as she was a creation of beauty.

The corset came free to bare beautiful full breasts topped with dusky nipples. Kinson folded the garment carefully and placed it over the arm of the huge chair, followed by the silk top she'd been wearing underneath.

She stood in nothing but sheer thigh-high stockings and a pair of sexy-ass shoes. Thick, curly waves had fallen forward to obscure one side of her face, and she peeked at him through those silky strands as if she held a close secret. A secret she wished for him to discover.

Kinson circled her like a shark looking to take care of some very specific dietary needs of the plump, fat seal variety. And she was the seal.

Fingers trailed over his skin as he walked around her.

He stopped at her back. "Spread your legs a bit." He paused, taking a moment to trace lazy circles over her bare ass, to tease the tops of the stockings. "Wrap those lovely long fingers around your breasts and touch them the way you want me to touch you."

Without hesitation, Madison palmed a swelling breast

with one hand while twisting and pulling the nipple of the other globe.

Her head began to fall back as she arched into her own touch.

"No. Keep those beautiful eyes on me in the mirror, Maddy."

Her lids snapped up to capture his gaze. And like the exceptional woman she was, she carried out every order with excellence and no half measures.

"Rub your thumb across your clit." And she did.

"Plump those pretty wet lips of your pussy." She did.

"Ease off." Done.

"Squeeze and pull your clit until you're on the verge of coming, but do not come until I say you can. Understand?" She nodded. It was a shaky endeavor considering her eyes were glassy, her breathing uneven, and her head practically lolled back and forth.

Even with her immediate compliance, Kinson was sure his wife had begun slipping into her favorite state—subspace.

"Tug harder."

"Yes, sir," she panted, though he hadn't required her to use the formal response.

When instructed, she dipped two fingers deep inside her heat and Kinson bit back a smile when Madison's eyes crossed. To her credit, the woman held on to her control. It didn't matter if that control hung on by a thread so thin it was almost non-existent. What mattered was her freely given obedience and the desire to please.

Knowing Madison's favorite thing to do was touch him during intimate moments, he deliberately kept out of reach as he tormented her by filling her lust-filled head with words of naughty promises.

"I'm going to fuck you, Madison. I'm going to give it to you hard and fast, just the way you like it. I'm not going to ride you through your second or third orgasm, baby. No. Instead, I'm going to stop moving, stop stroking my cock against your sugared walls while you come and come and come."

She bit her top lip but kept working her clit as she listened. A sheen of fine sweat now covered her skin, and her scent perfumed the air.

"And when, and *only* when you beg me to move, am I going to give you everything you're asking for."

Maddy opened her mouth to beg right then.

"No. You've got to make yourself come first." Kinson waited a few moments and then said, "Now!"

And just like that, her eyes widened and mouth froze on a silent scream as her climax crashed through her.

Legs trembled from ankle to thigh, yet her hand stayed where he'd told her to put it as her breathing continued to fly out of control.

"You can stop touching your pussy now, Maddy. Hold on to me." As soon as a hand touched his shoulder, he knelt and lifted a foot to remove first one shoe, and then the other.

Fine tremors continued to wrack her body. Knowing that she was so far gone drove his own need. Every sound she made impacted him, but he had a promise to keep before he allowed himself to get lost in her luscious body.

"Wrap those long, talented fingers around your ankles."

Madison bent at the waist and gasped as the first blow landed across her beautiful bare ass. He was sure to keep the blows light until her skin warmed. Then, and only then, did he increase the intensity and frequency of the blows, careful not to push her too far past the limit he knew was there.

And when she begged, earnestly begged for his cock, did Kinson give her what they both wanted, needed—immeasurable pleasure just on the right side of pain.

7

*I*t had always amazed her how he could manage to be so damn bossy, and so giving at the same time.

Sure, he'd taken her on a couple of dates to the movies, out to dinner, lunch, and the occasional mid-day interlude in one of the themed spaces upstairs, but he still shooed her out of her office if she'd been in there too long. He'd even taken the responsibility of scheduling all of their employees from her. Instead, he'd given it to one of the managers and forbade her from working a minute past ten hours a day.

Truth be told, she'd been putting in fourteen and sixteen hour days for so long, her body had forgotten what sleep was. And she loved re-learning that particular lesson given her husband woke her up in the most delicious ways.

It was tempting to go to turn in early every night just for the delightful two-in-the-morning nookie.

"Madison? Wake up, baby. We've got to go."

She stretched and yawned. A tilt of her head brought her clock into focus. Well, sort of, given the bleariness of her eyes. Wait, that couldn't be right. Six o'clock...on a Saturday morning?

"Come on, sleepy head. Time to get up." The voice sounded like Kinson's but it couldn't be. Kinson was being nice to her. Kinson was dating her right now. He wouldn't wake her up super early on a Saturday morning when they had nowhere to go.

She didn't move except to roll over. Knees drawn up to her chest, she shivered when the covers were yanked off of her body. Didn't matter. Hell, she'd been cold before. Big deal. She curled up tighter to her pillow. She was not getting up no matter…

"Holy shit! Are you kidding me!" she squeaked as her husband danced out of kicking distance with his handy dandy glass of ice cold water—water that had just been splashed on her.

"You. Will. Die!" she swore.

He laughed and taunted her with a "come on then" motion of his finger.

Energy filled her from out of nowhere and Madison stood up in the bed and sprung like a jaguar out of a tree after a big fat tapir.

Laughing, Kinson snatched her right out of the air and pulled her against his gloriously naked body.

"Oooh, well good morning, then," she drawled as the heat of his erection warmed the flesh of her stomach.

He nipped her nose and then planted a gentle kiss on her lips. "Good morning, lovely."

Keeping his arms around her, he carried her into the bathroom that was already filled with steam. Set on her feet, she immediately put her hair up and stepped into the shower. Ah, it was heavenly.

And when he stepped in behind her, grabbed her hand-made lemon soap and lathered her back, she tried to think of a word more awesome than "heavenly," but her brain had begun to shut down with the warmth and pleasure of his fingers as they slid over damp skin.

Since using one's brain early in the morning was over-rated, she let her thoughts go where they willed. Arms at her sides, she stood there in a near-stupor and let her husband work her over with those strong hands of his. It was a fruit-scented, sensual massage...with bubbles.

Fingers moved from her shoulders, down her back and over her sensitive backside. She moaned, sighed and moaned some more. God, it felt so good.

"You are becoming spoiled, woman."

"Is that bad?" she drawled, head falling forward.

"Not in my book. You've spoiled me plenty over the years. I can get your back sometimes, too. Just don't fall asleep."

His hands came around the front of her body and worked lather across her breasts.

Oh, yes. That was just wonderfully yummy.

"You like that, eh?"

"Mmmhmm," she sighed. Eyes closed, she didn't bother to move, knowing he would put her where he wanted her.

She didn't have long to wait.

Modifying the water from super-hot to just a hair past warm, Kinson rubbed his hands over her limbs swiftly. The cooling of the shower and the vigorous rubbing got her blood pumping and her energy flowing.

By the time he pulled one of the hand-held showerheads off the mount and rinsed her thoroughly, she was fully awake and more invigorated than she could remember in a good long while.

Wow. Must have been the ice water, she mused to herself.

Kinson's deep voice whispered in her ear from behind. "Sit down, baby. Let me see to you."

Madison started to tell him that he'd already seen to her plenty, but he was a stubborn man and she knew if she wanted to alter his plans, she'd just have to do it.

She sat on the wide bench embedded into the wall of the oversized shower. The moment her husband stepped in front of her, she knew he planned to go down on her and suck her clit into oblivion.

Before he could bend a knee, she reached out and wrapped her fingers fully around his engorged cock.

He hissed with pleasure, and before he could say another word, she put her mouth to this heated flesh. One pass, then another, and a third made sure he was good and wet. Then she took him to the back of her throat without preamble.

Her husband literally shouted as his hands slammed into the tiled walls to steady himself. She wanted to smile, and would have if doing so around his girth hadn't been impossible.

Madison put her whole body into the experience, wanting to give to him in this moment. Cheeks hallowed, tongue encircled, hands ran up and down the back of his thighs, nails scraped gently over his perfect ass.

Careful to never, ever put her teeth on his cock, Madison sucked him as if she loved nothing more than to blow his cock. The growls and groans that echoed around the bathroom turned up her own arousal until she was so ready for him that even though she was wet all over from the water, she could easily differentiate the honey flowing from between her thighs.

Slick, hot and ready should be her motto where her husband was concerned.

With his head thrown back, Kinson tightened the fingers that were already buried in her hair. After a few long, semi-controlled pumps, he looked down at her.

She recognized that look—her man was close. But close wasn't good enough. She pulled back and took him in her hand with a lingering lick. "Come for me, Kinson. Give it to me."

He removed her fingers, flipped her around and slammed into her body in a move so swift, it took her breath away.

And all she could think was, "More!"

Her man was built from head to toe, and everywhere in between. Kinson's muscles weren't only for show. He was a strong man, through and through, and his rod fit the bill right along with the rest of him.

Thick and heavily veined, his rock-hard cock paused at the tight-ringed entrance of her sex. The rim of the plum-shaped head parted her flesh.

Shallow digs followed by deep plunges had Madison panting, moaning and damn near demanding that he finish her.

And when had script flipped from her pleasuring him to Madison demanding that he fuck her instead?

Sly, sly man.

At Kinson's quiet chuckle, she knew she'd been had, but didn't give a damn. She was on the verge of coming. Yes, coming needed to commence right now!

"Work it out, Madison. Make it happen."

Without hesitation, she rubbed her fingers over the swollen bundle of nerves that had suddenly become the center of her world.

Kinson continued to plunge deep, then deeper. Fingers dug into the flesh of her hips as he plastered his body against hers, his shaft as deep as he could go.

He came with a shout. The pulse of his orgasm caused the tip of his cock to press against *that* spot deep inside her soaked pussy, once, twice, three times.

As Kinson's hot juices splashed against her core, Madison tipped over the edge and met him on the other side.

FULLY INTENDING TO FIX A BITE TO EAT FOR THE TWO OF them, Madison inhaled deeply and let out a breath—coffee and bacon already scented the air.

She and Kinson looked at each other, smiled and simply said, "Kuri."

Wrapped in fluffy warm robes and traditional slippers, they made their way to the kitchen and discovered that Kuri had indeed taken care of them.

But that was nothing new.

Madison's heart broke, filled with compassion and understanding. Kuri, a talented woman who was capable of running Twilight Teahouse's restaurant, was currently little more than a housekeeper in their home at this point. She was getting nothing that they'd agreed on when she'd come to serve Kinson, except a place to live, a generous salary, plus a job at Twilight Teahouse. But emotionally, physically? She was getting nothing. Just like Madison had been getting nothing.

But that had changed. Madison had her husband back.

Kuri had no one.

She sipped her coffee and ducked her head while pretending to get into the morning news on her reading device. But honestly, she was simply avoiding Kinson's keen gaze that seemed to keep itself plastered on her face.

Maybe he wouldn't notice that she'd gone from sensually satisfied to sad in two-point-three seconds? She couldn't help but feel bad on behalf of a woman who had become a very good friend to her over the past year and a half.

"Spit it out, Madison."

"Not now, but I will. Promise."

"Okay. Well, we're going out today so you can tell me what's going on while we're on the road. Deal?"

Shit. She hadn't wanted to set a timetable on when she'd

spill her ever lovin' guts. But he wasn't asking for anything unreasonable, so she agreed.

Madison rose from the table and at her husband's inquiring look, she simply said, "Be right back."

"Don't let your food get cold."

"Okay," she mumbled, grabbed her coffee off the table and took it with her to Kuri's room. And to her disappointment, though it wasn't unexpected, the other woman wasn't there. Where was she this early in the morning on a weekend?

Madison stood in the threshold of her friend's room and looked around.

Spotting a piece of paper folder on the nightstand with her name on it, Madison snatched it up and sat down for a moment. The little note simply said, "Made breakfast then took off with Rachelle and her riding club. Riding motorcycles up to Mount Rainier so left early. Not sure if I'm spending the weekend with her or not. If I do, I'll see you at work on Monday morning."

Sigh.

Madison hung her head, feeling so very sorry for Kuri. But at the same time she was glad that the woman was out doing things with others rather than just sitting around the house.

Kinson's voice came through the intercom.

"Hey, baby. Done eating. Getting dressed now. We're out of here in twenty minutes. Dress warm and casual."

Well, there was nothing she could do to help Kuri at this very moment, so she tucked the scrap of paper into the pocket of her robe, picked up her coffee cup and hightailed it back to the kitchen to finish her meal.

"Dress warm and casual?" she wondered aloud.

Well, that told her nothing about where they were going. They lived in the Pacific Northwest—in springtime, dressing warm and casual was the order of almost every day. Well, wherever he planned to take her, the last thing she wanted to be was late so with breakfast done, she jumped into a pair of jeans, yanked a cable knit sweater over her head and fluffed her curls just as she heard the garage door start to rise.

HALF AN HOUR LATER, MADISON LOOKED AT HER HUSBAND AND wondered what in the hell they were doing up at fourteen thousand feet in a luxury helicopter.

Glad he'd suggested she bring her camera, Madison made good use of it as they headed to wherever. For a person who didn't care for surprises, Madison was beginning to look forward to the next bit of "awesome" her husband had in store.

Madison knew herself well. Kinson's good looks, charm and brilliance weren't the only reasons she'd married him so many years ago. The man was an alpha, but so was Madison. She needed a man as strong as herself, otherwise she'd run all over him and then grow to resent him for not being able to balance or keep her in check.

She gave herself into his care because he was *capable*.

On the other hand, Kinson needed something similar.

He enjoyed time with submissives—loved flogging them, revving them up sensually, getting into their heads and giving them what they needed when it came to sensation play. But in the end, he *needed* Madison because she could give as good as she got, yet still *chose* to submit to him.

In that moment, she gave him what he needed—no holds barred, straight up truth.

As promised, she looked him in the eye and told him what she'd been thinking earlier about Kuri, and the note that she'd found on Kuri's nightstand.

Kinson listened without interrupting. He trusted her to

lay it all out for him, and she did. Basically, if she'd been disappointed in her husband after having years and years to get used to his ambition, how did Kuri feel after spending almost two years in the home of someone who'd been almost non-existent for half of that time?

"I think she's been scarce because she doesn't really know how best to deal with you being back. She's had plenty of time to build up resentment. But now that you're home, what is she supposed to do with all of that?"

"I've been thinking about it as well. I've wanted to talk to her since I got home but honestly, you're my focus. You're my primary. You're my wife. And that means we need to find a balance that works with all of us, or…"

He let the words hang in the air, and since this was something he had to handle, so did she.

The coast came into view and shortly after, they landed on a helipad near a bluff that overlooked the Pacific Ocean. It was still early, but the tide was out and the sun was up and sparkled off the water like little diamonds that rolled out to the deep.

As Kinson pulled a gear bag out of the chopper, a big blue SUV rolled to a stop near them. A handsome man with a bright disposition, and a literal spring in his step, hopped out and strode over to meet them. Dressed simply in a bomber jacket, jeans and what looked like hiking boots, he moved quickly in spite of the huge, heavy looking bag over one shoulder.

Two more people with equally gigantic gear bags were right behind him, grinning like crazy.

"Hi, are you Kinson Lee?" he called out while still a short distance away.

"Yep. You must be Braden Nile."

Madison looked back and forth between the two men, thinking that the stranger's name sounded familiar.

Kinson turned and motioned to her. "Madison, this is the photographer I told you about a couple of days ago. Braden, this is my wife, Madison Lee. We're thrilled to be participating in this project for Ms. Harvin's charity."

"And she's equally thrilled to have you. And I must say, Madison…may I call you Madison?" he inquired with impeccable manners.

"Absolutely," she replied with a smile so big, she was sure that all her teeth were showing.

"Ms. Harvin has heard some fantastic things about what Twilight Teahouse is doing. While it's known as a private adult establishment, news of the events you've been holding in your local community are starting to really get around. It's pretty damn impressive how you've brought sex positivity to Seattle, as well as highlight Japanese culture in a place where not everyone is Japanese. Inclusive rather than exclusive… while still being private. Not sure how you guys pull it off, but it seems pretty cool to me."

"Well, thank you," Madison said. It hadn't been easy to figure out a balance like the one they had at Twilight Teahouse. It was awesome that someone like Tamela Harvin had not only heard of their little piece of heaven, but that she actually knew what they were trying to accomplish.

"So, Kinson, you ready for your photoshoot? Do you need a place to change?"

"Yes, I'm ready, but nah, I don't need a place to change. It's just a matter of removing clothes. No big deal."

"Fantastic. Let's make our way toward the water and figure out where we want to set up."

Braden walked up and down the beach, judging the position of the sun and how shadow would play off of Kinson's body. He'd lit up like a Christmas tree as he declared that the light was such that he wouldn't need any backdrops or special props. In seconds of picking the perfect spot, they were ready to roll.

KINSON DROPPED HIS BAG IN THE SAND AND DUG AROUND inside for something he knew his wife would never expect— three bundles of soft bamboo rope. He plopped them into her palm and then began to strip.

With the first bit of clothing he removed, Kinson heard the click of the shutter on the photographer's camera and sent up a silent prayer that the man was attentive. Being a world famous yogi, he'd had plenty of pictures taken and knew that sometimes the best photos were completely spontaneous.

Besides, he would pay real money for a picture of his wife's mouth, wide open in shock as she stared down at that rope.

"Uh..." she stammered. "What am I supposed to do with this?"

It was a fair question considering he'd never been truly bound by her before. Ever.

"I'm going to get into a few different positions, and you're going to tie me into them. No yoga mats or equipment. Just you, me, the sand and this rope."

Braden's gasp made Kinson smile almost as much as the man's whispered, "Damn, that sounds hot."

"Ready?" he asked his wife, and pretended he didn't see the tears gathering in her eyes. He was just thankful they were tears of joy and not pain. After all, he'd caused her enough of the latter.

THE FLESH OF HER SEX WAS STILL SWOLLEN AND SENSITIVE

from their morning romp. The moment the rope landed in her palm, her entire body lit up with a sensual zing as well as a lump in her throat at the gift he'd just given her.

Yes, the charity calendar thingy was a huge present. But when Kinson, a man who was not into bondage in any shape, form, or fashion, placed the rope in her hand, Madison was undone.

Truly and completely undone.

It was a typical Pacific Northwest morning, blustery and chilly, but beautiful with the deep blue sea as their backdrop. Thoughts were immediately naughty and Madison could only shake her head at herself as she watched Kinson peel off his sweater, followed by his jeans.

In seconds, he stood there in nothing but a pair of black boxer briefs, contrasted against deeply tanned skin. As he stretched and warmed up in preparation of the positions he was going to pose, she stood there and watched, certain that she wore a deer-in-the-headlights expression.

Jeebus, the man's legs were so toned and tight, he didn't have to flex to show the muscles packed there. His chest was all sculpted pecs, cut shoulders and strong neck muscles. His arms, from shoulder joints to wrists, were chiseled as if the most talented sculptor had spent a lifetime designing him.

It just wasn't right to be so damn gorgeous.

And shortly, she was going to have her arms—and her rope—all over him.

Sure, she'd seen his body before—had seen it for years—but today she was taking the time to appreciate it in a way she hadn't for quite some time. At the same time, her mind pictured and then either immediately rejected or considered the different types of knots and designs she might want to use.

She hoped she wouldn't embarrass herself by drooling in front of these professionals she'd just met.

"Ready?"

Madison, Braden and both assistants nodded eagerly. Kinson went immediately down onto the wet sand at the very edge of the tideline and created his first pose.

Elbows in the sand and all of his body weight on his upper body.

"Tie my upper body in this position first. When you're done, I'll stretch out my legs into a plank position. There won't be anything touching the sand but my forearms."

Holy shit!

The strength it took to pull that off floored Madison. It simply brought home the fact that her husband's body, no matter how many times she saw him naked, was a tool made for action. Actions like picking her up and holding her entire body weight up against a wall so he could drive his beautiful cock into her willing body, and…

"Madison?"

"Huh?"

"Are you ready?" And the smirk from hell was plastered across his face. Damn, busted again.

"Oh, shut up," she grumbled.

"Not a chance," he laughed. "I'm happy my wife loves looking at me, but can we move it along, beautiful? My balls are trying to climb into my body. It's cold as hell out here."

She tied an intricate tortoise shell design that gathered in the middle of his back, but instead of binding his arms at his side, as she typically would when she was doing this particular tie, she did some fancy rope work around his biceps. Brayden muttered a few oh-that's-nice compliments as she worked, and mentioned that the design would bring attention to the muscles in his back and biceps.

When Kinson stretched out his legs, keeping them off of the sand and straight out behind him, Madison went still.

"How long can you hold this one?" she asked.

"For as long as you need me to." It was such a Kinson answer, she snorted, shook her head at him and got busy with the knots and bindings down his legs. When she was done, he looked so sexy she was almost panting.

Braden called for his assistants to pass him this or that camera, depending on the shot. He got so caught up in the beauty of the scenes, he even called Madison over to show her a few of the shots as he worked.

"Okay, I'm ready for the next post, Kinson," Braden said.

Madison hustled over and untied him, then rubbed his arms and legs swiftly to make sure his blood was flowing and that there was no numbness or pins-and-needles in any of his limbs.

He grabbed a towel, dusted the sand off of his forearms and then spread the towel across the sand. Kinson moved immediately into the next pose, and Madison worked her magic quickly. She didn't want him restrained too long and kept her eye on him to avoid any nerve or muscle damage.

Laying on his side, he stretched his arms over his head and reached back, while his legs went the opposite direction. The man had just turned himself into her own personal manly doughnut as he stretched his body in an almost perfect 'O'.

"You make a good vowel," Madison chided.

"Don't make me laugh in this position," he said, trying to hide the chuckle in his voice. "After I'm tied, ask Braden to help you turn me onto my stomach and I'll balance myself that way."

Firmly secured into the pose, Madison called Braden over.

To her man she said, "You, sir, are amazing."

"I know," he said with a smile so big she knew he was picking at her. So she picked back.

As she tickled him, he threatened her with all manner of

naughtiness. "No wonder you never let me tie you up before!" she squealed as he tossed a threat her way that had to do with blindfolds, ice cubes and spankings. "I can get into all kinds of trouble and you can't carry out any of those inventive things until I untie you."

His voice dropped an octave. "Madison Lee," he growled. A shiver traveled up her spine that had nothing to do with fear and everything to do with how sexy this man was. Would she pay for her shenanigans? Hell yes. But there was no doubt she'd enjoy it!

In the meantime, she bit down on her bottom lip to stop herself from laughing. He was still very much in charge, even though he was the one wearing the rope. Even still, Madison wasn't concerned about what he would do once she unbound him. They both knew he would never touch her in anger. Ever.

Suddenly, fog began to gather in a bank just beyond the tideline. And it couldn't have been more perfect as it rolled in.

Kinson was glorious. Skin shrouded in mist, he looked like some kind of sea god. At one point, Madison was sure she'd heard the photographer gasp in surprise as he looked through the viewfinder.

In one of the pictures, the fog wrapped around Kinson like a blanket that covered half of his body, while leaving the other completely brightened by sunlight. It was like watching a full moon shrouded by a half-eclipse with the wave-filled ocean visible through the 'O' created by Kinson's bowed body. It was...unearthly beautiful.

It didn't take long for Braden to get the shots he needed. As Madison untied Kinson, the photographer got straight to the point.

"That was the most unique and awesome photoshoot I think I've ever done."

The pleasantries were dispensed of quickly as a shivering Kinson dressed and Madison rewound the rope into neat bundles and stacked them into Kinson's gear bag.

Kinson turned to Madison and said, "Let's go."

She looked up into his eyes and went stock still. The bright orbs were changing color, which only happened during moments of strong emotion. Morphing from light brown to golden hazel with flecks of green, his gaze was hooded by thick lashes.

Oooh, that expression meant all kinds of delicious trouble for her. Of course she knew exactly where his mind was but she still asked, "You look pretty intense right now. What are you thinking about?"

"You. Naked. In that same rope." He motioned to the bag she'd just zipped up.

Oh my goodness.

She heard a shutter click and sucked in a breath as she broke eye contact and looked toward the noise.

Braden grinned and held out the camera. "Have a look."

To his credit, the photographer had captured Kinson's deep longing and that one photo conveyed everything her husband *hadn't* said. It was all right there, as if the camera lens had looked right into his soul.

Headed back to the helicopter that was perched like a sexy, sleek black and red dragon up on the bluff, Kinson reached out and relieved Madison of the bag she'd been determined to carry. Her now-free hand was wrapped up in his as they strode.

Settling in quickly, once in the air she only had one question for this man on the ride home.

"Am I going to make it into the house before you tear my clothes off?"

He pinned her with a gaze that took her breath away yet again. "Not likely."

---

8

*T*he man made good on his promise.

His hands had roamed as they drove from the heliport home. Long arms had given him the advantage as he'd expertly steered the sleek coupe with one hand, and played her body like a fucking stringed instrument with the other.

By the time they pulled into their garage just north of the city proper, Madison was panting like a winded horse and she needed to come so badly, she teetered on the verge of tears.

As the garage door came down, he was out of the car and around to her side. The door was yanked open and her shoes were history as he pulled them from her feet and tossed them to the backseat. Her pants and underwear were next.

He kneeled on the cold cement, put one of her legs up on the dashboard and went down on her right there with half her body still in the car.

It was fucking glorious...until he left her teetering even more precariously on the edge. With a deep groan, he pulled back and kissed the inside of her thigh.

"Into the house."

No need to say it twice. Madison moved, uncaring of the fact that she was bare-assed and shoeless.

Before she could get through the door that led from the garage into the house, Kinson took her by her shoulders and pressed her up against the wall next to the shop vac. His kiss was wild, urgent and as delicious as dark-chocolate covered pomegranate. When they came up for air, neither spoke. Instead, it was a race to the bedroom where Madison dove onto the bed and immediately took her favorite position—on her knees, luscious backside up and chest down.

Shoes and jeans went flying. Kinson didn't bother removing his shirt. Instead, he was pressed to her flesh and inside of her so quickly, Madison screamed in delight.

"Yes! Oh god, give it to me."

Her hair was still long enough for him to gather it tightly in a fist to angle her head the way he wanted. She gasped her pleasure at the slight sting when he pulled it just hard enough for her to understand how far gone he was, but not hard enough to really hurt her.

Oh how she loved that edge only he was allowed to take her to—just this side of pleasure, but that side of pain.

Kinson could be a demanding lover and Madison loved that her man didn't have to worry about breaking her. He could take her the way he desired—which happened to be the way she loved it. And he did indeed take her. Hard, fast and gloriously messy.

"Knees wider. Push back against me like you want it," he demanded.

She did. No hesitation.

At the muted buzz behind her, she squirmed with ripe anticipation as a toy landed in her hand, sending vibration from her fingers to her forearms.

"Don't change the setting," he growled.

Holy shit, the thing was as high as it could go!

Even though she hadn't orgasmed yet, Madison's clit was already so sensitive and swollen, she wasn't sure she could take the added stimulation.

Kinson leaned over her body, nipped her ear and said, "Oh you can, and you will, lovely."

Kinson pistoned into her body and she felt herself pulse around him. A few choice swear words ratcheted up her arousal when he combined them with, "Holy fuck, woman, you're milking my cock!"

When she balked at using the toy, he reached down and guided her hand toward her quivering flesh. Then it touched her clitoris and…

"Fuck!"

Her entire body shook as if she stood on top of a piece of concrete that was being pummeled by a jackhammer. Moments later, Madison went wild—scalp tingled, spine went taut, hips bucked and her already sopping channel gushed.

Their voices melded together into a harmony of shouts as they both yelled their completion to the rafters. And when he collapsed on top of her, she pulled him tight and wouldn't let go.

EASING OUT OF THE BED, KINSON SLIPPED INTO A PAIR OF pajama pants and grabbed his robe from the back of the door. Leaving Madison to sleep off her post-awesome-sex coma, he padded barefoot into the kitchen.

He entered through the door closest to the living room and brightened when he caught sight of a fall of coal black, super straight hair.

Kuri.

"Hey, you! I haven't seen you since I got home."

Kuri turned and looked him square in the eye.

Kinson's gut did a freefall. There was no smile, no words of welcome on her lips. Her face was expressionless, free of stress lines between her brows, no frowns and no tightness around her mouth. Yet she still managed to appear as hard as flint.

She didn't lower her thick black lashes nor slightly lean her head to the left as was her habit. No easing of her body into her favorite position—on her knees.

This woman might be a bone-deep submissive...but obviously not right now.

"Kuri?" He called her name quietly as he made his way across the room to stand in front of her. Kinson raised his hand to slide his fingers into her beautiful hair at the nape of her neck ...and met only air.

A swift side-step made it abundantly clear that his hands were not welcome anywhere near her skin. She blinked but didn't say anything. Didn't need to. The flare of defiance in her eyes screamed anger, hurt and totally "not submissive."

The freefall of his gut a moment ago was nothing compared to the blow to his pride, but he couldn't allow his ego to reign here. He needed to deal with the problems that he'd created for himself, even if it meant that it was going to hurt.

He motioned for her to have a seat at the kitchen table.

She didn't.

Kinson's temper was firmly in check, but his natural dominance began to slip the leash he'd cinched tight specifically for this conversation.

"Sit. Now."

Then she did something Kinson was sure he'd never seen. Ever.

"Kuri, did you just roll your eyes at me?"

Her eyes widened at his no-nonsense tone. When she continued to stand, his posture went rigid. His arms crossed over his chest and his head lowered enough to stare at her through his lashes. One brow hiked itself up his forehead as his body language morphed from patient-and-understanding Dominant to I-will-spank-your-ass Dominant.

With a huff, Kuri immediately parked her ass on the plush cushion of the chair and glared at the highly polished table-top. Kinson let his hand drop to his side. With a deep breath, he squashed his impatience.

Kinson shook his head at himself in disgust knowing that Kuri was the reason his house was impeccably spotless and the wood on this table held such a high sheen. She prided herself on taking care of him and his home. There was nothing she loved more than serving others. And in his case, serving *him* as his submissive.

And he'd failed her, just as he'd failed Madison.

Fuck.

"Okay," he said, "Kuri, spill it."

The woman took a deep breath of her own. "I want out of my contract and collar with you."

Madison's words rang loudly in his head.

How can she serve someone who is never here?

It made sense that Kuri was defying him for the first time in…

Wow, how long had it been? The fact that he couldn't answer his own question made it clear that it had been much too long indeed.

———

After speaking with him, Kuri had left the house and Kinson had headed straight to his wife's side. He hated waking her, but this was important and he needed his woman's opinion.

Her suggestion had been a homemade brunch, completely unhealthy snacks, and a matinee in front of the fireplace.

She even suggested a blow-everything-up movie he'd been wanting to see, but hadn't been available overseas. Nothing cleared a man's head like an action movie while spooning with the sexiest woman in the world.

Bundled up in sleeping bags, blankets and lots of pillows, Madison turned to face him as the final credits rolled across the screen.

"So what are you going to do?" Madison asked.

"I'm going to give her what she asked for. It's only fair."

"But...?"

God, he totally didn't deserve this woman who knew him so well.

"But," Kinson said, tracing the curve of Madison's hip, "I told her to think about what she needs and we'll discuss it, the three of us, in the morning. It's about more than just her collar."

"True," Madison said, "her job at Twilight Teahouse has nothing to do with her collar or you, so if she's leaves our home, she's not just left with nothing. And she can choose to stay here if she wants. I really don't mind. She and I have become rather close over the last year and a half."

While Kuri would have a say, Kinson understood that giving was such a part of Kuri's nature, he didn't think she could handle being in his and Madison's home while holding herself distant from him. Caring and giving was part of what made her who she was. Not being able to take care of him would eat at her, heart and soul, until she became resentful—or more resentful than she already was. And there was another very important thing on his mind.

"I need to be sure she's safe. If she's going to enter into another D/s relationship soon, it's got to be with someone who will treat her well."

"Has she agreed to that? I mean, is she going to allow you to protect her in such a manner?"

"I didn't discuss it with her, but I'm thinking that when we talk in the morning, she'll confirm that she's pretty much done with me. But she'll allow you to watch after her."

Madison sat up so quickly, the bowl of popcorn they'd been sharing went tumbling to the floor. "Me? Why me?"

Kinson knew that Madison's surprise was because of the gravity of what it meant to be someone's protector in the lifestyle. It wasn't something to be taken lightly, and was quite an honor in their particular circle.

"Because she *is* your friend, Madison. You two have taken care of each other. And if there's anything you do, and do well, it's look after those you love, those you call friends. And thankfully for me, those you call husband."

"So, it looks like we're beginning a new stage of our lives, eh?"

"Absolutely. How do you feel about that?" he asked her.

"Grateful to be walking into it with you."

"And to mark the occasion…" Kinson reached back to the couch and dug into the pocket of the robe he'd placed there earlier. He pulled out a wide, narrow box. Madison's breath caught in her throat when he turned it her way and flipped the lid open.

Inside was a bracelet of baby-blue chalcedony stones set in rose gold—the first he'd ever given her. Placed securely around her wrist, he snapped the clasp into place and took in the joy and sheer surprise that flitted across her face. In this moment, happy, grateful and humbled described them both.

"Here's to new memories and moments," he toasted, and

raised his half-empty glass of iced tea. With that, she straddled his hips and kissed the wind right out of his sails.

And he would make sure that she never again regretted
taking this particular journey with him.

ALSO BY AUTHOR T.J. MICHAELS

Carinian's Seeker, Vampire Council of Ethics Book One

Serati's Flame, Vampire Council of Ethics Book Two

Hatsept Heat, Vampire Council of Ethics Book Three

Seeker's Solace, Vampire Council of Ethics Book Four

Silk Road, Seals of Destiny

Spirit of the Pryde, Pryde Ranch Shifters

Niah's Pride, Pryde Ranch Shifters

Pursuit of Pride and Pleasure, Pryde Ranch Shifters

Shiftin' Sassy, Pryde Ranch Shifters

Winter Blues, Pryde Ranch Shifters

Jaguar's Rule

Forever December

Egyptian Voyage

On the Prowl

Entwined Hearts

Shards of Ecstasy

Caramel Kisses

Hide No More

Just Peachy

Juicy, Twilight Teahouse Book One

Luscious, Twilight Teahouse Book Two

Succulent, Twilight Teahouse Book Three

Gathering of the Storms Vol 1, Wind and Fire

Gathering of the Storms Vol 2, Reckoning

Some Naughty, None Nice

ABOUT THE AUTHOR

T.J. is an award-winning author of several romance genres, including paranormal, fantasy, sci-fi and urban fantasy romance. Writing like a madman, T.J. hasn't lost steam. Her mind? Yep, that's gone, but steam there is a-plenty! No matter the genre T.J. is penning, her favorite thing to do is build worlds. To take you somewhere extraordinary. To transport you to a place where you can close your eyes and slip into your fantasy...

Visit T.J. Michaels online at her Website
www.TJMichaels.com